THE HARLOT'S PREROGATIVE

THE HARLOT'S PREROGATIVE

Andrew Moncur

*For Mum, Muriel & Ed,
with all love,
Andrew*

September, 1997

review

First published in 1997
by HEADLINE BOOK PUBLISHING

A REVIEW hardback

10 9 8 7 6 5 4 3 2 1

British Library Cataloguing in Publication Data

Moncur, Andrew
The harlot's prerogative
1. English fiction - 20th century
I. Title
823.9'14 [F]

ISBN 0 7472 1745 9

Typeset by Avon Dataset Ltd, Bidford-on-Avon, Warks

Printed and bound in Great Britain by
Clays Ltd, St Ives plc.

HEADLINE BOOK PUBLISHING
A division of Hodder Headline PLC
338 Euston Road
London NW1 3BH

In memory of my father, Ian H. Moncur

'Power without responsibility – the prerogative of the harlot throughout the ages.'

Rudyard Kipling (1865–1936).

'They are engines of propaganda . . . What the proprietorship of these newspapers is aiming at is power, and power without responsibility – the prerogative of the harlot through the ages.'

Stanley Baldwin (1867–1947) stung by criticism of his government by press barons. Kipling and Baldwin were cousins.

Chapter One

The sea lavender carpeting the salt marsh was exactly that shade of smudgy purple-blue which so many girls choose for their first eye make-up. It was warm and still at the very edge of the marsh where the land finally lifted itself out of the creek mud and started to climb above sea level.

The grass stood tall at that point. It curved along in a narrow band between contour lines marked out clearly on the ground. The grassy strip lay above the flood tide level – shown by a ribbon of dross, driftwood, bottles and plastic fish boxes – but below the margin of gorse and dense brambles which grew on slightly higher ground, a prickly tangle scattered with pink and white blossom.

There was distant noise: the steady roll of the sea breaking on the sand bar. Nearby, over the hum of bees, came the fretful call of some bird, probably an oystercatcher. The sky was a pale wash stretching, cloudless, to the low horizon.

The marshland looked as though it had been left alone to drowse under the early sun. The faintest breeze crept in from the sea.

There was a burst of laughter, cut short. A man and woman were lying together in the thick, waving grass, safely hidden under the wall of impenetrable brambles.

The man pushed himself up on one hand. He was wearing a blue shirt, a sleeveless grey pullover and khaki trousers; his shirt sleeves were rolled up. He had a broad back and strong arms.

The woman's chocolate brown sweater lay to one side. Her blouse was unbuttoned to the waist and a fine white strap had slipped from her shoulder. He seemed to be reaching behind her. The woman arched her back, raising herself on her elbows and then lay back on the red tartan blanket.

She laughed again. The tall man was kneeling at her side and bending over her. He was doing something with her skirt. She had white legs.

1

Andrew Moncur

Her arms came up to his neck. Slowly she lifted her knees. A sleeveless sweater floated through the air, falling soundlessly beside the blanket. A leather belt was flung away to the other side.

There was perfect silence in the bird hide. It stood a little over fifteen yards away, across the fringe of the marsh, in direct line with the sheltered bank where the couple moved, rose and sank together in the long grass.

The hide's front wall was cunningly concealed by brambles, spikes of gorse, buckthorn and weathered bundles of old thatching reeds. Inside it was deeply shaded, the observation window a narrow oblong of brilliant light. The red-bearded man, leaning over binoculars on a tripod at the front of the box, at last allowed his breath to escape in a long wheezing whistle. He turned and jerked his head towards the slit of light and the scene outside.

'Well?' he murmured. 'What do you reckon?'

There was a lengthy silence as a second man, standing closer to the back wall of the hide, squinted through a telescope. He was wearing a hat in speckled jungle colours. At last he looked up.

'I'm shocked,' he whispered. 'At any rate, bloody surprised.'

'Did you notice the rump?'

'Could hardly miss it.'

'It's more than just pink. You wouldn't say pink, would you? I mean, pink . . .' The bearded man shook his head.

'Do they breed here, Nigel? Does that happen?' asked the man in the hat.

'It's been known.'

There was a hoarse, animal moan from somewhere outside the hide; it was followed by a series of moist, marshy sounds.

'I'm sure about one thing,' said the birdwatcher in the jungle hat. 'It's definitely not the twite.'

'Twite? Oh, come on. You can forget the redpoll, too.'

'That's true, Nigel. We can rule out the redpoll.'

He adjusted his focus, trying to fix his attention on a point beyond the blurred, rounded pale shape that kept rising into the circle of his eye piece. It fell away, only to rise again – and again.

'Are we agreed, then?' asked Nigel.

'The scarlet rosefinch . . .'

The Harlot's Prerogative

'The camera, Keith. Let's have the camera.'

At that moment there was a curious, piercing cry. It was quite unlike the wicka-wicka of the bar-tailed godwit, the nasal buzzing of the trumpeter finch, the strangled gargle of a grey heron, the high *tew-it* of the rosefinch or the call of any other known bird.

He was a council estate dog. He had the broad head and the small, hot eyes of a bear; the black and tan coat looked like a worn carpet – or as a worn carpet might look if only a carpet could raise its hackles. The dog's lips curled back in a nasty grin, baring all its teeth. Its snarl sounded like the grinding of bones.

The young woman pushed her hands more deeply into her coat pockets. She had at some time stored away the scrap of knowledge that when a dog threatens to attack this is the best and safest place to keep them. She was now clinging to the hope that there might be something in it. The dog circled, stiff-legged, keeping its head low. It had been following her since she stepped out of her car on the approach road to the block of flats.

It was an extremely old dog which should have made her feel better, but didn't.

'Good boy,' she said soothingly. 'You great, slobbering, mangy, good dog.'

The woman stepped briskly under the shelter of the porch, dipped her shoulder and threw her slight weight at the double doors – only to rebound with jarring force. Her spectacles tipped and slid dangerously down her nose.

'Oof,' she said, which upset the dog. She pushed against the doors again, keeping her eyes on the animal and her hands in her pockets. The doors of reinforced glass hung heavily, barely rattling against their bolts. Glancing around, she saw that the entrance was secured by a number-coded lock and an entryphone. The bare brick hallway, seen through the glass, seemed an unattainable sanctuary.

The dog stood off and barked furiously. It was actually barking its own front feet off the ground.

Sheets of newspaper blew across the footpath and the muddy grass towards the estate road where she had parked; three skinny boys in replica club football shirts had appeared from a patch of nettles and

3

bramble across the way. A strip of yellow plastic sheeting was fluttering like a flag from the concrete post at the corner. The boys – they had now been joined by a fourth – were loitering near her car.

She hesitated, looking from the boys to the large dog to the entryphone. Finally she bent and pushed the tip of her nose against a button on the panel beside the door.

There was an electronic burr.

'Er, Sherbet,' a voice seemed to say, crackling from the speaker.

'Mrs Howell?' said the young woman, bending again to the entryphone.

'Wor dosay?' asked the voice.

'It's Ellen Bright. You're expecting me . . .'

'Ooo?'

'Bright.'

'Wassat warkin?' the voice replied.

'Sorry. It's the dog. I've come about the body. You know?'

'Wor?'

'The body in the lift . . .'

'Fuggit.' The line went dead. The doors to the entrance lobby remained implacably shut. The dog glowered; it had German shepherd in it and possibly a little of what was originally known as the Rottweil butchers' dog.

'Why don't you push off,' said Ellen Bright in a conversational tone. She stepped nimbly to the left as he danced in, bounced on the spot once or twice and then backed away again, snarling. His muzzle was quite white.

Ellen looked more closely at the entryphone pad and then, squinting with the effort of keeping her target in focus, pushed another button with her nose. Her fists were still in her pockets.

Her fingers were entwined with what she knew to be a cotton sock. She could not understand what it was doing there in the pocket of her waterproof.

The television monitor picked up the Member of Parliament for Walsingham just as he yawned, stretched back against the green leather-covered bench, laid an ankle across his knee and inserted a pencil in his ear.

The Harlot's Prerogative

His manner seemed to hint at a certain lack of interest in anything the Minister of Agriculture might have to say on any topic, at any time, to anybody.

He actually showed none of those vital signs normally associated with a viable life-form as the minister rose and spoke, responding to a private notice question on the outcome of a recent meeting of the European Union's fisheries council.

The MP remained inert, seeming to register not one syllable of the reply. The words washed over him, as the waters of the Gulf Stream flow past the migrating eel. All the while his eyes remained wide open but unseeing; observed from the far side of the chamber he appeared to be staring abstractedly at the back of the neck of the Member for Argyll and Bute.

Maurice Lovelace had found in the course of almost twenty years' public service that the back benches of the House of Commons provided ideal conditions for the marshalling of creative ideas. He did not, of course, have in mind anything touching on the life of the nation or its government.

The Commons chamber during the droning hours was the perfect place to prospect for, mine and refine his little nuggets of journalism. He was composing even as the fish question was thrashed out. The TV camera and the debate had both moved on before he suddenly appeared to come alive. He leaned forward and began to pencil a note.

'On the motorway of life,' he wrote, 'we can all be left crying on the hard shoulder of adversity. But when the spark of hope fires the crank shaft of recovery, then we can say: The high road is my road again.'

At the foot of this uplifting paragraph he scribbled the byline which had become a household name and a source of quiet inspiration for thousands of women. It was a rounded signature familiar to the many readers who had seen it reproduced over the years in their weekly magazine: 'Yours truly, Constance Verity.'

Miss Verity was more than a mere agony aunt. She was an advice columnist, certainly, but also a thinker of heart-lifting thoughts; a belletrist, a poet, a sage of the weekly magazine trade. She was infinitely better-loved and far more widely known than Maurice

5

Lovelace, the all but anonymous backbench MP who was her creator and her alter ego.

The thin woman put down her cup of tea on the low table. She picked up the packet of cigarettes and a plastic lighter and held them in her lean claw, as though for comfort. She coughed in a gravelly way.

Ellen Bright, sitting in the other armchair, tried to catch her eye.

'So, you were up here on the seventh floor, Mrs Howell, with your husband? Your late husband, I mean.' Ellen was half-turned awkwardly in the chair. She was neatly built – light and dark, as someone had once called her. (He meant she carried no excess weight and her hair was almost, very nearly, but not quite black.)

'You were both up here then on – let me see now – Monday, 4 May, the day he passed away. That was Dennis, wasn't it? Dennis Howell?' she asked, raising an eyebrow like a little question mark.

Mrs Howell held a cigarette between her lips, unlit, and looked away towards the corner of the room where the television was purring loudly. A commercial filled the big screen. Liquid mud, or possibly chocolate, was being poured in swirls. The volume had been slightly reduced which made the picture the more mesmeric.

A car alarm started to wail, then stopped abruptly. It may have been something happening outside the block of flats or, there again, perhaps on the TV. It was difficult to tell.

Ellen leaned forward in what was meant to be an encouraging manner. She glanced down to check that her tape recorder was running and then smoothed the page of the reporter's notebook on her lap.

'I'm sorry. I realise this must be very upsetting. But what I want to ask you is this: how did the undertaker's men come to lose your husband – your husband's body, that is – in the lift?'

Mrs Howell remained engrossed in the television picture of a child, a little girl, playing with pots and pans on a miniature cooking stove.

'I'm sorry,' said Ellen. 'Now, your husband. I mean, the corpse – Dennis – was, if I have the story straight, going up and down in the lift completely unattended. On a trolley.' She looked at the older woman in an anxious way.

The Harlot's Prerogative

'Terrible,' said Mrs Howell.

'Yes, I'm sure it must have been . . .'

'Really terrible.'

'I'm so sorry . . .'

'Wicked. The price of kiddies' toys. Look at that.' She gestured at the television with her still-unlit cigarette.

'I see,' said Ellen, stroking her cheek with her pen.

'I'm sorry, dear,' said Mrs Howell, 'but which magazine was it you said you work for?'

Chapter Two

The offices of *Home & Beauty*, on the thirty-second floor of the looming Mameluke Tower, enjoy a view of the River Thames so far-reaching and panoramic that some visitors, on seeing it for the first time, are physically sick. Others suffer severe giddy turns.

Below this level, editorial staff toil on sixty-one other titles owned by the great publishing group. Above this point reside the corporation's much-feared financial control and corporate management teams.

Between the two, in this high-level frontier zone, lies the group's sixty-second magazine: *Home & Beauty*, the award-winning women's weekly. It is invariably described in this way. The award was actually won in 1978, long before the magazine came into the ownership of Mameluke – in actual fact, some years before that publishing conglomerate itself was born, thrown together as a result of upheavals in the print industry.

It is no longer mentioned in and around the magazine that the award was given by the British Domestic Science and Food Hygiene Council for excellence in recipe research. It was, like so much else in the history of *H&B,* a modest success.

The colour scheme on floor thirty-two is pastel blue with a thin line of red here and there. At first glance the entrance lobby combines all the glamour of a branch office of some provincial building society with the solid substance of a TV studio set designed to last for a single election night.

That particular shade of blue is supposed to convey a quality of purposeful calm. It helps to soothe guests kept waiting in this public area, often for prolonged periods, before seeing journalists and others on the magazine's staff. In some instances, members of the public have been left to sit there in perfect peace for entire days, unnoticed, without ever seeing anybody at all.

The atmosphere surrounding the editor's office had been, in

contrast, highly charged and crackling with anxiety for almost forty-eight hours. The first unmistakable feelings of tension had arisen with the release of the latest audited circulation figures for all national magazines, an event which had been followed by a number of visits from managers descending, grim-faced, from the higher reaches of the tower.

'There's a terrible sound in there of heads rolling. It's like a ten-pin bowling alley,' said Muriel Oliver, the editor's secretary, making arch gestures towards the inner door with her neck and shoulders for the benefit of her young assistant. 'Believe me, Juliet, I've seen it all happen before. There'll be some very well-known names passing through this office – and some of them will be for the chop.'

Juliet Neckles did not look up from her tray, filled to overflowing with newly delivered mail.

'Blood on the wainscoting, as my old boss used to say.' Miss Oliver flared her nostrils dramatically. 'And not before time, if anyone wants to know what I think. Which is, I'm afraid, all too rarely the case around here.'

The day's canteen menu had been tucked under her telephone and she now examined it closely. She could not understand why the baked potato with salsa and cottage cheese had been omitted again, despite the note she had delivered only last Wednesday for the urgent attention of the canteen manager.

'Here's another of those letters from that funny woman,' said Juliet, holding up an envelope marked with the House of Commons portcullis symbol.

'If you mean Constance Verity, Juliet, then I think the appropriate words you are looking for are: "highly", "valued" and "contributor". Although, mind you, the old girl has been given the summons to appear here. She'll have to show her face in the office for once – which is a turn up. A remarkable thing. Unparalleled.'

In all her days at the magazine, Muriel had not once seen Miss Verity in the office. Contact with the columnist had always been by exchange of letters or messages sent by fax; she had a telephone answering machine but showed no sign of coming to terms with the personal computer and the modem.

Now, in her mind's eye, Muriel made a heavy black cross against

Andrew Moncur

Constance Verity's name on the list of *Home & Beauty*'s regular freelance contributors. If the chop was going to fall anywhere then, she thought, why not on that particular neck?

Juliet was still waving the envelope over her desk. The editor's secretary waved in reply, making little cutting-scissor gestures in the air with her fingers.

'It will be her editorial copy for the magazine. Very uplifting. It always arrives in one of those letters posted at the Houses of Parliament. Open it up and let's have a look-see.'

Juliet tore open the letter and unfolded the pencil-written note inside. She began to read, slowly and clearly: 'To: House of Commons Table Office,' it began. 'Question to the Prime Minister. From: Maurice Lovelace, Member (Con.) Walsingham and the Snorings:

'To ask the Prime Minister what are his engagements today (Thursday). And (supplementary) whether he has any plans to visit the Snorings (Great and Little) and Little (or New) Walsingham and Great (or Old) Walsingham, in North Norfolk, and, if so, whether he will note the current rates of water abstraction from the River Stiffkey and the state of aquifers in the region.'

Juliet's little voice trailed away. There was a moment's silence. 'I'm sorry. I don't find that very uplifting at all,' she said at last.

Ellen Bright replaced the telephone receiver and exhaled with a little whistle. Her cheeks felt warm.

It was a small but not insignificant success. She had just, at the third attempt, fixed a meeting. She would call in tomorrow and see the commissioning editor in the features department at *Home & Beauty* magazine.

The purpose was to sell her work. Ellen Bright made her living as a freelance by trading in a valuable commodity, known in the business as TOT. It is in demand throughout the magazine industry.

Triumph Over Tragedy is a class of upbeat, uplifting magazine story which demonstrates the power of the human spirit to overcome adversity. Articles of this sort deal with brave children and indomitable mothers, battling grannies and plucky victims, cruel fate and stoical dignity. They score with the readers by describing pain, courage, fortitude and eventual triumph – always triumph – without descending chest-deep into mawkish sentiment.

Good TOT writers move their readers without burying them in an avalanche of slush. They know their way around public disaster and private calamity; they recognise hard knocks and ultimate success against the odds.

Ellen Bright was on her way to *Home & Beauty* with the moving first-hand account of a widow's loss. Specifically, the unfortunate woman had mislaid her late husband's dead body.

'Do we have a Member of Parliament called Verity?' asked the clerk in the House of Commons Table Office, leaning on a desk heaped with tottering piles of bound copies of *Hansard*, parliament's official record.

'Called what, Barry?' asked his colleague, taking a crunching bite of apple.

'Verity. Constance Verity.'

'Very familiar name. Sounds like one of the Liberal Democrats,' said the second clerk, chewing thoughtfully. 'Somewhere down in Cornwall. Truro – or Tweeddale, Ettrick and Lauderdale. That sort of bollocks. What's the problem, anyway?'

'I don't think Tweeddale's in Cornwall.' Barry sounded genuinely puzzled. 'In fact, I'm absolutely sure it's not . . .'

His colleague tossed the apple core towards the black waste bin in the corner of the room. 'Why do you want to know?'

'It's in the stack of members' questions. There's one signed by Constance Verity. She's bunged in a question about, well, motorway hard shoulders and spark plugs. Something to do with emergency breakdown services, I suppose . . .'

'Does it make any sense?' The second clerk raised a quizzical eyebrow.

'No, not really. But, then, precious few of them do,' said Barry, probing in his pocket for a handkerchief.

'In that case, put it down as a question for the Secretary of State for Transport. Mark it "for written answer" and push it through with the rest of the rubbish.'

Chapter Three

Maurice Lovelace had been a contributor to *Home & Beauty* for twenty-odd years, a connection which had survived through the more or less troubled reigns of nine editors (one of whom occupied the chair twice) and no fewer than three changes of ownership. On several occasions it had seemed probable that the magazine itself would fold; at other times his column appeared to be facing the chop. Yet both had gone on through thick and thin, good times and lean.

They had both been pushed about and, from time to time, knocked into an entirely new shape – sometimes for better, sometimes for worse. In that sense, Mr Lovelace liked to say, it was very much like any other marriage.

He had been offered his first break as a penniless graduate. It came about through an act of kindness and shameless nepotism.

The young Lovelace had precious few strings to pull. He had grown up in the unsettled world of the British colonial exile bobbing on the final ebb tide of empire.

Maurice sometimes described himself as the last outpost of the British Empire. His father had been a policeman, serving first in East Africa – at Zomba, in Nyasaland – and later in Fiji. Finally, after the Fijians gained their independence, he had been posted to Grand Turk, the seat of government in the British dependent territory of the Turks and Caicos Islands.

It felt to the boy as if his mother had been lost along the way which was, more or less, what happened. He had only the most imperfect memories of a young woman – he could see her in black and white, shading her eyes from the sun, exactly as she must have appeared in scores of faded snapshots. She had been there in Africa, which meant any time up to his sixth birthday. He remembered journeys by truck and by train; he could recall swimming with her although he couldn't say where.

The Harlot's Prerogative

But then she had no place in his memories of Suva, where he had arrived about three weeks before his seventh birthday. She had not been with them on the flight; his father had briefly explained that she was in England, resting. It astonished Maurice in later years that he had been so accepting of this extraordinary turn. In reality, it said something about the relative importance of the nursemaid and the mother in the life of the colonial child. If the amah had been mislaid, Maurice would have been distraught.

A couple of years later, when it was time to be sent 'home' to school in England, it was made clear to him that his mother had a new life and a new family. He should not expect to see her again.

Maurice's upbringing had been a series of bewildering twists. All the securities and certainties of home came to be represented by the compound, the shaded veranda, the smiling black servants in the kitchen yard, the tropical night sky. The miseries of exile had come to mean England and school and the straitened regime of his aunt's cold, draughty house in a street of unimagined dullness on the western outskirts of Birmingham.

The life of Aunt Dolly, his father's only sister, had contributed to his sense of lost bearings. She was a pretty, flowery, sweet-scented woman. On the other hand, her friend Georgina – known as George – invariably wore a neat little suit, the trousers with turn-ups; she had laced black shoes, a starched collar, a tie with a Windsor knot and a dark beret. At night she would walk around the house in striped pyjamas, bed socks and a towelling dressing gown in vaguely regimental colours. In the garden at home George smoked a pipe. Her smoke-blackened briar, like the brogues, the pyjamas and the suits, always struck the boy as a perfect, scaled-down miniature. Even as a child, staying there during holidays from his preparatory school, Maurice had known that his aunt's household occupied some point of risk.

Once, by mistake, he had called George 'Uncle'. Georgina had looked pleased.

As the withdrawal from imperial outposts became a wholesale retreat, so the boy's feelings of loss and expulsion grew greater – and the more hopeless became his attachment to faraway places of which he knew nothing. For him there could be no sense of coming home. He was a displaced person, a refugee in his own land.

The years of separation had made him a lonely young man. His father soon seemed a distant stranger. The solitary colonial officer yearned for an England which had probably never been; the lonely boy longed for a place in the tropics as it could never be again.

The distance between the two of them was starkly exposed in the course of a single afternoon during his first year at public school. Maurice Lovelace would never forget it.

His father was on home leave and had fixed to visit the school to give his boy a day's outing. He was by this time an increasingly anxious and irritable man, ill at ease with his fellow countrymen and their incomprehensible attitudes. He couldn't understand their haircuts, let alone anything else.

At the agreed time Maurice, a skinny thirteen-year-old, was hanging back, keeping watch from a first-floor window. He was observing the arrival of parents – always in pairs – as the Jaguars and Rovers streamed through the gates and wheeled across the broad sweep of forecourt. There was a fine drizzle.

He saw his father and with a painful leap in his chest recognised the change in that lean, darkly tanned figure. Mr Lovelace stepped out on to the gravel immediately under his window; he stood for a moment beside the car and looked across the First XI cricket pitch. He was ageing. His back and shoulders had become gaunt; he was starting to stoop.

Maurice was about to run downstairs but stopped, transfixed, as the little scene unrolled before him.

'Ah, there you are,' said his father, catching sight of a boy named Medlicott who was walking along the neat edge of the lawn.

'Me, sir?' said Medlicott, looking over his shoulder to left and right.

'Yes, of course. Got your coat?'

'Yes, sir . . .' Medlicott flapped his hands in his raincoat pockets.

'Then jump in and we'll find somewhere for lunch.'

'But, sir . . .'

'Don't argue, boy. Just get in the bloody car.'

'Sir. Oh, sir . . .'

'For heaven's sake. I can't bear hanging around damned schools

14

and school masters. Come on. Chop, chop. Let's go.'

'Yes, sir.'

And Medlicott, obeying the adult command and his stomach's pleas for the chance of a square meal away from the grim simplicities of the school's junior dining room, opened the passenger door and jumped in.

'Don't keep calling me sir,' said Mr Lovelace.

'Yes, sir,' replied the youth. 'Sorry, sir.'

Maurice Lovelace did not move as the vehicle pulled away and headed down the long, tree-lined drive.

It transpired that during his lunch Medlicott had eaten steadily and answered in monosyllables, responding to the familiar parental questions in the way expected. There had been, he explained later, only one sticky moment.

'Dolly's in very good form,' said Mr Lovelace.

'Has the farrier done her shoes?' asked Medlicott, dropping his guard for a second.

'Farrier?' said Mr Lovelace, giving the boy a hard look. 'What on earth are you talking about?'

'Dolly. At Easter her hooves needed, well, trimming,' said Medlicott, suddenly feeling the chasm yawning wide at his feet but for the moment being unable to see another way to turn. 'Is she in foal?'

'Don't be an idiot, boy. Your aunt's been endlessly good to you. You shouldn't speak of her like that. She sends her love. She's a very loving aunt.'

'Sorry. So many aunts,' said Medlicott airily.

'You have an Aunt Dolly and that's it.' He stared at the boy again. 'Apart from dear Stella in Suva – although she's not your proper aunt, of course.'

'Suva, sir?'

'Oh, for goodness' sake. I'm pleased to see you're eating cheese at long last.'

'Cheese, sir?'

'Yes, cheese. You never could stand the stuff.'

'Aahh,' said the boy, his mouth full of cauliflower with a cheddar sauce.

15

'Good show. Just proves what an English public school education will do for a chap,' said Mr Lovelace. 'Knocks a bit of sense into a man, eh?'

On his return, when he was confronted by Maurice, young Medlicott decently handed over the five shillings which Mr Lovelace had given him as pocket money on parting. Maurice returned two shillings and sixpence. The boys would remain friends for the rest of their school careers and beyond.

'Did he mention anything I should know?' Maurice had asked when Medlicott was back at the school after the unexpected lunch.

'Do you have a horse at home? Called Daisy?'

'No. No, we don't. Why?'

'Oh, nothing,' said Medlicott. 'That's just the name of my pony.'

'Did my father say anything, you know, important?'

'Not a thing. He mentioned something really weird about cheese – but otherwise he just wanted to talk about cricket results.'

Later that week Maurice Lovelace wrote to his father, thanking him sincerely for the enjoyable exeat, the splendid meal and the pocket money of five shillings. Next February, he said, that would be worth twenty-five new pence in decimal coin.

Chapter Four

Maurice Lovelace, in the comforting form of Constance Verity, made his greatest contribution to magazine journalism by developing what he liked to call the Agony Aunt's Three Way Formula, a response to every conceivable problem thrown up by the reader. He calculated that any one of just three stock replies could be used to deal with virtually every question raised. In really complicated cases it might be necessary to use them in combination, but otherwise they would answer individually.

They were as follows.

Response Number One: reassurance. The reader had no cause for alarm; the condition described was completely natural. It was meant to be there. It was supposed to look like that. It was a normal part of adolescence. No, it would not stunt the growth. Yes, it was safe to do it more than once a month.

Response Number Two: guidance. Had the reader thought of seeing a doctor/counsellor/lawyer (delete as necessary)? No, what the reader described was not a reliable method of contraception. No, the act the reader described was not a normal thing for a man to expect his wife to do. Yes, it was still against the law in many countries. No, medical and psychosexual experts were not easily shocked. No, they wouldn't laugh. Perhaps the reader might try using a little petroleum jelly?

Response Number Three: rejection. The reader was thanked for putting those interesting thoughts in writing/photographs in the post. Unfortunately, it would not be possible to publish them in the foreseeable future. What a joy it was, though, to have had the chance to see the items now returned.

Constance Verity's use of this formula had helped to build her reputation as a pillar of strength for the readership and a ready source of help and down-to-earth advice.

There had been disasters, of course, when clerical errors had led to people receiving Response Number One when they ought really to have had Number Two, and vice versa.

For instance, an embarrassed thirteen-year-old from Merseyside was given the clearest possible guidance – which she carried with her into her late twenties – that kissing with tongues was illegal in many parts of the world and she ought really to see a therapist.

A forty-seven-year-old lady from Edinburgh who submitted examples of her most heartfelt poetry, asking Constance Verity for her comments on this verse, received a letter saying it was completely ordinary and reflected no more than the usual experience of the sexually inquisitive pubescent boy.

The vast majority of readers, though, were helped over some of the trickier hurdles of life.

Ellen Bright had grown up in a house where women's magazines provided a window to the world. They had been a path to discovery; she had picked up a great deal of theoretical knowledge about cooking and colour coordination and breast feeding and diets and eye make-up and Hollywood and how to make your man moan for more.

She then went off and rejected most of it, just as she turned her back on the combined wisdom of her own parents. It was all part of the awkward business of growing up, as the magazines frequently said in advice columns which awkward teenagers failed to read.

Ellen had been a happy little girl. All the family pictures showed her with a gappy-toothed smile; she was frequently holding a teddy bear whose head was back-to-front. His name was Nelson.

Her father's name was Jon. He was a distant, amused, sometimes faintly bitter man whose detachment had sometimes unnerved his children. As teenagers, Ellen and her two brothers had shared the uncomfortable feeling that they had in some way disappointed their father. He could be oppressively silent; the weight of his quietness had crushed the joy out of what should have been happy days – on holiday outings or around the birthday tea table. But then, from time to time, he could surprise everyone by overflowing with good humour, clowning in a ponderous way and running on with a string of his own absurd, cock-eyed jokes. The children's shrieking response on these occasions helped to disguise the fact that he had unnerved them once again.

He was a builder by trade. It was perhaps his misfortune that he had also inherited the responsibility of managing the family firm. Worse, he had done so at a time when the state of the economy was driving building companies to a wall not of their own construction. Mr Bright had taken over a fairly large and successful business and presided over its development, with a good deal of hard work and worry, to the point where it had become a fairly small business struggling to make ends meet. It was typical of the man that he gave himself no credit for seeing to it that the firm had survived at all.

When she was still young, Ellen had written to her mother's favourite magazine. 'What can I do to make a man happy?' she had asked.

The reply came back remarkably quickly, signed by Constance Verity. Ellen was puzzled by the reference to petroleum jelly.

Maurice had emerged from his education ill-fitted for any very useful career. It was inevitable that politics and journalism should have beckoned.

The men who taught him were cast in a mould that was already antique before he was born. They spoke of service and sacrifice and the flag – while the real world had tacitly agreed to let the sweating white man lay down his burden. They believed in British power and influence even as the ensign was being hauled down, the battleships were under tow to the breaker's yard and the space race was leaving them rooted to the ground. The boy made their convictions and their regrets his own. Everything conspired to see to it that Maurice Lovelace would emerge as a throw-back to the values of a previous generation. He had a romantic desire to enter politics, not to bring about change but, if anything, to halt it.

This solitary young man had no very clear notion of how to make a living beyond a half-formed idea of finding a way into television.

Fortune was kind. His closest friend since school days was the favoured nephew of Chesney Brimlow, then proprietor and publisher of *Home & Beauty* and half a dozen other titles. His magazines were in those days housed on three narrow floors above a wholesale book store just around the corner from Fleet Street.

It was in all honesty a cramped hole. The top floor was shared by a boxing newspaper and a cycling magazine; squeezed into one corner was a tenant, the London staff reporter of the *Aberdeen Courier*. The middle level was given over to a couple of women's magazines rooted in the nonconformist self-help tradition and an altogether gamier little photographic journal. It carried black and white shots of naked women, usually in groups playing games with beach balls in sand dunes.

Home & Beauty enjoyed a relatively spacious pair of rooms at first-floor level. Two further rooms on this level were occupied by a journal which interested Maurice Lovelace and his college friends very much indeed.

The Brimlow publishing business, although by then visibly decayed, possessed one title which mattered to them. *The Savant* was recognised as a political weekly with influence far exceeding its tiny circulation.

Young Lovelace had been introduced to Lord Brimlow before lunch during a weekend visit to his friend's family home in Hampshire.

'This is Maurice Lovelace, uncle. I mentioned him to you the other day. We were talking about the *Savvy*. Do you remember?'

'Remember,' said Lord Brimlow, looking down at a bus ticket he had found in his waistcoat pocket.

'Maurice is interested in that sort of stuff. It's a rough old game, I tell him. But he's terribly keen, poor chap.'

'Chap. Poor chap,' said his lordship, plucking nervously at a button.

'He was very much involved at the university. Became a bit of a bruiser. Took on all comers at the union. In the blue corner, naturally. Of course, he's now hoping to fix himself up with somewhere half decent to fight. It'll mean the usual slog, going the rounds.'

'Rounds,' said Lord Brimlow.

'Sooner or later he'll get a chance to fight some god-forsaken, no-hope, useless sort of a prospect. I tell him, don't worry. Don't throw in the sponge. You show your mettle and eventually you'll earn a chance to take a crack at something winnable. Wait and see when he gets into the ring.'

'Ring,' murmured the publisher. He started to tug at a thread on his jacket.

'Meanwhile, uncle, he's looking for a way to employ his formidable talents.'

At that point Lord Brimlow had risen from his chair and hurried from the room. He did not put in an appearance at lunch, an absence which passed without comment.

Three days later Maurice Lovelace received a hand written card from the managing editor at Brimlow House, in Magpie Court, inviting him to call there at his earliest convenience 'to discuss possibilities'.

Rex May was a slight, sharp man with a restless manner. He greeted Maurice with a strong handshake and a cool stare.

'So,' he said, 'I understand you want to work for *Health & Discipline* magazine. Or, as it's known in the trade, the *Self-Abuser's Gazette*.'

Lovelace sat motionless without uttering a word for a full twenty-five seconds. Eventually he cleared his throat. 'No, actually,' he croaked. 'Actually, no.'

'That's very odd,' said the managing editor, shuffling some notes which had been tucked under the edge of his blotter. He took a Senior Service from the box on the desk and tapped it on his thumb nail. His lighter flared up like a burning oil well. 'Lord Brimlow himself told me that you were keen on naturism. Photography. That sort of nonsense.'

'I'm not at all sure how...'

'His lordship said he was sending along two young men who had been personally recommended to him. One was some kind of heavyweight boxing blue, full of fight talk. He was supposed to be a suitable case for a job on the *Boxing Standard*. That obviously isn't you, is it?'

He looked Maurice Lovelace up and down and raised an eyebrow. Twin plumes of smoke emerged from his nostrils.

'And the other chap was supposed to fancy himself among the nudists. Is that not so? Am I wrong? Or what?' Rex May cocked his head and gazed at the young man.

21

'There's been some confusion,' said Maurice. 'I had been hoping to work on *The Savant* . . .'

'Oh, dear me, no. Out of the question. But there's another possibility. Do you think you could make a go of it on *Home & Beauty*?'

'I don't know the first thing about women's magazines.' Maurice was looking increasingly uneasy.

'Don't worry. Life on the average women's weekly is only slightly rougher than the *Boxing Standard*.'

He was kind enough not to mention that the last young man to be thrown to the *Home & Beauty* editorial department had lasted only a day and a half. He went off to join the Royal Marines.

Maurice lasted a little longer. Within the month his first column had appeared under the title 'On the town', with a block showing the head and shoulders of a person unknown, faintly resembling Noël Coward in the 1930 production of *Private Lives*. Or possibly Neville Heath, Bournemouth's most notorious multiple murderer.

Maurice's initial effort had been flung back, heavily slashed and scored.

'There's only one thing wrong with this,' said a sub-editor called Janice. 'It's utterly bloody unusable.'

'Oh, is that all?' he said. 'I thought it might be something serious.'

'For a start it's about eight times too long. We need 650, maybe 700 words maximum. Secondly, it doesn't say a single thing about what's on in town. Third, it doesn't appeal to women. Fourth, it's grossly defamatory and almost certainly libellous. You simply can't say these things.' Janice hurled back the copy. 'Otherwise, it's terrific.'

He smoothed out the crumpled page.

'Supposing I took out the word "frightful"?'

'Look,' said Janice, rolling a fresh sheet of paper into the typewriter. 'I'll show you how it's done.'

Only one other obstacle remained.

'Could you be a woman instead?' asked Janice.

'If necessary,' Maurice replied.

'Then how about – let's see – Constance? Constance something. Something which suggests strength and trustworthiness.'

'Constance Eisenhower?'

The Harlot's Prerogative

'Not totally catchy, Maurice.'

In later years he came to believe that the reason Constance Verity's career lasted so long was that the author had stayed away from the office. For nearly two decades Constance had not set foot inside the place, preferring as far as possible to keep herself – and her true identity – strictly to herself.

Chapter Five

The blackbird tilted his head and poured a beakful of song across the shrine garden. He paused, turning a bright eye towards the woman who had now come to a halt on the path beside the lawn. Then he blinked twice and started to pick out his tune again.

The bird was singing, with great purity, the opening bars of 'These Foolish Things'. He appeared to be beating time with one horny little foot.

'That bird,' said Mrs Wade, taking three awkward, hobbling steps and catching at her husband's sleeve. 'That bird is whistling – oh, you know – that song . . .'

'Hold on,' said Mr Wade. He half turned, reached for her arm and placed his free hand confidently in the small of her back. It was a reassuring, habitual gesture; for a few seconds the couple looked like old time dance partners. Mr Wade glanced away over his wife's shoulder, staring at something in the remote distance. 'Gently, gently,' he murmured.

'No. It's that taxi song. It goes: Dee-da-dee something, something, dee-da taxi,' she said. Mrs Wade's head was shaped like a cottage loaf; she had a round, dimpled chin and her hair was caught up on top in a clump held in place by an elastic band. Her face was a patchwork of pink and white. Her shoulders and backbone were rounded – almost humped – and in an arc the pale skin there had been sunburnt to a painful shade.

'And, look! Look at him. Would you believe it? Now he's doing a little dance!'

Mrs Wade leaned heavily on her husband's arm. She had an uncomfortable gait, rolling from the hips and taking four or five small steps for each of her husband's. Her knees were swollen and around the thickened ankles her skin appeared mottled and tightly stretched. Her canvas shoes seemed inadequate for their burden. She was struggling for breath.

24

The Harlot's Prerogative

'It's a singing and dancing blackbird,' said Mrs Wade in a faint little voice.

'Really?' Her husband made a noncommittal throat-clearing noise and peered at his wristwatch.

The pair, arm-in-arm, turned the corner at the end of a hedge and came to a standstill. Three tall timber crosses, each set at a slight tilt away from the others, loomed up from a flower bed. Beyond the three crosspieces they could glimpse a figure of gold – an angel, almost certainly – perched on top of a tall red-brick tower with louvres. It was a gilded weather-vane. The tower itself was difficult to place. It might have been a church belfry in Tuscany or, possibly, a disguised factory chimney.

The angel and the crosses, closer to hand, were outlined against a sky of the brightest blue.

Mrs Hilary Wade and her sixty-two-year-old husband, Neville, had arrived at the twelfth of fifteen Stations of the Cross, symbolising stages in Christ's passion, which greet pilgrims visiting the garden at the shrine of Our Lady of Walsingham.

They had come in the hope of finding if not exactly a miracle, then some form of healing or relief. Hilary Wade eased her painful right ankle and took a shuddering, deep breath. Any fool could tell, and any doctor would confirm, that Neville was not a well man.

Duncan Murray unwrapped the tube of fruit gums and slipped the first, a black one, into his mouth. As he approached his car, parked in front of a half-timbered house in the Common Place, the vehicle's central locking system picked up his signal and threw itself open with a satisfying whine and a clunk.

It felt as though he had opened the door of an oven. He reached inside to drop his jacket and a blue folder on the passenger seat and then walked around to the far side of the car, tugging his damp shirt away from his back and loosening his tie. A blanket of warmth embraced him as he slid into the driver's seat, already reaching for the ignition to lower the windows. It was amazingly warm for a day so early in the year.

He pressed a button on the radio. The speakers bathed the car in choral music that he recognised but could not for the moment name.

Andrew Moncur

With one hand he wound back the sunshine roof; with the other he reached for his packet of fruit gums again.

It was another black one. What flavour was that exactly? He didn't know for sure what the taste was, apart from black. Smiling at himself in the rearview mirror, he took the fruit gum between his front teeth and idly waggled it.

Then he fastened his seat belt and, looking down, slipped the automatic into reverse gear.

He neither saw nor heard the nun step from the pavement and start to cross immediately behind his car. Her young face was partly obscured by her wimple. Her full black habit swished with energy as she walked rapidly towards the centre of the road running diagonally across the small square.

It was still and hot. Nobody else stirred. The nun's black rubber-soled shoes made no sound on the gravel strip or the tarmac as she reached the middle of the road. Sun caught the windows of the Shrine Shop and the row of ancient timber-framed houses lining the far side of the square. He touched the accelerator.

The impact was shocking. It was an appalling, sudden clap of solid sound. There was a terrible wallop of firm flesh on metal panels. Afterwards Mr Murray would be able to remember a cry, a high-pitched shout of anger, above the metallic boom.

He ducked, shrinking from the blow. One foot, unbidden, slammed down on to the brake pedal. The other simultaneously hit the floor. His knuckles tensed on the steering wheel and his elbows locked rigid, holding the wheel at arm's length. He was already staring into the mirror in alarm, drenched with surprise, before the reversing car had juddered to a halt with its rear end angled into the road.

The blue folder had flown open, throwing order forms and computer paper to the floor. On the back seat his neatly boxed samples slid into confusion.

The nun had brought down her open palm with a tremendous over-arm slap on the lid of the car boot.

Now she leaned into the driver's window. Her mouth was a line of compressed fury. For a moment the young man and the sister regarded one another, inches apart. Mr Murray realised at last that

The Harlot's Prerogative

Vivaldi's *Gloria* was playing on the radio. It was the soft and gentle *Et in terra pax hominibus*.

'Why don't you bloody well look where you're bloody well going?' said the nun at last, spitting out the words with concentrated anger.

'Thank God,' whispered the young man indistinctly. The last fragment of fruit gum was stuck to the roof of his mouth.

Chapter Six

The women sat plumply side-by-side behind a desk apparently moulded from pink seaside rock. One leaned back, resting her bosom on her folded arms. The other, younger woman was laboriously writing on a slant across a desk pad stamped with the Mameluke Magazines Corporation logo. Her lips made a tight little cupid's bow; it looked like a valve for inflating her soft, fleshy cheeks.

The older woman peered down and picked a cotton thread from her blouse. 'Then Nicola asks about the sex. She knew that Derek would like the cameo colour – but only if it was a girl,' she said.

'What name?' asked the younger receptionist, tilting her chin defiantly at the visitor standing before the counter. Maurice Lovelace noted that her eyes looked angry, simmering with some non-specific resentment.

'Verity,' he replied, bending his long frame slightly over the desk. 'Constance.' He gave her a generous, perhaps excessively generous, smile. The woman's perfect little mouth closed a fraction more firmly.

She bent over the pad again, her nose almost touching its surface. Her lips were moving silently as she wrote in a large, childish hand in the space reserved for the visitor's name: 'Verity Constance . . .'

'To see?' she asked. And then, slowly, as though speaking to an idiot: 'Who? Who have you come to see?'

The other receptionist at the desk cleared her throat and reached into her sleeve for a paper tissue. 'But they was all boys,' she said. 'The girl was grey and black which wasn't what Derek wanted. He wouldn't have the boys, not even if they was castrated. Good afternoon. How may I help you?'

The new arrival had erupted from the revolving door and burst headlong into the reception hall. She was barely holding on to an untidy armful of newspapers, magazines and a sliding bundle of manila folders. If anything, she seemed to be propelled forward by this heap. 'Sorry,' she was saying. 'Sorry, sorry.'

Her bag was dangling from one hand by its useless, broken strap. The pile of paperwork hit the desk top fractionally before the young woman herself smacked into contact with the pink moulded rim. A sheaf of paper and photocopies started to cascade across the counter before she could snake out a restraining arm. The man bent to pick up a file held together by a rubber band.

'Sorry.' She found a spare finger and pushed her spectacles back on to the bridge of her nose.

The tall man at the counter gave her a friendly smile and held out her file. She was momentarily disarmed. She had, like many women of the age, a range of prepared defences. She could chill with a glance; stop a runaway truck with a stare of concentrated scorn. Men, complete strangers, could feel disconcerted for days by a single look of pitying, withering contempt. And then this man smiled at her.

'What's the name, dear?' The receptionist dabbed at the pink tip of her nose with the tissue. Then she reached across to take the pad of entry passes from her colleague, who was stabbing at the telephone with a finger like a pale sausage.

'Ellen Bright.' She enunciated with the care born of a lifetime spent being mistakenly called Helen. She pushed the dark hair out of her eyes.

The receptionist's ballpoint crawled across the pad. 'L.N. Bright,' she wrote.

'I'm running late. Sorry...'

'Yes, dear. And have you come to see anybody in particular – or did you just drop by to chuck an armful of wastepaper around the place?'

Afternoon sunlight streamed through the immense glass panels and spread across the cool marble floor. The pudding-faced receptionist held the phone to her ear and coiled a length of hair around her index finger. She glanced up at the waiting man and looked away.

'Muriel?' she said into the mouthpiece at last. 'Reception here. Are you expecting a visitor? It's a – where are we?' She stretched out to retrieve the desk pad. 'Oh, all right. I'll do that small thing. All part of the . . .' She suddenly held the phone away from her ear and glared at it angrily. 'Rude cow!'

She ripped the pass from the pad with venomous force. It was folded with four slamming movements into the clear plastic envelope of a lapel badge. This in turn was thrust at the tall, dark-suited man as though it were meant to do him an injury.

Maurice Lovelace clipped it to his jacket pocket and, without looking back, stepped briskly across the grey marble floor towards the distant line of lift doors.

The sound of voices – of one voice, at least – was audible before the lift opened. The noise level rose as the doors slid apart, heaved on their way by a large hand sparking with brilliant-cut stones, a gold chain and nails polished like fat beads of newly drawn blood.

'. . . this side of the uterus. Don't take my word for it, I told her. The man's a complete aboriginal.' The woman, giving the door a final impatient shove, stepped out of the lift. She hitched the patterned shawl over her shoulder and at the same time swung her briefcase with a solid smack into the thigh and groin region of the short man who followed her into the lobby.

'Yes, Gwen,' he said. He was a sandy, pale shadow of a man and the low blow seemed to make him buckle at the centre.

'Remind me to give Sheila a bollocking,' boomed the woman, surging ahead. 'If there's one thing I can't abide it's carrot cake. Moist sawdust.'

'Right, Gwen.'

Ellen Bright had recognised the voice long before its owner came into view, following it across the marble entrance hall. There was something overwhelmingly solid about Gwen Lightsome's figure; densely packed corned beef, she thought. Ellen ducked her chin, hoping to avoid eye contact.

'Helen! Darling!' the large woman bawled.

'Oh, Christ,' Ellen murmured.

'Helen! What brings you here?' She was bearing down rapidly, bullocking towards the front desk. The two receptionists exchanged sour little mouth-pulling faces then pointedly looked away.

The Harlot's Prerogative

'It's Ellen, Gwen. Ellen. Not Helen.' She smiled diffidently.

'My sweet! It's been ages. What are you doing here at the House of Correction? Something intelligent, I hope.'

'Oh, you know. I'm freelancing now. I've come to put a few feature ideas to . . .'

'How long is it, darling? Four, five years? God, how time flies. I want to hear exactly what you've been doing.' She was looking beyond Ellen's shoulder to the point where her taxi should have been waiting.

It had been just over five years since they worked together on the evening newspaper in Liverpool. It had been Gwen Miller in those days, a name which had spawned a thousand weak jokes about big bands. As Gwen Lightsome, her married name, she had been reborn. She had gone on to become one of the nation's more forthright agony aunts, with a full-page advice column in *Woman's Week* and her own late-night television phone-in.

'Gwen,' said the pale, freckled man at her elbow. 'We're running late.'

'Thank you, Reggie. Busy, busy. Rush, rush, rush.'

'You must be going full pelt all the time,' said Ellen.

'I'm sure you know what it's like, darling. Bloody telly. Book-signings. Radio. Desert wretched Island thingies.' Gwen adjusted her shawl again. 'Still, people expect you to put yourself on the line, don't they? They want you to give a little.'

Ellen shrugged, a helpless sort of gesture.

'Look, my love,' boomed Gwen, touching her on the wrist. 'My dear. Terrific to see you. We really must have lunch.'

'But it's nearly twenty past four . . .'

There was a prolonged and uneasy silence.

'No, I mean we must have lunch – sometime.'

'Oh, I see,' said Ellen, grateful to know that they would never, in fact, be required to eat together at all.

'Give me a call, won't you. We can have a proper heart-to-heart. You can tell me about . . . all about everything.' Gwen was already heading for the street door, followed by the bobbing figure of wispy Reg, her husband and the iron hand behind her thundering success.

She stopped just short of the door and turned to call across the

Andrew Moncur

---

hallway: 'Love everything you write, Helen. Keep reading your byline.'

'Balls,' said Ellen quietly, waving in reply. Then she patted her visitor's badge, picked up her bundle of papers and turned towards the lifts.

When Ellen Bright arrived by lift at the pale blue entrance hall, on floor thirty-two of the Mameluke Magazines' office block, she was still fighting for control of her bundles of newsprint and her files packed with research notes.

She stepped out of the lift, holding her chin clamped hard down on the pile of paper; her view was restricted to a narrow glimpse of the landing's short-pile carpet which, she noted, had been woven in an extremely soothing shade.

She took half a dozen steps to the left. Then, catching sight of a low sofa at the extreme range of her peripheral vision, veered back to the right. She dropped the entire armful on to the seat with relief. Then she looked up and took in her surroundings for the first time.

It was unfortunate that she was, at that moment, facing the enormous window and its unbroken view over the rooftops, the fabulous spires and towers, of the Palace of Westminster and then far away across the south-eastern reaches of Greater London. The huge panorama stretched under a dramatic sky towards the Thames river flats and the distant commuter towns, motorways and fruit orchards of Kent. The entire world just fell away at her feet. All her senses plunged into this awful chasm, gaping endlessly before her. Any trust in the tower block to provide a secure foothold instantly deserted her. She was in mid-air, battered by the wind and teetering over cloud-rimmed space.

Ellen fainted. There and then, with all of London at her feet, she fell down in a heap. It was as if her slender legs had simply given up the struggle against the forces of gravity.

Far below, in a street of Victorian terraced villas and relatively new yellow brick maisonettes near the Elephant and Castle, a horse-drawn carriage arrived precisely at its appointed time. It had come to pick up from his embassy and official residence His Excellency

32

The Harlot's Prerogative

Dr Seraphim Anchaos, the newly appointed ambassador extraordinary and plenipotentiary of the Democratic Republic of
Tartaristan to the Court of St James.

Dr Anchaos represented the interests of his nation, the former
soviet republic, from a semi-basement flat halfway along on the
left, or north, side of Lammas Street. The embassy lies almost exactly
at the point where Newington meets the Borough, a district not
generally favoured by members of the diplomatic corps. In fact, it
is safe to say that this locality remains unknown to every other
accredited diplomat in London, with the exception of both staff at
the legation of the Republic of Nauru.

They happen to use a shoe repair shop and heel bar across the
way on the far side of Lammas Street.

The reason for this arrangement has been long forgotten by all
concerned.

The explanation is, in fact, that the first native Nauruan to visit
the United Kingdom, after the island was declared a British man-
dated territory in the immediate aftermath of the Great War, became
romantically attached to the elder daughter of the then owner of
the boot repair shop.

The islander was unable to prolong his stay or his suit but
continued for several years to post parcels to his friend in London.
He wished to send her recognisably Nauruan gifts but unfortunately
the island's sole export was then, as it is now, phosphates. So,
instead, he regularly posted to her tins of Australian pineapple
chunks.

This traffic had to be halted during the Second World War when
shipping was disrupted; rises in postal charges made it prohibitive
to start up the parcel service again when peace resumed. But later,
when Nauru was admitted to membership of the Commonwealth,
the faithful islander – by now a distinguished elder – arranged for
the infant republic's representative in London to deliver by hand
one more consignment of tinned fruit.

This good man made his way to Borough High Street – only the
second Nauruan in recorded history to venture on this journey –
and eventually found the cobbler's shop. Sadly, the original owner
and his daughters had departed many years before; the woman

who had been the object of this long-running attachment had married, of all people, the postman and moved to Stevenage New Town.

The bearer was unable to present his gift of pineapple chunks but did, however, take the chance to have new heels fitted to his black slip-on shoes. Succeeding members of the legation staff were, in turn, informed of the cheerful service available at the shop. They continued to patronise it down the years.

His Excellency Dr Anchaos, the Tartaristani ambassador, had in contrast never visited the shoe repairer's although it was just across the road from his residence. Indeed, the heel bar staff had an excellent view of the horses, the carriage and the liveried coachmen arriving at his door.

Dr Anchaos was on his way to present his credentials at Buckingham Palace.

Chapter Seven

The Golden Gong children's bravery awards ceremony had been taking place throughout the afternoon at St Margaret's, Westminster, only a stone's throw from the Mameluke Tower. The guest of honour was Her Royal Highness the Duchess of Kent. Word quickly spread through the small crowd gathered outside the north gate that a major celebrity was inside the church.

As the duchess led the guests from the building, cameras started flashing and a television crew was soon trampling on the flower beds. They homed in on the greatly loved figure one onlooker described as 'a real, dignified lady'.

'Gwen! Gwen! Look over here, love,' the photographers shouted. Gwen Lightsome, the celebrated agony aunt, smiled for the cameras in an unassuming way.

The awards ceremony was organised every year by *Woman's Week*. It was a way of acknowledging the outstanding courage of a couple of dozen boys and girls – they had, in almost all cases, behaved bravely in the face of domestic disaster or terrible illness – while also bumping up the flagging circulation of the women's magazine.

'Dear me,' said the duchess to the large woman on her left while the photographers snapped and whirred. 'Those television people seem to have knocked over that very unfortunate little boy with the runny nose . . .'

'Yes,' said Gwen Lightsome, glancing at her list of child award winners. 'He hasn't got a caliper on his leg, has he? No. Here we are. That's Liam, the have-a-go hero from Doncaster.'

'He doesn't look very heroic at the moment, poor lamb,' said the duchess.

'I expect he's overawed by the occasion.'

'Shouldn't somebody do something about him?'

'Of course, ma'am. Right away,' said Gwen, turning and fixing her personal assistant with a terrible glare.

'Kirsty,' she hissed as soon the young woman had hurried to her side. 'Kirsty. Get that snivelling little specimen cleared away immediately, will you. It's ruining the picture line up. Quickly now.'

'Thank you, my dear,' said the duchess, touching Gwen's wrist as the weeping child was enveloped and swept out of sight.

'Oh, no. Thank you, your Royal Highness. Thank you so very much for pointing out the – I mean, yes, the problem.' Mrs Lightsome was bending so low she practically rested her nose on the pavement, as one of the picture snappers later put it when describing the events of his interesting day.

Chapter Eight

Maurice Lovelace, the visitor's pass clipped to his breast, felt the lift floor rise at express speed beneath his feet. His stomach experienced a moment's faint misgiving.

Half turning, he examined his reflection in the lift's mirror wall. His eyes looked more and more like boiled sweets these days. It suddenly occurred to him that given long legs, a lean frame and a dark pinstripe suit a man could easily be mistaken for a walking bar-code. While his figure was no longer exactly boyish, he could at least describe himself as being in a state of controlled decline. And yet, if this was the way a parliamentarian was supposed to look, then it was a parliament which had been through too many all-night sittings.

He stared at the ceiling. Then, feeling himself safely unobserved in the flying wardrobe of a lift, he danced a few steps and pulled a face like a horse. 'Absolutely marvellous,' he boomed out loud. 'Why not? Why bloody not?'

As Constance Verity had put it so very succinctly in a recent magazine piece: *'If you can't laugh at yourself, don't worry. Everybody else will.'*

It was an extremely rare and so exciting event for Miss Verity to get out and about in this way, making herself available for a meeting with her editor. Throughout the years of her successful career in print she had preferred to conduct all transactions at arm's length. Her alter ego had no notion why this urgent request had now been made for her to appear in person.

His decision had been spontaneous. Why not take Miss Verity up to town for once? They had never before set foot inside the Mameluke building; it was a visit long overdue – and it would be a wonderful surprise to introduce the magazine staff to the true author of the column, so devotedly followed by their readers.

The real identity of Constance Verity had once, in the dim and distant, been known to an editor of *Home & Beauty*. But over the years, with the arrival of each successive holder of that post, Maurice had become less and less inclined to trouble them with tedious details about Miss Verity's life beyond the magazine. After a while they came to believe that she was some kind of hermit enjoying her seclusion. Her copy always arrived on time and to within a word or two of the agreed length; she made no demands, had no temperament, threw no tantrums. Everybody was happy.

He had telephoned the editor's secretary the previous day, told her that he was calling on behalf of Miss Verity and confirmed that she would be pleased to visit the office. In person. His message had been received with gratifying sounds of surprise and pleasure.

What was the meaning of this summons? Possibly it meant an offer of some new deal; another book, maybe. Constance had enjoyed modest bordering on notable success with *A Lot Of Kisses On The Bottom*, her anthology of love letters. She had made the best-seller list with her collection of inspirational *mots justes*, *Come Inside, Love*.

The lift hissed on its way towards the extreme heights of the tower block.

'What's her name, Juliet?' asked Miss Oliver.

Her assistant was kneeling on the blue carpet in the *Home & Beauty* reception area, looking down at the young woman who lay there, motionless, on the floor. The body was stretched out between the waiting-room sofa and the big window with its amazing view across the London skyline.

'No idea,' said Juliet. 'I've never seen her before in my life.'

'The name's on the visitor's badge. On her lapel, Juliet. Yes, that's it.'

'It says Verity Constance,' whispered Juliet, as though afraid of waking the woman from her swoon. 'Wasn't he a country singer? Or did he play cricket?'

Muriel Oliver gave a little snort.

'It's a woman,' said the youth from the post room. He had found the visitor in a faint and raised the alarm; now he was loitering at the scene.

38

The Harlot's Prerogative

'Thank you, Troy. I think we had noticed that. Yes, we've taken a second opinion and, you're right, she is a woman. Well done.' Miss Oliver made elaborate eyebrow-raising, face-pulling and strangling gestures visible only to the kneeling Juliet. The young woman lying on the floor stirred and moaned softly.

'This is a VIP,' said Muriel. 'Or at least an MIP. And, I'm telling you, I am amazed. She's incredibly well preserved, considering . . .'

'MIP?' said Troy.

'A moderately important person, Troy.' Miss Oliver rolled her eyes at Juliet.

'Let's move her into the ladies'. Pick up her spectacles. There, by the wall. Right. Here we go . . . No, we can manage very well without your help, thank you, Troy. Haven't you got some post to deliver?'

The lift with its solitary burden was climbing up and away from the editorial floors housing *Woman's Sphere, Hiya!, Perfect Home, New Slimming Express* and their sister magazine, *Country Wife.*

Swiftly and unseen, it passed in succession the cluttered offices of *Practical Fretworker, True Passion, Poultry Farmer's Times, Top TV Chat, Horse & Garden* and *Mother's Own,* a weekly journal so elderly in style, content and readership profile that the words 'orgasm', 'sex romp' and 'ten ways to make him moan for more' had started to feature prominently on its front cover only within the past eighteen months.

Their first appearance had come at almost the exact moment the magazine's more aggressive rivals had finally decided to ditch sex as their paramount topic and, at long last, to try exploiting something else in their restless pursuit of sales and market share.

This did not, however, mean that sex had stopped happening altogether. From time to time, passion and intrigue, full-blooded enough to interest even the readers of *Mother's Own,* occurred within the great Mameluke Magazines' building itself. At present, for instance, the chief sub-editor of the *British Pig Breeder,* a bimonthly, was widely known to be enjoying steamy sex romps with the associate editor of *Vegetarian Digest.*

The affair had been uncovered because of their injudicious

exchange of intimate messages on the editorial computer system, usually in the form of anguished queries about where they might possibly get together to eat. And what.

The lift ascended, gliding by corridors and landings worn smooth by the passage of hurrying art editors, page-planners and cookery picture arrangers. In stairwells and behind fire doors furtive smokers heard the whine of the lift's motor and the murmur of its passage.

Each floor had its own waiting room and reception area decorated in more or less stomach-turning colours chosen by design consultants and hung with framed covers of the magazines which were created there. So *Classic Saloon Car's* glossy artwork was displayed beside the muted – or, indeed, camouflaged – title pages of *Rod & Field Weekly. Country Home Beautiful* tried hard to outshine its neighbours.

One floor above, *Gardener's Realm* lived in a state of uneasy truce with *Geewhiz*! One floor below, *Caravanning Week* rubbed shoulders with *My Date* and beyond that, in a particularly untidy office which seemed always to be drenched with the scent of almonds, *Hairdressing & Styling Today.*

The lift gave a final surge, slowed and gently came to rest, opening its doors with a sigh.

Maurice Lovelace peeked out, uncertain whether he had in fact arrived at his intended destination.

The reception lobby was decorated in a slightly bilious shade of cooking-apple green. Framed title pages looked down in a blaze of shining eyes and teeth. He recognised none of them.

'Here to see the boss?' The young man's receding hair was pulled back into a pony-tail; his pointy teeth and round spectacles gave him a rodent-like appearance. He was wearing a pale yellow linen jacket and trousers which might have been made from black plastic bin liners.

'Well, yes, I suppose . . .' Maurice placed one highly polished shoe on the landing in the way of a swimmer putting an experimental toe in the water. The boss-word was still capable of bringing him out in a clammy sweat; it had done so since the period he still privately called the Thatcher Terror. He had never been able to

The Harlot's Prerogative

understand the boss; she had shown no interest whatsoever in understanding him – at that time a junior backbencher. In one three-year period she had spoken to him on only a single occasion, upbraiding him in public during a party conference with the puzzling words: 'You were wrong on every count about Spitzbergen. Wrong, wrong, wrong!'

This had worried him greatly at the time. He could not recall ever having expressed an opinion one way or the other about Spitzbergen; indeed, he wasn't entirely sure where Spitzbergen was, beyond knowing that it was a winter sports resort somewhere in the Alps. He had felt compelled later that day to visit the reference library in Bournemouth, close to the conference centre, to look it up in an atlas. Maurice had been astonished to discover that in actual fact it was a Norwegian island group in the Arctic Ocean.

It was later suggested by friends that the prime minister had mistaken him for the political editor of the *Sunday Telegraph* who had an obsessive interest in Nato's northern flank. Ever after, the same friends made a point of greeting Maurice by saying: 'You know, you were utterly wrong about Spitzbergen . . .'

'Capital skiing, Prime Minister!' he would reply – as he had done in the first instance, all those years before, when originally taken to task by Mrs Thatcher.

They had been long years during which his political career had not prospered; a Sargasso Sea of ambition, as he used to say to close colleagues.

The change of regime, when it came, brought promotion and the sweet burdens of office for another set of rising stars. For Maurice Lovelace MP the front bench, the ministerial car, the call to the *Any Questions?* panel and the *Newsnight* studio had all remained elusive dreams.

'I'm considerably bothered by gilt, you know,' John Major had said to him once when their paths crossed by chance in the House of Commons tea room.

'Oh, you don't want to worry yourself about that, PM. We all have a bad conscience about something or other. Some skeleton in the cupboard. Usually a woman,' Maurice had replied with a great rush of kindly feeling.

'I mean the gilt market. Gilt-edged securities,' Mr Major had said, giving him a strange look.

And so it had gone on; a slow process of experience triumphing over hope.

'Hey. You come from that madhouse across the river?' The young man with the pony-tail was now up on his feet.

'Yes, I have. In a manner of speaking,' said Maurice.

'And you're the Conservative, elder statesman type?'

'Well, you could say so. Yes.'

The rat-faced man visibly brightened. 'Praise the Lord. I've been stuck here over an hour waiting for you to show. Would you mind moving your arse, as the bishop said to the actress. This way.'

'Now, hold on . . .' said Maurice, following him through a pair of doors and into another apple-green corridor. He bridled at being ordered around in such an offhand way by this young person. He was, after all, a long-serving if not especially prominent, or even known, Member of Parliament. More to the point, and in this building of all places, he was the man behind one of Britain's most celebrated bylines. He *was* Constance Verity. He had come to see the editor, as a senior, respected contributor. And here he was being told by this vole-faced youth to move his arse. The mother of all parliaments herself had been referred to as a madhouse.

He could feel his gorge rise. He started to become aware of his spleen; his gall and very probably its attendant bladder began to be vexed.

'Do you know who I am?' he asked. He had never knowingly used the words before and surprised himself by doing so now.

'Do you know who I am?' This time he said it more firmly.

'No, can't say I do,' the young man called over his shoulder as he hurried on. 'But I know your agent, of course.'

'You do?' Maurice Lovelace was genuinely astounded. Old George Tatham had been a political agent for almost thirty-five years. He was well known and respected in East Anglia, naturally enough, but it seemed incredible that his reputation should extend to London's media fleshpots. George was a large, shambling man, a pipe smoker, fond of dogs; in fact he bred rather good cocker spaniels. He had been informally engaged to the same woman for at least fourteen years.

'How on earth do you come to know him?' Maurice asked as they moved smartly along.

'He supplies us with lots of girls. He's particularly good for the lingerie end of the business. Boobs, bums, suspenders, naughty knickers, leather – you know the sort of thing.'

Maurice Lovelace stopped and reached out to touch the corridor wall. 'Girls?' he repeated in a hollow voice. 'Suspenders?'

'That's right.'

'Leather? Leather *knickers*?'

'Models, models, models. Can't get enough of them. They pass through here like a sausage factory. Which is why we need good reliable blokes like your man.' He had hurried ahead and was waiting by the door.

'Are you absolutely sure?'

'Oh, come on. He has good girls on his books. And, of course, boys – including older ones like yourself. The distinguished look. Hah!' He pushed open the door, revealing a bare cubicle. 'Right. If you'll just dive in here and get your clothes off, I'll let Jenny know you've arrived.'

'Hello,' said Juliet, the assistant secretary, dabbing at the young woman's temples with a soggy paper tissue. 'Do you know where you are?'

'Oh, God,' said her patient. 'There was a terrible drop in front of me. I thought I was going to fall.'

'And who are you? What's your name? Do you remember?'

'It's Ellen Bright,' said Ellen Bright, sitting up straight and brushing down her skirt.

'No. No. Your name. That's not right,' said Juliet, a note of anxiety creeping into her voice. The visitor's badge was quite clearly visible.

'I've got a great story. About a corpse being abandoned in a lift. Going up and down like a yo-yo.'

'Oh, dear,' said Juliet, wishing that she had paid more attention at her first aid course to the needs of people suffering memory loss and, quite possibly, brain damage.

Andrew Moncur

* * *

'Can we just run through this again, sir?' said the overweight man in the navy blue uniform of the Mameluke Magazines' internal security staff. He had loosened his tie but the bristling rolls of chin still spilled over his collar. 'Now, you deny being a male model? Am I right?'

'Yes, that is precisely correct . . .' Maurice Lovelace ran a hand through his hair, which was looking increasingly dishevelled.

'Despite the fact that you talked your way into *His* magazine in the first place by claiming to be a . . .'

'I didn't have the faintest idea it was his magazine!'

'No, not his magazine. It's *His* magazine.'

'Well, I certainly didn't talk my way in anywhere,' said Maurice in a pained voice.

'Let's say you gained access. You gave him to understand you were here as a model in a photo-shoot for – what was it, Simon?' He turned to the rodent-faced young man, who was leaning aggressively against the door with his arms folded.

'Executive men's shirts,' said Simon. 'We had booked a model called Nigel Carlton, right. Then this bloke turns up, telling me he's been sent here by his agent.'

'That's not true . . .' said Maurice hotly.

'Hold on, sir. Did you or did you not discuss your agent in some detail with the young gentleman here?'

'Well, yes, I suppose so. But you don't . . .'

'Thank you. You then told him that you're not a model at all but, in reality, a Member of Parliament? Name of Lovelace.'

'That's right . . .'

'The MP for Walsingham?'

'And the Snorings . . .'

'I see,' said the security officer. 'Walsingham *and* the Snorings.'

'Great and Little,' said Maurice.

'Great and Little?'

'Snoring.'

'Ah-ha. But when I arrived on the scene, you claimed that you were, in fact, a magazine writer called Constance Verity . . .'

'Yes, you've got it. That is totally . . .' Maurice looked relieved.

The Harlot's Prerogative

'Miss Constance Verity, of *Home & Beauty* magazine? Right here in this building.'

'Correct. Although I can see, of course, it's a little difficult for you to appreciate the . . .'

'Miss Verity. A woman?'

'Yes.'

'But then we look at your visitor's admission badge, issued today by the receptionist down at the front counter. And it says, quite clearly, that your name is L. N. Bright.'

'I'm sorry. I'm unable to explain that. It makes no sense to me.' Maurice Lovelace seemed, at last, to be grasping the complexity of his situation.

'No. It doesn't make any sense at all, does it. I'm going to have to ask you to stay here for a moment while I make a couple of phone calls. Will that be all right with you, sir?' the security man asked. He allowed a significant little pause. 'Or is it madam?'

'I think you should take a look at Verity Constance, Muriel,' said Juliet, the assistant secretary, peering round the plantation of Tiger Paws begonias which reared up on Miss Oliver's desk.

'It's Constance Verity, Juliet. You're going to have to get that right, you know. She's a very big name round here.'

Juliet leaned closer to her boss in a confiding way. 'Well, she's been taken peculiar,' she said in a loud whisper. 'She's forgotten her own name and I don't think she knows where she is. She's talking about dead bodies in lifts.'

'Right,' said Muriel. 'I think it's time to give her a whiff of telephone cleaning fluid. It usually does the trick.'

The young man in the pony-tail stared at the ceiling in a non-committal way. He had not, to be honest, called in the gestapo because of any serious fear that the gent in the striped suit was a dangerous intruder loose on the premises. He thought he had discovered, if anything, a slight case of mischief: a little in-house espionage of the kind that was rife throughout the building.

Individual titles within the Mameluke group devoted quantities of energy and low cunning to trying to discover and plunder each other's editorial plans. Only recently the *His* feature-writing staff had pulled off a coup against the detested *HQ* magazine, three floors above, by successfully hijacking their schedule setting out details of six weeks' worth of planned features.

It had involved borrowing a canteen tea trolley, with its entire cargo of sandwiches and buns. A reporter was dressed in a white overall jacket and a paper hat and sent in to cruise *HQ*'s corridors and unguarded offices, seeking crumbs of information. During his tour he not only lifted the schedule but also sold fancy cakes worth £14.60.

Woman's Week had once, notoriously, been accused of placing a young reporter on the staff of *Perfect Home* to spy on its editorial plans. *Perfect Home*, tired of finding its brightest feature ideas appearing on the rival's pages a week or two in advance of its own intended publication, finally unmasked the traitor – but only after using her to feed duff information to the opposition, unwittingly, for at least eight weeks. It was during this period that *Woman's Week* was tempted into running as an exclusive a story claiming that HM the Queen was putting Balmoral Castle, in Aberdeenshire, up for sale.

It's one of those strange things about journalists, that they should choose to expend so much energy doing down their closest colleagues. Within the Mameluke building they paid hardly any attention to the real opposition employed by the other great conglomerates, PanInternational Publishing or the Cochon-d'Inde magazine chain, preferring by far to score over their nearest neighbours working under the same roof.

'Madam?' said Maurice Lovelace a full three minutes after the security officer had left the room. 'Did he say *Madam*? What on earth did he mean by that?'

Chapter Nine

The cookery editor emerged head down, walking briskly. There was something wrong – an awkward angle in her back and shoulders; a shuddering, half-muffled sound rising moistly from somewhere in her thorax. It dawned slowly on those who saw her depart. She was crying.

Once outside she darted off, looking to neither left nor right. Her heels clipped away along the corridor. There was a moment's embarrassed silence.

The door to the inner office swung open again. The woman who looked out was surprisingly small, pale and finely built. Rosie Maguire, editor in chief of *Home & Beauty*, was also younger and far more ferocious than visitors, in virtually every instance, expected her to be. They were moved by the wispiness of her frame and the almost childlike innocence of her face, and it followed that they were all the more shaken by the extraordinarily abrasive fury of her attack when it came. She stood in the doorway now, peering out and frowning.

Daphne Chapman, who had been waiting in the outer office with a folio of page plans and art work on her lap, looked up and realised that the next fifteen minutes were going to be at least as sticky as she had feared – and probably far stickier.

'Ah, Daphne,' said the editor, switching on a bleak little low-wattage smile and turning it off again immediately. 'Come in . . . but do me a favour first of all.'

'What's that, Rosie?'

'Chuck that lot in the bin.' She indicated the prepared art work with a dismissive wave. 'We're making changes round here.'

'Bin it? What, all of it?' Daphne tried to subdue the rising note of distress and horror which she could hear wailing somewhere deep down inside herself. The pages on her lap represented weeks of work; they had been prepared in time, but with no great margin of error, to keep pace with the relentless treadmill of approaching deadlines.

'The whole bloody works. Chuck the lot. I want brighter. I want fresher. I want younger. I want sexier. I want braver. I want immediater, nower, todayer. I want newer. I want . . .'

'You want a bunch of fives up your throat,' thought Daphne. She kept her mouth tightly shut. All editors threw these wobbly turns from time to time. In her experience, all of them knew exactly what they wanted – but not necessarily in advance of publication. This was a drawback. They only knew *after* the event, with the benefit of perfect hindsight, precisely what they had had in mind in the first place.

Daphne Chapman described this process as retrospective forward planning. She had been in the magazine business long enough to know that editors were unusually gifted at explaining their wishes clearly – but only after the event, when it was far too late for anybody to act upon them. When they issued orders in the first place, with ample time to spare, nobody had the foggiest idea what they were going on about. It followed that the editor's clearest guidance was always issued afterwards in the form of a rebuke.

As dear old Constance Verity had put it in *Home & Beauty* only – when was it? – yes, last Easter: *Look ahead along life's Tube, on the Circle Line of destiny, running into the dark tunnel of the future, and all we see is where we've been.*

'Muriel,' snapped the editor, turning to the corner desk where her secretary was working, head well down. 'Where's bloody What's-her-face Verity, for God's sake? Should have been here by now. Find out what's happening, will you . . .'

'Constance Verity? Oh, don't worry. Everything's under control,' Muriel Oliver replied in a sort of soothing, sing-song, kindergarten voice. 'She's having a little lie-down in the ladies' loo. Poor Constance. She's being looked after by Juliet, the new girl. She seems very capable, by the way.'

'Constance Verity? Lying down in the ladies'? What on earth for?'

'Fainted. Out there, near the lifts. She went down with an awful wallop.'

'Hot flushes, I suppose.' The editor was sounding dangerously snappy. 'Is this young? Is this immediate? Is this bloody now? Or is it fundamentally menopausal?'

'Very attractive woman,' said Muriel. 'Lovely dress. Full skirt. Monsoon, I should say, if anyone wanted to know my opinion . . .'

The editor raised a pale hand and brushed her fringe of straw-coloured hair out of her eyes. 'Muriel,' she said, turning a commanding gaze on her secretary. 'I want that woman revived, hauled back on her feet, marched to the nearest lift shaft and . . . Hold on. Wait one second.'

An idea was starting to take shape in Rosie Maguire's tough and immensely sharp professional mind. There were, of course, as in so many things, certain financial implications.

'On second thoughts, Muriel,' she said softly. 'Perhaps you might check on the state of the casualty, give poor Constance my very best regards and ask if, just as soon as convenient, we might have a little word here in the office.'

Daphne Chapman, her features editor, watched this abrupt change of mood with interest. If anything, Rosie sounding sweet was even more menacing than the brutal alternative.

'Righty-ho. Will do,' said Muriel. 'I'm really looking forward to meeting her properly. She's my fave.'

Rosie Maguire stared at her secretary for a full minute; her face was working but no words emerged.

'Come into the office, Daphne,' said the editor at last. And she turned rapidly on a long, black heel.

In the shrine garden dedicated to Our Lady of Walsingham a cuckoo turned his unblinking, yellow-ringed eye towards the sun. Like few other birds, he had distinct eyelashes. The bird shuffled, then gave voice to his unmistakable call.

'Listen to the turtle dove,' said Mrs Wade, cocking her head and raising a cupped hand.

The sunshine caught Neville Wade's upturned face, filling it with a surprising radiance, as he stepped from the shaded doorway of the shrine church. There was a greater brightness around his eyes than could be accounted for in the light of a normal summer day – even in Norfolk, where the sky is vast and the clarity can be intense,

Andrew Moncur

touching every tree and stone with a sort of internal, inside-out light.

'Are you all right?' Hilary Wade's round spectacles caught the sunlight, too, as she stepped a little closer to her husband. She looked into his strangely luminous eyes and frowned. 'Is everything behaving itself? Is it, you know . . .?'

'It's fine,' he said, smiling beatifically. 'Everything's just fine.' His voice seemed to come from a distance. 'I feel – what's the word? – transfigured.'

'Oh, dear,' said Mrs Wade.

'I'm a new man, Hilary. A new man.'

'Do you think it was that water?'

The couple had just, with some difficulty, climbed the flight of seven steps from the Holy Well, the subterranean spring head of ancient construction whose waters are regarded as a sacramental by many making their pilgrimage to the Walsingham shrine.

'What's lupus?' asked Mrs Wade, leaning on her husband's forearm.

'It's the Latin for wolf. Or is it rabbit? I can never remember which. Why do want to know?' Neville Wade was wearing an expression which his wife would recall in years to come; it was, she thought, a look of serene satisfaction.

'It says here,' she said, flourishing the booklet she had picked up on the way to the shrine. 'It says that great miracles of healing have been wrought in bodies and souls by sprinkling at the Holy Well, including the cure of lupus.'

'Well . . .'

'Why would they want to heal wolves? Or rabbits for that matter? Tell me that, Neville.'

Her husband had turned to face her. He hesitated briefly, his mouth working, then he spoke with great urgency.

'It's gone. I mean the pain has gone, Hilary.'

'The pain?' Mrs Wade's stared up at her husband's thin face. The skin around his eyes and nose was, she noticed, violet and quite translucent.

'I don't like to say it out loud, but something – some sort of alteration – has happened. I can feel it inside myself.'

The Harlot's Prerogative

The couple had reached the low brick and flint wall which marks the boundary of the shrine's grounds. They walked blindly on to the pavement. Sunlight formed an aura around their grey heads as, holding one another tightly, they stepped out into the road, looking neither right nor left.

'It's a miracle . . .' Mr Wade started to say.

At that precise point there was a squealing of brakes and rubber being laid on the road. Almost instantly came a double heavy blow, the shattering of glass and a long drawn out scream.

Duncan Murray, the salesman – or marketing executive, as the job had been described three years earlier in the situations vacant columns of the *Daily Telegraph* – had been only too happy to turn his car out of Common Place, setting off to leave Little Walsingham. The nun was still standing, hands on hips, chin out, in the middle of the road. In his mirror, to his relief, the black figure was abruptly hidden from view. There was a saucer shaped dent in the car's boot lid.

The young man had already turned down the volume of the radio and reached for his car phone.

'Jessie?'

'Yup?' Reception was poor but that half-bite of a word called up the image of his girlfriend's very smooth, very brown face. He smiled into the mouthpiece.

'It's me. I nearly ran over a nun.'

'God almighty!'

'Afraid I missed. She got away.'

'Typical. Useless.'

The car gained speed as he passed the sign of the Hospice of Our Lady, Star of the Sea. He caught a glimpse of something ahead, some sort of emblem standing at the roadside. It looked like a gilded – what was it? – an arrow piercing a six-pointed star.

'Where are you?' Her voice was clearer now.

'Norfolk. Village called Walsingham. It's the holy place, remember? I'm just . . . Jesus Christ!'

The couple leaving the shrine of Our Lady simply walked off the pavement and stepped into the path of the oncoming vehicle. The road is particularly narrow at that point.

The young driver, holding a phone, could only swing his wheel desperately, pulling hard to the offside and away from the inevitable impact. Oddly, he kept the handset to his ear even as the car made violent contact with and then ricochetted along the high, unyielding flint wall on the right hand side of the road.

Every stage of the noisy destruction of Mr Murray's company car was relayed by telephone directly to his girlfriend's waiting ear: the breaking glass and shattering plastic; the tearing metal and buckling of wing, door and frame; the tiny bound of a mirror pinging off and somersaulting away along the gutter. She even heard the inflation of the driver's air bag and the stifled cry of Mr Murray as he was hit on the side of the head by a cardboard box containing one of a range of highly polished titanium cups used in hip replacement operations. She could not have identified accurately the landslide of samples or the collapse of myriad fragments of windscreen, showering inwards.

One hubcap spun, more and more rapidly, in the middle of the road. A single artificial finger joint in plastic and steel bounded away, skipping across the pavement near the main entrance to the shrine.

Duncan Murray, pinned in his seat by the inflated airbag, could still see his crooked rearview mirror. A nun, holding up her black skirts, was high-stepping round the corner. He could not be expected to know that it was Sister Sigebert Buckley, of the tiny house of the Mildredine Little Sisters, who was lifting her knees and pounding towards the crash scene and the site of so much potential suffering.

'Bugger,' said Duncan in a small, wheezy voice.

The hubcap came to rest. In the brief silence that followed, it was possible to identify the clear voice of a blackbird. He appeared to be singing a familiar but momentarily elusive tune.

It was understandable that Jessica Matthews, having heard the accident taking place at long range, should herself have been thrown into confusion. Few people, even today, can claim to have witnessed – however obliquely – a traffic pile-up happening roughly 144 miles away on the other end of the telephone.

There was not a moment's doubt in her mind that a crash had occurred or that she had been a particularly helpless party to the accident. The link to her boyfriend's car appeared finally to have been severed. She could swear that a single disconnected word had come through – it sounded strangely like 'bugger' – before the phone fell silent.

Jessie's first reaction was one of numbness approaching paralysis. The ill-fated call had come through to her car phone as she was driving along Albert Embankment towards Lambeth Bridge, with the Houses of Parliament bright in the sunshine ahead and to her left.

The sheer violence of the sounds she had heard, car-to-car, stunned her into an almost robotic state. For a while she remained on course, driving in a mechanical, unseeing way; she carried on, approaching Lambeth Palace, changing gear and signalling correctly to turn on to the bridge; only her astonished face showed that her mind was elsewhere.

By now she had crossed the Thames. She spun the wheel to turn into Millbank, heading towards Parliament Square – but instead just then she jerked back to wakefulness and the full shock of all that had happened.

She swung left without warning, aiming directly across the line of traffic and at the same time hitting the accelerator. A gap opened and she tore through, standing on the brakes as she approached the kerb. At least one horn blared.

If she noticed the horse-drawn carriage at all it was only for a fraction of a second. There was nothing to tell her that it was out on royal household business. In the time available there was barely an opportunity for its coachman to gather his double reins and bring the pair under control.

Bunker and Smartie, both half-Cleveland bays crossed with Oldenburgs, bred at Hampton Court, rolled their eyes and plunged ahead in a great surge of panic. The coachman in his black silk hat and drab coat was very nearly thrown from his high seat. The footman on the box never stood a chance.

It would probably have been the case that even a regular footman, schooled in the traditional way at the Royal Mews, would have found himself in trouble as the bow-fronted Clarence mounted the pavement and rocked over on its springs.

As it was, the man on the box was no liveried member of the royal household but a police officer from the Scotland Yard diplomatic protection squad. His nineteenth-century uniform, down to the white breeches and riding boots, was merely a cover. Intelligence sources had suggested that his passenger, His Excellency Dr Seraphim Anchaos, the Tartaristani ambassador, was at some risk, particularly while travelling across London in something so slow moving as a four-seater carriage drawn by two horses. The civil war had, after all, been such a bloody and very recent affair.

Further, it amounted to an additional security risk that the palace had seen fit to provide by way of a carriage, for the sensitive task of conveying the diplomat through the very heart of one of the world's most open and cosmopolitan capital cities, the 200-year-old Clarence with its front-facing bow window of sliding glass panels.

The shiny little carriage bucketed forward. His Excellency was lifted and thrown bodily across the deep-buttoned, black leather seats as the nearside wheels mounted the pavement. His head twice thumped against the box-cloth ceiling. Dr Anchaos assumed that he was under attack and reached for the weapon he invariably carried in his waistband.

Chapter Ten

The security guard's phone call to the editor's office at *Home &
Beauty*, up on the thirty-second floor, was confusing and ultimately
unrewarding.

It did not serve to clarify which of the four or so alternative
identities – and which of the two available sexes – should properly
be attached to the stranger found in the building. The conservative-
looking, well-tailored person who had been reported on the
premises of *His* magazine, ten storeys below, was still being kept
under observation there.

'Hello. Security calling. Can you help me?' the officer asked,
having been put through to the editor's secretary. 'I have a man, or
possibly a woman, here.'

'Shall I put you through to *Family Medicine*'s reader helpline,'
Muriel Oliver asked politely. 'They might give you some guidance.'

'Guidance?'

'About how to tell the difference.'

'No, no. That's quite all right, thank you,' said the security man,
a little too hastily. 'Are you expecting a visitor called Bright at all?'

'No, I don't believe so.'

'Well, somebody called Lovelace then?'

'No.'

'A male model called Carlton?'

'Certainly not. Look, I have a great deal of . . .'

'This won't take a moment,' said the officer. 'Are you expecting
a Constance Verity?'

'She's already with us. In fact, she's in the ladies' lavatory at the
moment with my assistant. That's Juliet. Miss Neckles.'

'Are you absolutely sure?'

'Of course I'm sure. I've seen her birth certificate.'

'What?'

'Juliet Heather Neckles. Born 2 March, 1980. Is that all you want to know? We have a very busy day here . . .'

'I just wanted to inquire, is this Verity person a Member of Parliament?'

'It hadn't crossed my mind to ask,' said Muriel. 'She seems a perfectly normal, rational human being, which tends to suggests the contrary. But she will be coming along to this office shortly and I will put your question to her in person.'

'One further thing, Miss. Is this Constance Verity a *man* by any chance?'

'A man!' Muriel snorted. 'What a preposterous question.'

And having said that she put the phone down with a fine crash.

'Rude cow,' said the security man to the now silent receiver.

'I'm so sorry. Really dreadfully sorry.' Ellen Bright was deeply embarrassed. She hadn't fainted since she suffered a nose-bleed at Brownies when she was aged eight. They had given her a badge for it, she seemed to remember. This time the experience was far worse, possibly because these days she had further to drop. She couldn't imagine what had come over her. 'I'm sorry,' she said. 'So sorry. But what's happened to all my papers?'

Juliet, the assistant from the editor's office, explained that they had been found in the reception area, safe and sound, and had been put aside until she was ready to retrieve them.

Ellen filled her palms under the running tap and dipped her face to splash it with cold water. She brushed her hair and retouched her lips and her eyes. She could have done without this nonsense. She was, after all, trying to make an impression.

Ellen Bright checked herself in the glass once more. She was surprised and touched that Rosie Maguire, the editor in chief, should have sent good wishes and asked to see her. Freelance writers are not used to being treated with this sort of consideration.

There is an extra dimension to the offices occupied by editors. For a start they are larger and several degrees more extravagantly furnished than those allotted to staff of lower rank and perfume. The rooms, poky cupboards in reality, set aside for the next band of employees, the deputy and assistant editors, can be especially squalid, a staff relations practice probably picked up from some of

The Harlot's Prerogative

the more oppressive and corrupt rulers of the Ottoman Turks.

Interestingly, the contrast in the relative quality of accommodation is often most marked in the case of editors of the democratic, egalitarian kind; those who insist they are great mates with the underlings they hire and from time to time, however reluctantly, fire.

From these conspicuously plush, even downright opulent, offices issues a flow of austere editorials – their tone barely muted at all by the depth of the carpet's pile – calling on governments and employers to provide fair dos for all.

Editors' offices often bear all the hallmarks of having been designed. That is to say, they haven't happened by accident. They are deliberately done that way; often papered and painted with a flagrant disregard for taste or the welfare of those who have to work there or visit them. They may have vast desks in odd shapes, built as though to emphasise with appalling starkness just how seldom the editor actually writes anything.

Similarly, the window with its splendid view of the city and its myriad people merely serves to remind everyone how rarely the editor actually goes out and meets anybody.

It was with a complex mixture of emotions that Ellen Bright, now fully recovered, followed her guide along the corridor towards the office of the editor in chief of *Home & Beauty*. She glanced to left and right over the fabric-covered screens, not quite at head height, which separated the passageway from the features section and the sub-editors' room.

She glimpsed a familiar scene: desks crowded together and almost lost under teetering piles of paper, lava flows of glossy print, directories, overflowing wire trays, computer monitors and keyboards, haphazard rows of books, heaped newspapers, telephones, cascades of reference files, plastic cups, shopping bags, outdoor clothing, postcards, sandwich wrappers, facetious headlines clipped from other journals, frocks on loan for fashion shoots, notebooks and copies of forgotten memoranda from the managing editor warning in the strongest possible terms that in future desks must be kept tidy and free of rubbish. Here and there a face stared boldly around an improvised space divider or a coat stand.

Andrew Moncur

There was a scream of laughter from the far side of a row of dark blue filing cabinets. As she rounded the corner, Ellen saw a distant hand raised in a wave and she caught sight momentarily of a face which, across the length of the room, seemed vaguely familiar.

She pushed up her glasses to take a second glance but it was too late.

Then she almost collided with the large figure of a woman who was waiting in the outer office of the executive suite, one hand resting on a familiar stack of cardboard files.

'One question, if I may, dear,' said Muriel Oliver, holding up an arm like a police officer on traffic duty as the visitor approached. 'You're not by any chance a Member of Parliament, are you? No, I felt sure that you couldn't be – but I did say I would ask. You look far too sensible. That's my view, although my opinion doesn't seem to count for much around here, I can tell you. Dear me, no. Who cares what I think? You may well ask.

'Still, what was it you yourself had to say only recently on that very selfsame topic? *The last person to be asked may be the first with the answer while the first is often the last to know.* Or have I got that the wrong way round?'

Ellen Bright nodded and smiled, hoping that this strange person was not, in fact, the editor in chief.

The security man pressed the lift button and they felt it start its long descent through further strata of magazine production.

Maurice Lovelace pictured in his mind's eye a vast nest where editors, reporters, photographers, puzzle compilers, even astrologers strove together like so many ants.

It wasn't hard to imagine that here and there throughout the great tower savage editorial decisions were being taken. A palace coup was probably in progress on *Monarchy Now*. They would be arguing over the whole page make-up of *Beauty Care Review*. Stormy internal rows were almost certainly buffeting *Yachting Day*; in all probability the cover story for next week's *Successful Personal Finance* was being torn up and binned at crippling expense. They might well have decided to drop *Crochet Stitches* and kill *At Rest*, the journal of embalming and funeral home industries. As for the future

The Harlot's Prerogative

of *Bumper Crosswords*, who had a clue?

For certain, nobody paid much attention to the learned journals: *Prosthetics Quarterly*; *Thermography Review*; *Climatology Proceedings & Abstracts* and so on. This was partly due to the fact that they were produced from a cubby hole tucked away behind the *Woman's Week* cookery laboratory. Not one member of the group's financial management staff had visited this tiny office since the mid-eighties.

The lift threw open its doors and the security officer stood aside, allowing Maurice Lovelace to step once again into the marbled hallway. Maurice led the way as they walked together towards the street door. A car horn wailed outside on the busy road.

He paused at the main reception desk. 'Good day,' he said, with dignity. 'Would you kindly pass a message to the editor of *Home & Beauty*. Tell her that Constance Verity has departed, extremely upset – distressed, in fact – about not being able to see her.'

The plump receptionist stared at him with her tiny mouth opened like a fish's.

The secretary, Miss Oliver, had tapped at the editor's door and ducked inside with the sort of dramatic flourish of an actress leaving or, in this case, entering the stage.

'I have Constance Verity outside in my office waiting to see you,' she said.

The editor turned and stared at Muriel Oliver with pale eyes which were not for the moment properly focused. She had just finished shredding the page proofs for a fashion spread as well as the unhappy fashion editor who presented them for approval. The unfortunate woman was sitting – shrinking, in all honesty – on the bench seat beneath the window.

'What?' said Rosie Maguire, as though from a great distance. The adrenalin surge of her savage outburst was still coursing through her slight frame. 'What did you say?'

'Constance Verity is here to see you,' said Muriel.

'I'm surprised the poor old dear can make it here unaided.'

'No. Sorry, but that's not right,' said Muriel, opening the office door and beckoning the attractive young woman who was standing in the outer waiting room.

Andrew Moncur

'And who the hell is this?' Rosie Maguire asked, her eyes narrowing to slits.

'Constance Verity,' said the secretary.

'Ellen Bright,' said the visitor herself, almost simultaneously.

'Holy shit,' said the editor.

The security man held open the door. Maurice Lovelace stepped out on to the pavement. He was almost immediately run over by the nearer of a pair of wild-eyed matching bays. They were pulling at frightening speed and completely out of control an early nineteenth-century carriage containing His Excellency the Ambassador of the Democratic Republic of Tartaristan, attended by a coachman and a footman of the royal household.

There was little he could have done to avoid it. The carriage came bucketing across the pavement with a great clattering of hooves, a whanging of ancient springs and whooping cries from its horsehair-padded interior. Maurice Lovelace MP saw a flash of foam-flecked tooth and highly polished brassware; there was a moment's glimpse of a flared nostril and a strangely foreshortened knee and splint bone. It could have been Bunker; it might have been Smartie. Something black and maroon shot past his face and he saw, as though in a frozen frame, the nearside wheel and – above it – the extraordinary spectacle of a footman detaching from his perch on the back of the carriage and becoming airborne, starting slowly to turn a somersault in mid-air.

At this point he was struck a most violent blow which seemed to begin at his right temple and extend the length of his body. He spun sideways and fell at full length, face down, with his head towards the imposing door of the Mameluke Magazines building. The royal footman, describing a perfect arc as he flew through the air, landed with a dreadful smack on top of the prone form. A black silk top hat rolled into the gutter.

Somewhere in the background a piercing scream cut through the clatter as the carriage and horses demolished an architect-designed display of evergreen shrubbery and tore off along the footpath in front of the great glass tower. It was impossible to identify the source of the cry of anguish. It had come from either the ambassador himself, inside the runaway carriage, or from the young woman whose car had slewed to a standstill in the nearside traffic lane, causing the bays to panic in the first place.

In any event, right there – on life's urban freeway – a writer was cruelly cut down. Maurice Lovelace had become the final victim of a road traffic accident which began almost 150 miles away at the exact centre of his own parliamentary constituency in Walsingham.

Chapter Eleven

He was lying on the pavement in a widening pool of blood when Ellen Bright stepped out from the Mameluke Magazines building, swinging two carrier bags crammed with her papers. A company security man was on his knees beside the outstretched figure; a mobile telephone lay on the ground nearby. The street was strewn with a trail of broken plants and scattered black soil.

A uniformed footman was sitting at the kerbside, holding his head in his hands and rocking gently back and forth. Ellen was sufficiently alert to notice, to her surprise, a large black pistol emerging from the holster at his waistband.

The figure on the pavement remained motionless. Ellen saw the fallen man's feet first of all; she noticed that the toes were turned in which, for reasons she could not have explained, seemed painfully, almost laughably, pathetic. The security officer looked vulnerable as well, kneeling there. His blue uniform clearly did not extend to his socks, patterned in an ugly mixture of grey and green. His shirt had pulled free from the waistband of his trousers. It made him look less like an official figure of authority, more like somebody's father under strain.

As she approached, an ambulance had come weaving through the traffic. It now backed across the pavement to reach the casualties and stood with its rear doors open and its blue lights flashing, feverishly reflected in the windows of the office block. The hurt footman was on his feet, nursing his elbow and probably a collar bone.

Ellen fumbled with her bags and reached up to straighten her spectacles. The security officer ducked his head towards the man lying on the paving stones; he appeared to be straining to catch a whisper.

She was unable simply to walk by. She felt instinctively that she knew the injured man; she had at least seen him before.

The Harlot's Prerogative

It might have been her, lying injured there. Poor Maurice Lovelace had been escorted off the premises only minutes before she left the building, her interview with Rosie Maguire, the editor in chief, having been abruptly curtailed.

Muriel Oliver's face was a picture of shock and distress.

'We've just had some terrible news from the front counter. They say that Constance Verity has been run over by a horse . . .'

Rosie Maguire looked at her secretary with complete incomprehension. 'What? What are you saying?'

'Constance Verity has just been run over by a horse and cart right in front of the main entrance. The accident was witnessed. It was seen by that rude woman on the reception desk.'

'God. Is she hurt? Badly hurt?'

Muriel nodded like the great tragedian she was. 'I'm afraid so. And there's something else.'

'Oh, no? Not . . .?'

'There had been a message left for you at the desk. Miss Verity wanted you to know she was extremely distressed not to be able to talk to you. It must have been the last words . . .'

'Oh, for God's sake.' Rosie Maguire made directly for her drinks cupboard.

'That man. Who is he? Was he?' Ellen Bright touched the security officer's arm. He was still watching the ambulance as it pulled away down the road, its siren echoing from the surrounding buildings.

'Poor sod,' he said at last.

'Yes. But what's his name? I feel as though I should know him.'

The security man shrugged. 'He had three or four,' he said. 'I don't know which one was his real name. Probably this one.'

He handed her the clear plastic badge used to identify visitors to Mameluke Tower. The space for the guest's name had been filled in with tiny, neat lettering: L. N. Bright.

'Was he conscious?' Ellen Bright asked. 'Did he say anything to you? After the accident? I thought, maybe . . . I thought I saw him speaking to you . . .'

'Only for a minute. It didn't make any sense.'

Andrew Moncur

'What didn't?'

'He said something. It sounded like, well, strange.'

'Tell me,' said Ellen.

'He said it was important. "Please remember," he said, "the glory of England lies in Martha's field." That's what it sounded like.'

'Not England's glory?'

'No, the glory of England. What can it mean?'

'I've really no idea,' said Ellen. 'Not the faintest.'

'And that wasn't all. He said some very peculiar things . . .'

'I think you should tell me everything,' said Ellen.

While Maurice Lovelace was carried away, horizontal, in the speeding ambulance, fighting for life in the laid-back way that his friends would have expected, armed police were surrounding a cafe in a depressed street behind Victoria Station.

A man, described as being middle-aged, of Middle-Eastern appearance and of middling height and build, armed with a large automatic pistol, had taken refuge in Delwyn's Coffee House where he was believed to be holding at gunpoint a number of customers and staff. He was understood to have shot and fatally wounded a cappuccino coffee machine.

The hostage-taking situation was reported by a patrol of traffic police, an officer of the mounted branch and an inspector of the Royal Society for the Prevention of Cruelty to Animals who had variously been called out to deal with a road accident involving a horse-drawn carriage from the Royal Mews. The carriage had careered through several major road junctions, a pedestrianised shopping precinct and a street market before finally coming to rest with its shafts impaling a costermonger's barrow; Bunker and Smartie, the matching pair of bays, were grazing the fruit and vegetables on this stall. One man had been run over and seriously injured by the bolting horses and their carriage. A footman from the palace had been less badly hurt; further information about the exact status of this person was being sought from the duty commander of the Metropolitan Police diplomatic protection section. In addition, four elderly women in the market had needed treatment for shock.

The Harlot's Prerogative

The armed suspect, reportedly a passenger in the crashed vehicle, had fled from the scene. The gunman, having taken over the coffee shop, then claimed diplomatic immunity. Officers of the same embassy protection squad were therefore requested to attend the incident.

In a shouted conversation with a mediator, crouching in the doorway of the neighbouring newsagent's shop, the suspect had described himself as the ambassador to Great Britain of the Republic of Tartaristan. He claimed to be under attack by assassins and threatened to shoot an unspecified number of hostages and the mediator unless he was promised passage to a place of safety under the protection of units of the British Army.

The confrontation was still unresolved when the proprietor, a Mr Delwyn Swingewood, arrived at the premises and, being unaware of the security alert, walked through the police lines and into the cafe.

He struck up conversation with the suspect and found that they had a common interest in bird watching and the Scouting movement.

They were exchanging photographs of their respective families when police marksmen burst into the cafe, shouting orders to the frightened staff and customers.

'Armed police! Don't move! Flat on the floor! Throw down your weapons while keeping your hands above your heads and your legs apart! Don't move! Armed police!' the officers had screamed.

Mr Swingewood, the proprietor, either refused to comply or found himself on the horns of a logical inconsistency when faced with these contradictory commands. He was accidentally shot through the foot by a Constable Malarkey.

He was then pinned to the floor at gunpoint while other armed police escorted to safety all others found, safe and sound, on the premises. Mr Swingewood was later said to be in a comfortable condition at St Thomas's Hospital, where a bullet, several fragments of leather, a wool/nylon-mixture sock and a corner of photographic paper were removed from his right heel.

The whereabouts of the gunman remained unclear, although there was speculation that he was among the hostages escorted from the premises by police officers in order to receive counselling, sweet tea and milk chocolate digestive biscuits at an emergency victim support centre set up at Cannon Row police station. No arrests were made.

The Commissioner of the Metropolitan Police subsequently received a note of thanks for his handling of the incident from the Minister of State at the Foreign Office; another letter, similar, was sent to New Scotland Yard by the Marshal of the Diplomatic Corps.

The Marshal of the Diplomatic Corps is a member of the royal household who ranks below the Gentleman Usher to the Sword of State but some degrees above the Hereditary Carver of the Queen's Household in Scotland, the Keeper of the Jewel House, the Painter and Limner, the Chief Binder, the Bargemaster, the Master of the Royal Bee, the Swan Warden and the Swan Marker.

Constable Malarkey, who fired the shot, received a commissioner's commendation for his brave conduct. He was then transferred to the dog training establishment at Keston, close to Biggin Hill on the outermost southern edge of the metropolitan police area. Sometimes, on a clear day, he could make out a far distant landmark: the aircraft navigation lights flickering on top of the vague smudge which was the Mameluke Magazines' tower.

'You realise who he is, this Maurice Lovelace, the man knocked down by the carriage outside your office?' If Ellen Bright sounded a little impatient it was because it had taken forever to get through on the direct line.

'Hold on,' said Daphne Chapman, the features editor. 'I thought it was our Constance Verity who was supposed to have been hit . . .'

'Well, it was – in as much as they're one and the same person. This Maurice Lovelace *is* Constance Verity. Your Constance is a man! He's been writing under that pseudonym for years. He told the security officer all about it immediately before he left the building and got run over. Of course, the security man didn't understand what he was talking about. But he repeated it to me, word for word, afterwards.'

Daphne Chapman hooked her bag with her toe and dragged it out from under the desk. This was a good excuse for smoking a cigarette.

The Harlot's Prerogative

'It's possible, of course,' she said. 'Nobody ever saw Miss Verity. Her copy always arrived by post. If we wanted to get in touch with her it had to be the fax or a message on her answering machine. We simply accepted it; it had always been that way.'

'The other thing about all this is he's a Member of Parliament. Maurice Lovelace, I mean. His parliamentary seat is Walsingham in Norfolk, the pilgrimage place. You know it?'

'I've heard of it,' said Daphne, shaking her lighter in the vain hope it might be made to produce a flame.

'Look,' said Ellen. 'I would like to research Mr Lovelace. It struck me that there might be something in it, quite apart from his double life. It could be a good piece: the fight for life in the land of miracles. That sort of thing. What do you think?'

Chapter Twelve

Mrs Legg sat at the kitchen table with her back to the garden door. She kept her knees wide apart and her generous thighs overflowed the seat of the mahogany dining chair. She was an unusually tall woman with strong shoulders and powerful, long arms. A little glaze of moisture stood out above her upper lip; sweat trickled in the small of her back. The temperature remained bearable so long as there was a through current of air, from open door to window, dispelling the solid heat of the oil-fired cooking range.

She was wearing nothing, virtually nothing, beneath her pale green polyester and cotton overall coat.

Veronica Legg was writing in a black-backed ledger. It was that time of day, the peaceful period when breakfast had been cleared away, the bed sheets had been vacuumed, the beds had been made and the guests' rooms cleaned. As was so often the case, the occupants, quite unbidden, had left the house early; they would stay away until late. Those departing had paid and bade farewell.

Mrs Legg was writing what she hoped would be the essential text book for the bed-and-breakfast industry. Her working title: *The Full English Breakfast*?

'Departure of Guests.' She underlined the heading.

'Unless you can be sure of their loyalty, do not leave it to your guests to fill in the guest book, particularly those comment columns where visitors are invited to make remarks.

It is far more convenient – and more encouraging for those following on behind – if the hostess herself enters comments in the guest book on behalf of certain visitors. In this way she can be sure that remarks are positive and convey what guests would wish to say if only they were able to find adequate words of gratitude.

In such instances the book must, of course, be removed from

public view until the visitors have departed.

The guest book is not the place to air petty grievances. Complaints are best handled in private (see entry: Barrack-Room Lawyers). The golden rule is to keep these guests' comments brief and very grateful.

Example No 1: Superb. Tasty cooking and ambience. We shall return!

Example No 2: Five-star delight. Heartfelt thanks for our wonderfully peaceful stay . . .

She paused while an Air Force jet screamed along the valley, hugging the contours and passing low over the line of poplar trees. The fighter passed to the east of Walsingham, heading for the North Sea. Veronica Legg looked down the slope of her lawn and caught sight of a lean figure in black, framed for a moment in the gap between the white lilac and the gatepost as he cycled slowly past.

She turned again to the ledger and started writing once more in her sloping hand. Across the corridor a tumble-drier bumbled away, churning a mixed load of towels, pillow cases and strange green doilies.

Father Bugloss cycled slowly along beside the snowdrop wood. He thought of it in those terms although the huge drifts of snowdrops and the creeping yellow flowers of the aconite had, of course, long gone by this time of year. The priest had once preached a Rogation Sunday sermon at St Mary's and All the Saints touching on the annual blossoming of that woodland – in which, he seemed to remember, he had become somewhat bogged down in the botanical differences between the winter aconite and the monks-hood and the wolfsbane, *aconitum napellus* and *aconitum vulparia*, respectively. Father Ursell had made some scornful remarks about weeds amongst the corn.

Father Bugloss wove his front wheel away from the roadside potholes. The lane at that point follows the boundary – as if the mapmaker's dotted line had been run along the crown of the road – between Walsingham Magna and Walsingham Parva, which was how he liked to think of the two parishes. With a similar attachment to the old form, he chose to describe himself as a clerk in holy orders.

He was a pale man; his skin was almost blue in those places where it was not obscured by an extravagant sprouting of black hair. His nostrils and ears sheltered dark little thickets and his razor fought a losing battle with the sheer whiskery day-round energy of his throat and chin. Even his eyebrows seemed to advance on one another, like a pair of hairy caterpillars responding to a mutual attraction. It was less immediately apparent that his chest, shoulders and back were alive with dense coils of the same black undergrowth. At prayer, he often showed a glimpse of pale, hairy leg between his sock and the hem of his surplice. Only on the very top of his head was the hair cover sparse and inadequate.

As a parishioner had once observed during his years as a curate: 'If they thought Esau was an hairy man, then they never met our Neil.'

The priest, at first glance, looked stooped and aged. It was a false impression, made the more convincing by the angular lines of his frame and by the drab green-black of his ancient cassock. He was in actual fact gifted with unusual physical strength; it was as though the strange angularity of his limbs made them into powerful levers.

He was reflecting on the relics of the true cross which are venerated at the shrine church in Little Walsingham. One is kept at the Altar of the Nativity, the other in the Chapel of the Death on the Cross, dedicated to Our Lady of Victories and St John the Divine. He thought of precious blood and holy sweat; of Gismas and Dismas who also died at Calvary. He turned his mind to the mysteries of sacrifice and to the rosary, the joyful, sorrowful and glorious mysteries. Neil Bugloss was a good Catholic in the communion of the Church of England. If asked to explain his life's work, he would say he was called to serve the holy house at Walsingham.

The wind was cutting in from the north-east with a terrible persistent heartiness, although at the same time the morning sun warmed the priest's back and the sky remained an unwaveringly perfect blue. It was in every way a beautiful day.

Father Bugloss had lived in Norfolk for slightly over seven years but he had yet to come to terms with the fact that it was possible to have, at one and the same time, strong winds and good weather.

The Harlot's Prerogative

He had exactly the same sort of difficulty in grasping that the sea lay to the north; at some visceral level within his hairy breast he felt it was only right and proper to travel south to the seaside.

It was, of course, part of the indelible legacy of boyhood. There had been a laurel-hedged street in a London parish; the houses were almost theatrical, and often darkly forbidding, in their high Victorian style. It looked as though the builders had made them up as they went along. The church had been modelled on Trinity College, Cambridge, by an architect with a slightly defective sense of proportion. Had Neil Bugloss ever examined his geographical prejudices he would have found that Littlehampton lay nearly, but not exactly, due south of that ugly London street. In childhood the sea was always down there, at the foot of the map.

They had travelled south to the Sussex coast as a family, an oddly stiff little group, making day-trips by train to sit on the shingle and picnic in their cardigans. A wind had always been the indicator of a change for the worse, which was the only way the weather ever seemed to turn when he was a boy. He liked now to use the word 'lad' in sermons, a term he had never employed in the seaside-visiting days of his own youth.

Littlehampton had been an unremarkable little town. It could make not only Bognor Regis but also Worthing seem exciting.

'Mornin', vicar,' called a short, broad man standing at a field gate with a terrier at his feet. 'Hev' come on warm, hen'tit?'

'Quite so. Splendid, splendid,' sang Father Bugloss, pedalling on with his lips pursed in a bright little smile.

'Bloody ol' fool,' murmured the man to his dog. 'Soft as bullock's lights. Let's goo an' hev' a cup o' drink.'

A camper van passed by, giving a wide berth to the black-coated figure on the bicycle. Its rear end bore a message in large white letters. 'Life is 4 living,' it said. 'Get a life.'

Neil Bugloss repeated the words aloud: 'A life. 4 living?' He searched for the significance of the number. The gospel makers? Perhaps it was a reference to the Four Last Things depicted in the church of St Mary the Virgin at Great Snoring: death, judgement, heaven and hell. As for the living? What could it mean? His living was in Walsingham these days.

71

Andrew Moncur

Each day he prayed for the conversion of England and for a greater devotion to our Lady among his fellow countrymen. He prayed, too, for the repentance of sinners and the reunion of Christendom.

Today, as he freewheeled down the hill towards Little Walsingham and the Anglican shrine, Father Bugloss was also hoping for a further miracle.

'Four,' he shouted out loud. The wind blew the sound across the sheep pasture.

Harry Green walked along the old railway line, devoutly hoping that he would not be called upon this morning to witness any miracles. Visions, apparitions, unsolicited messages of a prophetic nature, encounters of a supernatural kind or of some religious interest – he could do without them. As for appearances by deities, members of their immediate families or their handmaidens, their chariots of wrath, their saints, archangels or angels of lesser rank, whether in hosts or individually; all of them, so far as he was concerned, should be actively discouraged.

The theodolite tripod was bearing down painfully on his shoulder. His gingery, freckly face was pink with warm exertion.

Harry Green kicked a stone, hurting his big toe through the heavy boot. This reluctance to have anything to do with a visitation did not signify any absence of belief on his part; indeed, the fact that the idea crossed his mind in the first place was in some way an acknowledgement of faith.

It was more a British response to events: a matter of wishing to avoid embarrassment. 'Imagine,' he said to himself. 'Imagine what it's like afterwards, having to decide whether to tell anybody. People keep quiet about winning the lottery – so who's going to breathe a word about getting a personal visit from a divine messenger?'

He could picture the scene in the bar at the Oxford Stores, just off the Friday Market place, back in Walsingham. 'Good morrow, gentles,' he would cry. 'It's warm for the time of year – and, by the way, I've just had that Archangel Gabriel appearing to me in a vision. He was rising up in a pillar of flame from an altar of incense on the Snoring road. Now, landlord, draw me a foaming flagon

The Harlot's Prerogative

of your best ale to slake my thirst . . .'

It was a tiresome habit of Harry Green's to pepper his conversation with these mock medievalisms. He would never ask a friend to join him for a beer but, invariably, to sally forth to quaff a tankard or twain of ale tapped by yon buxom wench.

He would, in addition, corrupt these archaisms to make a language of his own which was if anything even more hard to endure. Let us sally fifth, he would say. The weather doth not seem three bad, doth it not, squireen?

It seemed to him probable that over the centuries for every miraculous vision recorded, to the wonder of the world, there must have been at least three which remained unreported. People would have been reluctant to cause a fuss or to make themselves look ridiculous – or worse. It stood to reason that approaches were from time to time made to quite the wrong people. If he knew his countrymen, then in some cases the green man from the woods, or the angel from the realms of glory, must have run the risk of being pelted with mud and sticks.

There were one or two puddles along the bed of the railway where it curved out of Little Walsingham through a deep cutting. To the south of the village the tracks had long ago been torn up and the line itself remained as little more than a rough path edged with brambles; but a path running dead-level through the rolling country on high-sided embankments and defiles.

To the north the track bed had been granted a new life. A narrow gauge railway still ran up to the coast at Wells next the Sea; open trains were hauled by the Norfolk Hero, a scaled-down steam locomotive built for the line.

The original railway engineers had sliced through entire hillsides and stopped up valleys to push the line through. It beggared belief that anybody could have reckoned the cost of these works might ever be repaid by a railway line linking Walsingham and a handful of its neighbouring villages to the outside world.

Looking back, Harry Green could see the golden onion-shaped dome rising over the tiny bell tower planted on the old railway station, a vision in its own right. The building had become a place of worship. It was, he thought, probably the only station anywhere in the history of world transport to have seen service both with British Railways and with the Russian Orthodox church. What had been declared redundant by the one had been consecrated by the other. Harry imagined the waiting room and the ticket office, bedecked with icons rather than timetables while bearded patriarchs, metropolitans, beatitudes and archimandrites rumbled the foundations like the steam trains of old with their *basso profondo.*

He started to whistle a little march. A mile ahead, beneath the bank of the railway track, in the valley of the River Stiffkey, stands the Slipper Chapel. It played a part in the system of pilgrimage which developed during the first 470-odd years of Walsingham's fame.

Medieval pilgrims travelling from the south would stop at the little flint-stone chapel to receive their absolution before entering what the devout called the holy land of Walsingham. Many would remove their shoes and go barefoot on the final mile of their journey to the holy house.

The entire picture was laid out before him now. In the valley bottom, where the lane curves along beside the river and its shelter-ing cover of trees, a small column of walkers was moving steadily towards the Slipper Chapel. A squat, carved figure was being carried shoulder-high at the head of the procession. Harry Green, even from that distance, could make out the white gloves of the bearers and hear their repeated chant. It was the *Hail Mary.* They were pilgrims returning from the centre of the village.

He lifted up his eyes and looked across the valley, beyond the stream and the sheep pasture, towards the neat, square tower of the church of St Giles in the hamlet of Houghton-in-the-Dale.

Something was moving rapidly over there. A red car, briefly visible, was heading north-east towards Little Walsingham. Going a goodsome gallop, as Mr Green described it to himself.

Sonia Marks was clearing the table in the window of the tea shop. Looking across High Street she could see into the shaded arch of the gatehouse, one of the remaining fragments of the once great medieval priory at Walsingham. She swept a line of cake crumbs into the palm of her hand.

The Harlot's Prerogative

Her life had not been easy. It seemed to her, looking back, as though she had been ill-used from the start. It had been hard at primary school; she could still remember the boy – his name was Scott – who had been the first.

'Sonia Marks?' he had piped at the top of his voice.

'Yes?' she had replied, looking across the row of yellow pine desks.

'Sonia Marks!' He was gleeful. 'Get set! Go!'

It had been the refrain of her life. The strange thing was that anybody should believe even now that the joke had never been made before.

She tipped the handful of crumbs into the flower pot on the window sill. The twining shoots of morning glory seemed to thrive on dregs of tea and table sweepings. Sonia wiped her hands on her red apron, smoothing it over her hips. She tucked a strand of dark hair behind her ear.

'Something Y, something Y, something Y,' said an older woman sitting at the table near the foot of the stairs, looking up from her newspaper. 'Four across. Six letters.'

'You've obviously cocked it up.' Sonia pushed her tightly-clenched fists into the pocket of her apron.

'Syzygy,' said the woman. She filled in the letters and then glanced up and smiled.

The newsagent over the road had changed the billboard on his shop door. 'Tragic MP fights for life,' it said. At least, Sonia assumed that was what it meant to say. In actual fact the bill read: 'Tragic MP fights for live'.

She put a fold of her cloth between her teeth and bit hard. There was nothing that she could do, as she had been telling herself since the previous morning. At the same time she automatically tried to complete the sentence on the billboard: fights for live what exactly? Live yoghurt? Live bait?

'Come on,' said the woman, rising and folding her newspaper. 'It's not the end of the world.'

A red car slowed and passed the open door at little more than walking pace. The driver appeared to be feeling her way through an unfamiliar place, looking for a landmark or a helpful sign. The ancient houses hug the kerb at that point. A few upper floors are jettied out over the street; most other houses have flat-fronted Georgian facades. The car crawled by the Martyrs' House and the Abbey Arch where a dark, lean man was weaving along on his bicycle.

Coming abreast of the car, he caught the eye of the young woman driver. She saw that he was wearing a clergyman's collar, a black biretta and a curiously patinated cape.

'Excuse me,' she called, leaning from the side window. 'Excuse me, Father . . .' She used the title without a second's thought. It was as though that priest's hat, so un-English, had awoken memories of Mediterranean and, above all, Roman Catholic society.

'Sorry,' she said. 'I'm looking for the Gideon's Well guest house. A Mrs Veronica – yes – Veronica Legg.'

Sonia Marks, catching the words through the door of the tea shop, made a hoarse sound which it was not immediately possible to interpret.

Chapter Thirteen

Mrs Legg ran a finger along the top of the switch and held it to the light to examine it minutely. She pursed her lips and made a tiny mewing noise. Through the open window, beyond the landing table and its bowl of hyacinths, came the full-throated voice of a song thrush.

'Listen,' said Ellen Bright, raising her hand. 'It's that tune. He's singing that – you know – that tune.'

'Yes, dear,' said Mrs Legg in that flat, tired-of-trying voice used by the English to discourage children and foreigners. 'Yes, that's right, I'm sure.'

The landlady held open the door and allowed the younger woman to enter the bedroom. In a single sweep of cool-eyed appraisal she took stock of the new guest. She weighed up and costed her clothes and her shoes, her suitcase and her handbag, her hair, her wristwatch, her perfume and the simple gold studs in her ears. She even added into her sum the likely price of acquiring the now-faint tan; the tennis-player's muscle tone; the manufacturer's name on the tortoiseshell frames of the spectacles.

She assessed her diet and her general health; placed her to within a point or two on the complex scale of the British class system; made informed guesses about her age, her place of origin, her education, her occupation and her income, her marital status, her religious persuasion, her politics, the newspaper she would most likely read, her general temper and her credit-worthiness. She reserved judgement solely on the question of the relative quality of her sex life. The entire assessment required all the time it had taken for Ellen to walk two paces into the room; only her back view was available, or indeed needed, for Mrs Legg's inspection and the completion of her inventory.

'What a very . . . a very interesting room,' said Ellen, looking at the bay window – or, rather, the portion of the window which remained. A partition wall had very obviously been built right through the centre of the original bay and down the middle of what must have been one big bedroom. It had left a curiously shaped space, taller than it was wide.

The moulded coving ran around only three sides of the room. Half of what once must have been an elaborate, central rose of plasterwork remained visible, sliced through.

The room was oppressively dainty. Little glass animals with spindly legs of what looked like boiled sugar stood on every available surface. There were bunches of dried flowers in the grate and on the mantelshelf; another crisp posy stood in a china pot on the bedside table and rose buds had been stitched around the brim of a straw hat which hung on the wall over the bed. Ellen couldn't understand these hats. There was another one hanging by ribbons on the back of the door and a third arranged on a small table in the window. Each of them was sprouting with a different type of dead flower.

There were china figures of dancers and cats and winsome dogs and birds. More dried flowers, leaves and grass emerged from a pair of small white-ribboned ballet pumps – or, possibly, babies' shoes – which called to mind Victorian funeral keepsakes.

It looked as if the stock of some gift shop had somehow found its way up the stairs. Ellen had the panicky feeling that it was impossible to turn round without sending glass giraffes and flower petals flying. How could that great, tall woman move without doing damage? The room was drenched with the smell of pot-pourri.

Tiny framed pictures of wispy flowers and cottages and women in crinolines choked up the fireplace wall. Little cushions with frills, lacework and ribbons had been scattered around the room. A pale green towel was laid, folded, on the foot of the bed.

There was a sense of reckless abundance about the curtains. They cascaded in layers, bunched themselves up in festoons, tumbled in a froth of lace; they had rope-like tie-backs and gilded rails with pulleys and draw cords. More lace had been laid over the bedside table.

In the corner, on a low stool, was a tea tray with a kettle and a handful of tiny plastic pots of long-life milk. Boxes of tissues had been left here and there around the room.

'Is there a phone?'

'You'll find a coin box in the hall. The bathroom is across the landing, the door on the right. The hot water takes a little time to get through to the taps there – but it's perfectly all right, eventually.' Mrs Legg smoothed the bedspread. 'We ask guests to be very careful with the toilet. The handle needs to be held down for a tick and then sort of rotated firmly up and down. I'll show you.'

Ellen put down her case near the foot of the bed and laid her handbag, with its newly-repaired strap, on a heap of cushions.

'You'll be a pilgrim, dear?'

'I beg your pardon?' Ellen thought for a moment the woman had mentioned pilgrims.

'Anglican, I imagine. The other lot tend to come in coach parties with priests. And they need white gloves.'

'White gloves?'

'For carrying the Virgin. They're very particular about that. There's a lot of stink if they don't wear the gloves. Oh, yes.'

'As a matter of fact . . .'

'And what time will you be wanting your breakfast, dear? We serve breakfast any time you like between seven thirty and nine o'clock. We always say the choice is yours. What time would suit? Not too early, I hope.'

'Well, shall we say eight o'clock?' Ellen ducked her head in a questioning way.

'Sorry, dear. I have two other guests coming down at eightish.'

'Oh, then – let's say half past.'

'Could you make it eight forty-five, dear? Thank you so much.'

'Mrs Legg, I was just . . . I was wondering if there might be any chance of having a sandwich now? Only a quick bite. I had an early start, you see, and . . .'

'Can't say one way or the other, dear. I shall have to ask Chef,' said Mrs Legg, stepping to the door. 'He's in one of his moods. But I will at least inquire for you.'

Ellen walked to the window and leaned on the sill. To the left she saw at first only the slender leaves of the wisteria. And then, with a leap of surprise, she was looking into the pale blue eyes of a jackdaw.

Andrew Moncur

Veronica Legg ran her thumb between her blue-white breasts and scratched briskly. She blew on the page in the visitors' book where she had just made an entry on behalf of her new guest. The young lady had paid such a nice tribute to the decorations in the Rose Room.

Mrs Legg slid her black ledger across the table. She took a bite from her ham sandwich, dropped it on the plate and sat chewing thoughtfully for a moment before starting to write.

'It is, in my view, important that every bed-and-breakfast establishment should have a member of staff of, shall we say, an uncertain temper,' she wrote.

It is a good idea to let all guests know that he or she is a difficult personality who may very well be unobliging.

In this way, the visitors will come to understand that their requests and wishes are unlikely to be met – but no blame attaches to the bed-and-breakfast landlady herself.

If this ill-tempered member of staff is totally fictitious, so much the better.

Mrs Legg picked up her sandwich again. Young Miss Bright had not shown a moment's surprise when she was given the bad news that Chef was not prepared to make a snack for her.

'So sorry, dear,' Mrs Legg had explained. 'He's throwing things around in the kitchen. When Chef's in this mood there's no talking to him.'

The beauty editor, a strangely unattractive woman with bad skin and a gum condition which sometimes made her look like a horse, left the editor's office in a fury, slamming the door behind her. She swore savagely at Troy, from the post room, who happened to be standing in her way.

'Well, really,' said Miss Oliver, secretary to the editor in chief of *Home & Beauty* magazine, having witnessed the entire scene. 'That b-woman. Lend a hand, will you, Juliet. Poor Troy's mail has gone all over the floor. Miss Piggy the beauty queen has walked on some

of it in her size twelves. Wouldn't you think she'd have the decency
... Oh, hello there. And what can we do for you, Daphne?'

Daphne Chapman, the features editor, indicated the inner door
with a nod and raised an eyebrow. She was chewing a wooden
cocktail stick.

'The editor is still in conference, I'm afraid,' said Muriel Oliver.
'She's been screaming at Sarah from beauty and that Vicki what-
d'you-call-her from promotions and special offers.'

'Ah, yes,' said Daphne. 'The cock-up with the neck firming
cream . . .'

'We're not supposed to be talking about that,' hissed Muriel,
making great arch gestures to indicate secrecy, flapping ears, panic
and alarm.

'I need to know what we're doing about the Constance Verity
slot.'

'Poor, poor Constance,' said Muriel, adopting the sort of expression Queen Victoria would have worn when speaking of her late
Albert. 'It seems that it wasn't only a case of being run over by a
pair of wild horses and a carriage. The woman in reception said
that what really did the damage was being knocked down by a
flying postilion in a top hat. Poor lamb. She never stood a chance.'

There was a prolonged pause while Daphne scanned Muriel's
open face.

'She?' Daphne asked at length.

'Constance. Miss Verity.'

'I think you mean 'he', don't you, Muriel? Constance Verity is
really a man. A chap called Maurice Lovelace . . .'

Muriel Oliver let out a terrible hooting laugh, then covered her
mouth with both hands. 'Oh, Daphne! You are wicked! You're
always teasing . . .'

'No. Look. Really.' Daphne held up her hand and, frowning,
looked at the vacant space between her fingers where a cigarette
should have been lodged, comfortingly. 'Oh, shit,' she muttered as
her pager started to bleat.

'Look, I can't stop,' she said. 'Remind me to fill you in some
time. And I need to have a chat with our gallant leader just as soon
as possible.'

Andrew Moncur

'I'll give you a buzz,' said Muriel. She was already eagerly picking up the staff restaurant menu which Troy, the post boy, had left on her desk. 'A man!' She whooped again. 'Dear, oh, dear.'

The hospice of Our Lady, Virgin Most Clement, administered by the Little Sisters of St Mildred, lay on the Friday Market square in Walsingham, across the way from the Black Lion Hotel. It was a small house or, rather, two houses linked by doorways knocked through on the ground and first floors. One house provided beds in twin rooms – plainly, even starkly furnished – for half a dozen sick or aged pilgrims. The other cottage, beyond the wrought-iron garden gates which had been fitted on the landing and in the hall, was occupied by the chapel and the quarters of the Mildredine nuns.

In the guest bedrooms elderly women turned uneasily on their thin mattresses as the thin strains of an electronic organ seeped through the corridors. The superior, four sisters and a novice were saying the office of compline, the service for the last of the canonical hours of prayer.

'Look down, O Lord, from thy heavenly throne, illuminate the darkness of this night with Thy celestial brightness, and from the sons of light banish the deeds of darkness,' the nuns prayed.

They looked like newly-made beds, with crisp white sheets turned down over their foreheads and pale, pinkish faces where the pillows ought to have been.

The novice stared up at the ceiling of what had been the parlour, on which Sister Augustine Bradshaw had painted scores of stars and an improbable number of new moons. Sister Sigebert Buckley had illuminated the fireplace wall with a vividly coloured and anatomically detailed painting of the Sacred Heart. The alabaster figure of Our Lady was a foundation present from the mother house in Worcester. The brass bell hanging in the hall had been a gift from the Orthodox Community of St Sepharvaim and St Pithon, in the nearby village of Binham; it had been annointed with oil and chrism and was now the special joy of Sister Christopher Bagshawe, who polished it daily.

The applique wall-hanging over the stairs, depicting the Annunciation, had been embroidered by Sister Thomas Figge.

The Harlot's Prerogative

Sister Sigebert had said unkindly that the angel Gabriel looked as though he was wearing a baggy brown dressing gown.

There was a crucifix on the wall. Beside it was an image of St Wilgefortis, a saint of dubious provenance who enjoyed the rare distinction of being martyred because she was a bearded lady.

The virgin martyr had long been adopted by the Mildredine Sisters who made a point of honouring her feast day, 20 July.

'O let no evil dreams be near, nor phantoms of the night appear; Our ghostly enemy restrain, lest aught of sin our bodies stain,' recited the novice, who had never in her life committed a sin worth mentioning but who had read about some of them in magazines.

Her name was Stephanie Beard and she had until recently worked at Barclays bank in Wisbech, Cambridgeshire. Wisbech, curiously enough, is the site of the Fenland stronghold where recusant priests were held in the turbulent years of see-sawing loyalties after the dissolution of the religious houses, including Walsingham's.

The sisters prayed that they might be made to abound in sorrow for their sins. Sister Sigebert looked particularly grave at that point. They then joined in their final amen.

'Oh, good,' said Sister Augustine. 'Cocoa.'

'And chocolate digestives,' said Sister Thomas.

'Oh, for God's sake,' snapped Sister Sigebert, who then crashed upstairs in her black lace-ups with the commando soles.

Chapter Fourteen

A furious debate was taking place among the staff of St Wilfrid's Medical Centre within twenty-four hours of Maurice Lovelace's arrival. The injured MP had been transferred to that private hospital at the earliest opportunity, although he was in no condition to enjoy his pleasant single room, the views of the river and the tasteful uniforms in pink and grey worn by the nurses. They were dressed in a calculatedly old-fashioned style, with starched caps and elaborately-worked silver belt buckles; this seemed to reassure patients who wanted a twenty-first-century hospital with nineteenth-century trappings.

The clinical argument revolved around the question of whether the accident which so grievously punctuated Mr Lovelace's career represented a mere comma, a more serious semicolon or a terminal full stop in the sentence of his life.

Opinion was divided. Mrs Freda Chung, the senior cleaning lady in charge of a team of three looking after the nine bedrooms, two consulting rooms, a nurses' office and the reception area on the third floor, expressed the view that it was merely a case of short-term unconsciousness. It would, naturally, lead to nothing more than a touch of cerebral concussion and retrograde amnesia.

Mr Evangeltine Hopkin, the porter on night duty in the Nightingale Wing, insisted that coma was now established, the patient having lost his reflexes, an objective sign of disturbed neural function. He went on to demonstrate the patient's lack of response to the stimulus of touch on the eyelash and the eyeball itself. He also whistled, pulled a hair from the exposed chest, blew in an ear and tapped on the patient's forehead, all without provoking a reaction.

The manager from the catering department, Mrs Santinelli, disputed these findings, claiming that there was no compelling evidence of either direct damage to the brain or intracranial bleeding. She attempted to perform the classical test of Babinski's Reflex, stroking the sole of the patient's foot with a canteen spoon. This procedure proved disappointingly inconclusive.

The late-duty telephonist, Marie Lloyd-Jones, a single parent and part-time employee, raised what she described as the sixty-four-dollar question. Namely, the problem of establishing whether the patient was in a persistent vegetative state or merely behaving exactly as every other perfectly average backbench Member of Parliament behaves any day of the week.

She suggested that were Mr Lovelace to be diagnosed as comatose he might gain some promotion to ministerial rank and even, if his condition were hopeless enough, to ermine and a seat in the House of Lords. At very least – just as long as he continued to lie around with his eyes closed, letting rip every so often with those horrible snoring noises – he could confidently expect to be made a member of the select committee on Welsh Affairs.

In any event, Maurice Lovelace remained in a state of deep unconsciousness and was hooked up to a drip for artificial feeding. A bulletin describing his condition as 'poorly' was issued to the Press Association. The news release led to a front page story (with picture on page five) in the *Eastern Daily Press*, Norwich, and another in its sister *Evening News*. Political staff at *The Times*, the *Daily Telegraph*, the *Guardian*, the *Daily Mail* and the *Express* all developed the story as a further crisis for the government, its wafer-thin majority put in jeopardy. They all speculated, in their brazen way, about the prospects for an early by-election – assuming the MP had been bounced along the road severely enough. The *Independent* described Maurice, inaccurately, as 'a former Tory Foreign office minister'.

In fact, his childhood travels aside, Mr Lovelace had an extremely limited experience of foreign affairs. He had once attended a meeting of the parliamentarians' assembly of the Western European Union, held in Berlin shortly after the demolition of the notorious wall. Maurice had been pleased to carry home a fragment of concrete, plucked from the rubble with his own hands. It enjoyed a prominent place on the desk at his flat in London, remaining on display there for a full three days.

Andrew Moncur

On the fourth day his cleaning lady, Mrs Canty, threw it away. She protested later that she couldn't be expected to polish properly if he was going to pile up dirty rocks all over the furniture.

It was probably for the best, then, that Maurice Lovelace could in no way be aware of Mrs Canty's self-appointed role in the days following his accident with the royal coach. While his secretary at the House of Commons coped admirably with official business, messages of goodwill from the constituency and so on, his cleaner took it upon herself to impose some order upon the private world of his flat. She had always previously been forbidden to handle his papers and now itched to sort out the untidy piles which covered so many surfaces. To her surprise, her employer had accumulated vast numbers of women's magazines – some of them ancient, most fit only for the rubbish bin.

Mrs Canty was unable to resist dusting in some depth the expanding files arranged in a line on the desk top. Hundreds of letters and postcards were tucked inside, bundled together with rubber bands. She noted the most bulging compartments of one file were marked 'Health', 'Marital' and 'Sex, general'.

When compelled to pick up a couple of letters which had somehow, there and then, become scattered on the carpet, she saw that they were both signed by women. They were framed in what she thought were most intimate terms.

Mrs Canty pulled a face and tucked them back in the gaping file. She wondered, but only for a moment, why both letter writers had addressed their remarks 'Dear Constance'.

It was in the course of rearranging his desk drawers that Mrs Canty came across an unfinished manuscript. She quickly discovered that Mr Lovelace had been working on a history of Walsingham, the ancient place of pilgrimage standing at the very heart of his parliamentary seat. 'England's Lost Treasure: A Mystery,' said the topmost page.

She made a cup of strong tea, helped herself to a Rich Tea biscuit, kicked off her shoes, climbed on to the sofa and started to read.

'The hand of history first made its way across the softly undulating country of North Norfolk to touch the Saxon village of Walsingham

The Harlot's Prerogative

Parva in the years of political tension and religious ardour immediately before Duke William of Normandy led his knights in the conquest of England in 1066,' the handwritten manuscript began.

Of course, this seemingly tranquil corner of England had not entirely escaped the great movements of the ages: the coming of Roman, Saxon and Dane; wars and rumours of wars; pestilence, plague and religious strife; druid, pagan and saint. The broad land of the North-folk was not, so to speak, placed on one the cul-de-sacs of history. But it is not difficult to imagine that the Walsinghams, and the neighbouring Snorings besides, escaped most of the flails of time's threshing machine. For the ordinary people, the slow pace of the pastoral round and the steady demands of cultivation must have continued uninterrupted, season by season, through the generations. The villein tilled the soil, whichever master might hold the manor. Ploughing, drilling and harvesting took place at their appointed seasons. Time must have ticked away according to the flight of the honey bee, the migrating goose and the long-awaited harvest home of barley, potato and sugar beet . . .

At this point a pencilled note appeared in the margin: 'Query eleventh-century potatoes.' Mrs Canty sipped her tea.

It was in 1061 that events occurred here which were to place the village at the centre of religious life for many centuries, with a significance extending beyond England's shores and throughout Christendom. It is no exaggeration that Walsingham, as a place of devotion, came to be discussed in the same breath as Rome, Canterbury and Santiago de Compostella.

Indeed, such was its position in the religious experience of the country and so great its importance as a place of pilgrimage – unrivalled in its power to draw the devout – that the Milky Way itself became known as the Walsingham Way, believed to point its starry path towards the shrine. Truly, Walsingham found itself as the destination on life's galactic highway.

Andrew Moncur

The story begins with the lady of the manor of Walsingham, Richeldis de Faverches. She was married to a Norman . . .

Here another margin note appeared: 'NB. Not – repeat, not – Norman de Faverches.' Mrs Canty, whose husband *was* a Norman – Mr Norman Eric Canty – gave a little sniff.

It is my belief that this landowner had settled in England in the years before the invasion which was shortly to throw the land under the yoke of the foreign oppressor. The pious woman, his wife, is said to have received while at her prayers three visions of the Virgin Mary.

Richeldis believed that in a trance or dream she was taken to Nazareth and shown the little house where the Annunciation took place. That is to say, the house where, we are told, the Angel Gabriel came down to inform the Virgin that she would conceive and give birth to a son. In her visions she saw this humble dwelling, where Mary and Joseph would have raised the infant Jesus.

The lady Richeldis, acting in obedience to the command she had received, resolved to build a replica of this holy house in Walsingham. She did so, but not without some initial difficulty.

According to one version of the story, she ordered that the little building should be raised on a site by a fresh spring which broke surface in the water meadows of the Stiffkey valley; this was taken to be the sign. But the carpenters were somehow prevented by mysterious forces from following her instructions. This is possibly the first recorded instance of the builder's time-honoured excuse cast in this particular form. However, after a night's prayer Richeldis found that her holy house had been erected on a different site nearby by some sort of miraculous intervention. Eventually the legend grew with the telling, to the point where it was believed that the actual *Santa Casa* from Nazareth had been transported to Walsingham by angels.

In any event, she raised a little timber building to what she thought to be the exact dimensions of the original house in Nazareth: twenty-three feet six inches by twelve feet ten inches. The original building had only one small door and a single window.

Within the holy house an image of Our Lady was set up. It was to be an object of veneration for the succeeding 500 years. The house Richeldis built would become a place of pilgrimage, the most frequented and without question the richest shrine in all England – not excepting the shrine of the martyred St Thomas à Becket in the Trinity Chapel at Canterbury Cathedral, even at the height of its fame, as Geoffrey Chaucer described it in the prologue to the *Canterbury Tales*. Walsingham itself would soon come to be known as England's Nazareth.

It was a wonder of the medieval world. Over the centuries of its existence it was to be visited by virtually every king and queen of England. Some say that the line began with Richard I, the Lion Heart, others name Henry III, the pious king who rebuilt Westminster Abbey. His son, Edward I, is known to have made the pilgrimage a dozen times and his body is believed to have been brought to rest in Walsingham for six months before his burial place was made ready in the south ambulatory at Westminster.

For certain, Walsingham's glittering cavalcade ended with Henry VIII. The king made at least three pilgrimages to the shrine – walking barefoot in penitence and to pray, forlornly, for the survival of a sickly son – before finally visiting it with its utter destruction.

The rapid rise to fame of the shrine can be ascribed to a number of factors. The plight of the Saxons, under their harsh Norman masters, would have created an early need for spiritual support. Another great force was the zeal of the western Christians to recover possession of the holy places of the biblical lands, by then long held under the sway of Islam. The first Crusade would lead to the capture of Jerusalem from the Muslims in 1099 and the ensuing two centuries were to be years of struggle with the Saracens for dominion over the Holy Land. The journey to England's Nazareth would in those times have had special importance for the devout who had little realistic chance of seeing the holy places of the East.

Mrs Canty took another biscuit. It must have been a Mecca for pilgrims. In those days, of course, Mecca did not automatically mean bingo. Or ballroom dancing, as it had when Mrs Canty first met Norman. Sighing, she returned to the text.

In the days of its fame the Walsingham shrine would stand at the heart of a richly endowed religious foundation and at the hub of a great enterprise catering for an army of pilgrims. The village of New or Little Walsingham was created to serve the visitors' needs. In the fifteenth century there were at least twenty-one hostelries for pilgrims.

The tiny wooden holy house was enveloped by a sheltering chapel built of flint and stone. A great Augustinian priory rose beside it, the black-robed canons acting as guardians of the shrine and its riches. Later a Franciscan friary was also created, its grey friars at the service of the sick and the poor pilgrims.

It is not difficult to picture the way the shrine itself grew rich. Fabulously, wonderfully wealthy; laden with the gifts, the votive offerings of the faithful, the innumerable revenues of the all-powerful church, the tithes and rents of the farmer and the peasant. When kings were numbered among its most ardent supporters, then fortune indeed showered upon the holy house.

A noble might present jewels and plate. When a great man fell ill he sent his own weight in wax as an offering; a lady would give rings and velvet gowns to the shrine. Walsingham was richly endowed with land and property holdings, like many religious houses – only more so. By the late thirteenth century the priors had possession of property in no fewer than eighty-six parishes throughout Norfolk.

Other religious houses set out to attract the faithful by displaying some relic, perhaps a piece of the true cross or a phial of the holy blood. Walsingham would lay itself open to charges of preying on the credulous by displaying a crystal reliquary supposed to contain mother's milk of the Virgin Mary.

The canons had to find a use for all the money that passed through their hands. Their defenders will stress that there was no welfare state, no poor law in medieval England; it was the monks and nuns who gave bread and alms to the needy, the lepers, the blind, the orphans and poor widows, the victims of plague.

Their opponents insisted that the monks eventually waxed fat, wallowing in wealth, superstition and decadence. Their tithes and land rents were often collected by agents, the monks having lost all direct contact with those on whose toil they ultimately depended. They were accused of every sort of sexual licence and of accumulating an unbelievable share of the nation's assets. One pamphleteer told Henry VIII that the bishops and abbots 'have gotten ynto theyre hondes more then the therd part of all youre Realme. The goodliest lordshippes, manors, londs and territories are theyrs . . .' As for begging friars, they were described as a 'gredy sort of sturdy, idell, holy theves'.

Reformers were critical of the troops of servants employed in the larger monasteries – typically, three or four for every monk. It is perhaps significant that Desiderius Erasmus, the Dutch humanist scholar who cast a critical eye over the church in the early sixteenth century, had himself been raised as an orphan in a monastery, witnessing the life of the monks, and had in youth entered the religious life, only to abandon his vocation. Erasmus always described himself as a faithful Catholic. He was admired by leading churchmen, like the high-minded Sir Thomas More, and despised by Dominican and Franciscan friars who preached against him.

He visited Walsingham in 1511, almost certainly staying at an inn called the Falcon, and described the village as the most celebrated place throughout all England.

Erasmus left an account of the richness of the holy house: tiny, sweet-scented, lit only by wax tapers. 'When you look in you would say it was the mansion of the Saints, so much does

91

it glitter on all sides with jewels, gold and silver . . . it is not easy to find a man who ventures to reckon prosperity unless he yearly salutes the Lady of Walsingham with some small gift.'

He reported that the canon in charge brought out treasures from beneath the altar: figures of kings in gold and silver and other offerings so numerous that it seemed impossible for them to be stored in the available space.

Within twenty-five years all of this ancient and fantastic scene would be overthrown by Henry VIII. Imagine the impact. This venerated place would suffer not merely suppression, but almost complete erasure. Consider how shattering a blow it must have been. And yet it took place without bloodshed remotely comparable to the personal suffering associated with other revolutions. It did not take long; a little over five years from start to finish to suppress the English monasteries – rather less to obliterate the holy house at Walsingham. In two or three years the cumulative wealth of architectural beauty, centuries in the making, was destroyed. It has rightly been described as the most sudden and wholesale transformation wrought upon English social life from the Norman Conquest of 1066 to the present day.

At this point Mrs Canty turned down the page to mark her place and pushed the document aside.

'He should query eleventh-century sugar beet, if you ask me,' she said aloud. Then she rose and put on her shoes once more.

Chapter Fifteen

Gwen Lightsome, who liked to describe herself as the agony aunt's agony aunt, was showing signs of being in agony. 'Oh, Christ,' she cried. Then, with an expression of anguished concentration stitched across her face, she started to stretch out her arms and legs – radiating out like the limbs of a particularly powerfully built, four-pointed starfish.

'God. Oh, God.' The words were torn from deep in her throat, or possibly somewhere down in the lungs. There were beads of sweat on her upper lip; her mouth was pulled into a grimace. Lying on her back like that, with her out-thrust legs and arms taut, quivering with effort, she had assumed the position of someone pinned at full stretch on a St Andrew's cross.

'Please, God!' Her eyes fluttered open, but only the whites were visible; her breathing had become harsh and loud. She was panting in a rhythmical way, making a sound which called to mind a steam locomotive pulling away from a platform and gathering speed. She arched her neck, the cords standing out in her throat as her chin came to rest, tucked tightly in and pointing towards her breastbone.

The slightly built man bouncing on the white pillow of her stomach seemed to be clinging on by his fingertips as the muscular pillars, drifts, billows and generously rounded slopes of her body thumped and walloped against the surface of the office desk.

His naked body was lean and shockingly pale with a fuzz of reddish hair blurring the outline of his chest, shoulders and fore-arms. A mottled patch the colour of ripe plums had spread across his neck and face. There was something of the boy and the dolphin about the desk-top scene – or perhaps Captain Ahab at the moment of his final entanglement with the great white whale.

Reg Lightsome's eyes were tightly closed but his lips were working furiously. He was saying something under his breath. A lip-reader might have been able to follow the words. 'He sinks into thy depths with bubbling groan,' the keen-eyed watcher would have discerned. 'Without a grave, unknell'd, uncoffin'd and unknown . . .'

Gwen's large white feet began to shudder. 'Yes,' she started to moan. 'Yu-u-us.' She took a mouthful of his shoulder to muffle the cry that was rising from some point in her abdomen.

At that moment the telephone bleated its electronic call. Once, twice it rang. The slapping of flesh on tooled leather became more urgent.

'Hold on,' said Reg.

'I ca-aan't. Not noo-ow,' Gwen groaned, thrashing her hips with immense power.

'No, not you,' said Reg, who had propped himself on one elbow and was being tossed about violently. He turned back to the telephone. 'Could you hold on for one minute please, caller?'

'Hello? Is that Mrs Lightsome's office?' said a distant, tinny, familiar voice.

'Please. Just one moment,' said Reg.

'No! Not now! Don't stop,' hissed Gwen.

'Is anything the matter?' asked Miss Oliver on the far end of the line. 'Is somebody hurt?'

'No, nothing. Everything's fine. Just hang on a tick.'

'No. No-ooo! Oh, Jesus!' Gwen's voice rose in volume and climbed vertically through two octaves.

'Hello? Hello? Is anybody there?' Muriel Oliver, phoning from the editor's office at *Home & Beauty*, was sure now that she could hear the cries of a person in pain.

'Yes?' Reg murmured.

'Ye-ee-es! Now. Yes.'

'Hello? What did you say?' asked Muriel.

'I'm just coming,' said Reg into the mouthpiece.

And then he did.

A trumpeting and whooping, picked up and conveyed by way of the phone connection all the way across town and under the River Thames, was instantly audible in the high-altitude office of the women's magazine. A long, juddering sigh could also be heard.

There was a moment's silence.

The Harlot's Prerogative

'Hello?' said Muriel Oliver at last. 'I'm trying to contact Gwen Lightsome. Hello? Can you hear me?'

'Ping-pong,' said Reg Lightsome in a sing-song voice. 'There is nobody here to answer your call right now. We will get back to you. Please leave your message after the tone . . .'

Then he held the telephone handset towards his wife.

'Bleat, bleat, bleat. Beep,' she said.

And so it was that Gwen Lightsome received her invitation to meet at her earliest convenience Rosie Maguire, editor in chief of *Home & Beauty*, to discuss future career prospects made possible by significant changes of personnel at that magazine.

The message included the priceless item of information that a replacement was being sought for, of all people, Constance Verity, *Home & Beauty*'s longest-serving contributor.

Ellen Bright had walked through the streets and squares of Little Walsingham in a state of permanent surprise. It was unlike any village in England that she had previously known. No-one looks for plaster saints and icons on sale in the high street shops of everyday towns in the English counties. Butchers and greengrocers, by all means. But not one country shop in ten thousand is filled with sugary-sweet images of Our Lady. How many market town high streets in England have a religious vestment workshop?

In the window of one shop alone, in the middle of Walsingham, Ellen counted seventy-four different statues and busts of the Virgin Mary offered for sale. She was quietly disappointed to find that most of the plaster saints were not made of plaster at all, but plastic. The images identified as Our Lady of Walsingham – a crowned figure seated on a throne, with child on knee – were, she discovered, as likely as not to have been made in Italy.

Nearby there were racks of rosaries and prayer cards printed in quaint typefaces; framed homilies; half a wall of crucifixes, a choice of almost 120 crosses in different shapes and sizes. Ellen picked up a shrink-wrapped pack of six drinks coasters – 'resistant to 80 degrees C', the label said. Each mat bore a different colour picture, including Our Lady of Walsingham and some colourful shots of her shrine.

Other shops along the main street were selling boxes of incense and finger-sized plastic nuns: framed paintings of the Sacred Heart; portraits of Jesus and his mother, with oddly northern European fair skin and follow-you-round-the-room blue eyes; copies of medieval pilgrim badges; ecclesiastical copes; black shirts with priest's back-to-front collars; even the odd bishop's, or perhaps abbot's, mitre studded with chunky paste jewellery; palm crosses in bargain-priced packs of fifty; nativity sets in moulded plastic, with model donkeys and wise men; and reproduction icons, shining with brand-new old gold. They were selling statues of black virgins, dazzling white virgins, simpering virgins, virgins at the centre of happy family groups, Barbie doll virgins. There were hand-painted models of saints and unpainted model Last Suppers; altar frontals at reduced prices; improving tracts, bibles and prayer books; and everywhere – absolutely everywhere – images of praying hands. Praying hands in china, bronze, stained wood, plaster and plastic; praying hands reproduced on canvas; praying hands in framed prints and praying hands on postcards.

In the time it took her to walk the length of High Street, she counted eight priests and four nuns; the women were barely noticeable in their cut-down blue headscarfs-cum-veils. There were knots of visitors standing at every corner and outside many of the shops; the majority were women of middle age, often grouped around a black-jacketed priest. Five grey-haired women with Liverpool accents were gathered at the door of a souvenir shop, opening paper bags and comparing their new purchases. Each of them had bought a mounted and framed copy of a prayer of St Francis of Assisi.

One priest in a cassock walked into the centre of the road and halted there, looking at the sky and taking a deep pull on his cigarette. He was only a young man with close-cropped hair and a full moustache.

At one point she saw a nun, who was muttering angrily as she made her way round a group of elderly visitors at a street corner. Ellen had time to notice that the sister was in full ankle-length, black habit with – what did they call that thing? – a coif. She had vaguely thought that all nuns had abandoned this sort of conservative full-dress uniform some years earlier.

The nun threw a final angry remark over her shoulder as she

turned into a garden entry. Ellen caught only a couple of words, a fragment of what she had said. They sounded like 'king' and then 'tourists'.

Minutes later Ellen was at the far end of the street, looking towards open country, when a group of pilgrims came into view. At the head of the crocodile was a man in a green fluorescent jacket, who appeared to be marshalling the walkers, and another holding up a cross. Four women were carrying on their shoulders a statue which she took to be an image of the Virgin Mary.

Ellen had heard the group before she had seen it. She now understood why. At the centre of the column marched a woman with an amplified megaphone slung over her shoulder. At a distance it had sounded like a solitary chant booming out but as they approached the thinner sound of individual voices became audible. The raincoated woman was leading their singing of – what was it? The *Sancta Maria* perhaps.

Ellen, if she had thought about it at all, would probably have described her approach to the church as generally in line with the attitude of Lord Melbourne, Queen Victoria's first prime minister. 'While I cannot be regarded as a pillar, I must be regarded as a buttress of the church, because I support it from the outside,' he was supposed to have said. She had been brought up as an Anglican, with a native sense of unease about enthusiasm and a mistrust of the extreme.

No, that wasn't quite true. She simply didn't want to take things to extremes herself; she was no more likely to become a proscriptive puritan than she was to bear witness to weeping statues and rocking virgins. Fervour was all right for other people. She rather admired the brilliant, jostling exuberance of Hindu festivals. The world might be a brighter place, she thought, if the walls of Salvation Army citadels teemed with erotic carvings.

She had, come to that, always known there was something pretty interesting about women Salvationists in black stockings with seams.

Ellen's father had been a steady and unspectacular churchgoer, secure in his faith, so far as his daughter could tell; if he was unwilling to play a more active part in church life it was probably because he did not care to take a very active role in life itself. Ellen's mother was a teacher and an optimist. She had, in a late-blossoming

Andrew Moncur

career, become head of a junior school and a dynamic force, throwing herself into new technology and computing with the energy of a terrier launching itself at a rat.

Mrs Bright was a dark, attractive woman with an impatient, quick mind which was capable of rushing her into misunderstandings. As a little girl, Ellen had sometimes found her mother wanting in sympathy, a little too brisk. She had the teacher's tendency: speaking to adults as though addressing a classroom of bright but slightly deaf nine-year-olds; speaking to children as though their life was meant to be a perpetual assault on one of the trickier faces of Mount Everest.

In her, faith and commitment to religion meant reliably taking a turn to arrange the flowers in church and helping to dress small shepherds for the nativity play.

Where her children were concerned, she had high expectations which had been, to a degree, fulfilled. It was a family joke, but a rueful one for Ellen, to recall that the little girl had on several occasions when trying to attract her mother's attention called her not Mummy, but Miss.

Ellen Bright sometimes felt that in her work she was still trying to attract her mother's notice.

'You're always very busy,' a man had told her. 'Yes, but we busy people are the ones who get things done,' she had replied. She had decorated the bedroom of their flat – well, his flat really. She had painted the stupid, flaking ceiling and all the woodwork. She had hung the wallpaper. She had chosen the fabric and, despite her chronic inability to put two stitches in a straight line, she had made the curtains.

And after all that it hadn't worked out.

'We'll be closing in a minute,' said the woman in the red apron, reaching across the table to pick up her cold teapot. 'Was there anything else you was wanting?'

'Sorry,' said Ellen. 'So sorry . . .'

'Pilgrim?' asked the tea-shop woman, in a neutral way.

'Sorry?'

'Are you in Walsingham on a pilgrimage? You know. Our Lady and all that.'

98

The Harlot's Prerogative

'No, I'm a – well, I'm here on business.' Ellen smiled brightly.

'What, you mean sort of business business?'

'Up to a point. We call it TOT.'

'Tea-oh-tea?' The woman frowned.

'That's right. I'm really in the writing business.'

'Oh, that's nice. It makes a change. People come here looking for miracles, you know. Was there anything more? Another pot? Don't let me rush you.'

Ellen made a more careful appraisal of the – what was she? Waitress? Owner? In any event, she had a fine generous figure. She might have been Italian: dark haired, dark eyed and she looked, now that Ellen came to think about it, dangerously close to flashpoint.

'Did you . . . do you know Maurice Lovelace?' she asked. The question had arrived with no pause for reflection. 'That's Mr Lovelace the . . .'

'Let's be having these, then,' said Sonia Marks. She scooped up the plate and cup from the table and turned away.

'Do you know him?'

'Not at all,' snapped Sonia, walking briskly round the end of the counter and disappearing into the kitchen.

Ellen was wide awake enough to know that her response was a lie. This, she felt reasonably sure, was a sin.

Across the road, an ancient black bicycle stood propped against the brick wall beside the sweet shop. A plastic bag, with black lettering on a turquoise background, had been pulled over its saddle. A yard to the left, a man's figure was visible through a plate-glass window. Father Bugloss was holding up a hand sprouting with black hair; he appeared to be beating time in mid-air.

He was reciting a passage of scripture: '*And Moses and Aaron took these men which are expressed by their names. And they assembled all the congregation together on the first day of the second month, and they declared their pedigrees after their families, by the house of their fathers, according to the number of the names, from twenty years old and upward, by their polls. As the Lord commanded Moses, so he numbered them in the wilderness of Sinai . . .*'

As it was, not a soul heard a word that passed the priest's lips.

Chapter Sixteen

'Bloody Rosie's still laying waste to civilisation as we know it. She reminds me just now of Genghis Khan in his Flail of God mood. She'll calm down in a little while, of course, but first we have to put up with the terror – and some dreadful youth-is-strength nonsense.' Daphne Chapman, head of the features department at *Home & Beauty*, cradled the telephone on her collarbone and drew another matchstick figure on her pad. This one she impaled with a large dagger.

'She's employed some child as a page designer on the strength of his art college degree in graffiti studies. Something like that. I tell you, he's spent the last two years underground in dank places. He's closely related to humankind but not quite one of us, if you see what I mean. You know the kind of thing: haircut like a hedgehog in an accident; pubic beard; mouth hangs open. We gave him "A Doctor Writes" to play around with and he came up with a logo which looked like two words sprayed on a wall.'

'And what were they? What were the words, I mean?' asked Ellen Bright. She was sitting on a field gate, her portable phone tucked under her chin.

'Tubular organs.'

'I see.'

'Do you?'

'No, not really. What does it mean?'

'Don't ask me. It's young though, isn't it?'

'Very young.'

'We don't know quite how it will play with our advertisers in the personal fragrance line. I liked your body-in-the-lift piece, by the way,' said Daphne.

'Thank you. That's what I wanted to know. I hoped you would make it a sort of campaigning thing.' Ellen felt her neck and shoulders relax.

100

The Harlot's Prerogative

'Sorry. Our beloved editor isn't very keen on campaigns right now. She thinks they're old, dull. She wants all the youth stuff – but don't worry. We'll get your piece in. After a month or two it'll dawn on her that kids don't buy *Home & Beauty* anyway. Not even if you give them whole pages of tubular organs.'

A passing car braked as a pheasant ran headlong across the road in its path.

'So, tell me how you're doing,' said Daphne.

'I'm in Norfolk. It seemed sensible to start at Walsingham.'

'Does Lovelace have a house there?'

'He's got an apartment in a sort of barn conversion. It's not much more than a holiday cottage. I'm still trying to get a feel for the man. He's a bit of a loner. I looked up his library file: there's amazingly little. He once tried to do something to protect the badger – otherwise damn all worth mentioning.'

Perhaps he had put his creative drive into the Constance Verity column which, as Daphne was all too well aware, would soon be missed by *Home & Beauty* readers.

'Our Rosie was almost upset after the accident; she bawled out her poor secretary in quite an emotional way. It was very moving.'

'The last time I met your editor – how can I put this? – we didn't exactly hit it off,' said Ellen.

'Oh, come on. She didn't bite you, did she. Or maybe she did. Let us know how you're getting on anyway.'

Ellen Bright looked away towards a wooded hillside, a smoky blue in the fading light. Silently a barn owl beat across her line of sight with slow strokes of its gold-dusted wings; its prey – some small creature – hung limply from its talons. Soon it was a pale shadow swallowed by the twilight.

For the mouse is a creature of great personal valour. For this is a true case: Cat takes female mouse . . . male mouse will not depart, but stands threat'ning and daring. If you will let her go, I will engage you. As prodigious a creature as you . . . Mrs Legg sang the solo in a mezzo-soprano voice of immense power, with a vibrato of such earth-shaking proportions she might have been bodily attached to a pneumatic drill or a runaway spin drier.

Andrew Moncur

The conductor tapped his music stand, attempting to halt this wall of vibrating sound.

There was a snort of laughter on the left hand side of the choir. A bearded man had leaned forward from the tenor section to whisper something to the pair of blonde women in the centre of the second row of the altos. '. . . down the walls of Jericho,' he said loudly into the sudden silence which had fallen across the room.

'Thank you, Clive,' said the conductor. 'Now, Mrs Legg – Veronica, dear. I'm not hearing every syllable. You're swallowing the mouse. Let's hear the mmm. The mmm. And the ess. Yes, the ess. Let's do that again and remember, fast and light. *Presto, leggiero.* Thank you, Elsie.'

'From the top, Father?' Elsie Marks, seated at the piano, made a pencil mark on her score and then repeated the opening bars.

Veronica Legg slowly craned her large head and directed a piercing glare, as cold as frozen fish fingers, towards the tenors.

Then she turned back towards Father Bugloss, rehearsing the St Mary's Priory Singers in, as he liked to put it, his capacity as principal conductor. His raised hand emerged from a sprouting cuff of hair around the sleeve of his black jacket. Mrs Legg opened her mouth and released another wobbling outpouring of sound.

'For the mer-mmmouse-sss is a creature of great personal valour,' she sang, like a harnessed earth tremor.

The bearded tenor, Clive, was gesturing with both hands, looking as an over-excited Leonard Bernstein might look if such a thing were remotely imaginable. Finally, he clapped his palms to his ears and bent over as though yielding to a gale force wind.

Neil Bugloss loved his music. He had once written a monograph on Ethelwold, the tenth-century Benedictine bishop of Winchester, who built the greatest church organ of its day: 400 pipes, thirty-six bellows and two monks required to take it into action, playing at full pelt.

The sound escaping from the Oddfellows' Hall, in High Street, was altogether less memorable. It might not have been immediately recognisable even to Benjamin Britten. The singing was momentarily drowned by the purposeful throb of a diesel engine. The last of the day's parties of pilgrims was departing Walsingham, bound for

The Harlot's Prerogative

home in an ageing coach which smelled of oil, cigarette smoke and damp plastic.

The priest in the first row of seats, nearest to the door, looked choleric; his nose and cheeks were veined the colour of communion wine. By the time the coach passed the remains of the ancient friary, on the edge of the village, a smile of great sweetness had dawned on his face. Within another quarter of a mile he was fast asleep and dreaming of birching nuns to the roar of mighty organs.

It was silent in the bedroom. The large window, overlooking the darkened Thames and the distant Palace of Westminster, was at least double- and possibly triple-glazed; the lights of ceaselessly moving traffic made it flicker like some private cinema screen, running a movie with the soundtrack turned off.

There was a faint click of heels. A person unseen hurried by outside the door to the private single-bed hotel facility, as the staff at St Wilfrid's Medical Centre liked to call the rooms where their patients lay in varying levels of drug-induced torpor or in self-sustained pools of anxiety or nervous excitement.

The excitement was mostly felt by those who had saved long and hard and now, at last, awaited the new nose, the altered breasts or the enlarged penis which they had ordered from the surgeons, confident that they could improve upon nature's first rough draft. The scars, stitches and discomfort were just part of the price these people were prepared to pay.

Maurice Lovelace registered no feeling, made no movement, uttered no sound, sought no change, displayed no emotion at all. He made no demands, lodged no complaints, expressed no preference, invited no visitor, regurgitated no meal, shed no blood, cracked no joke, argued no toss. He was, in short, the perfect patient. If only he could have found a way to roll himself to left or right on the hour, every hour, so sparing his nurses the task, he would also have been the most popular patient on Nightingale Wing.

He lay in a coma, untroubled by the passage of time or the briskly impersonal ministrations of the medical staff. A length of milky-white plastic tubing emerged from his left nostril, the only outward

103

sign that he was not an ordinary, well man simply enjoying a well-earned sleep.

He knew nothing of the nightly calls paid by Mr Hopkin, the late-shift porter, who had adopted the unconscious MP as his own case ever since diagnosing his condition on admission.

'Of course, the PM had no choice but to pass him the pearl-handled pistol and leave him alone to do the decent thing,' said Archie Miller, the chief whip. He was sitting at the bedside with his elbows on his knees and his large hands dangling between his wide-stretched legs. He had been there in Maurice's room, talking steadily, enjoying the complete absence of contradiction, for a good hour. He was recalling the highlights of his day in the labyrinthine back corridors of the House of Commons.

'After an entire morning had gone by without a sign of any letter of resignation – not a peep – the prime minister was starting to get a little short, as you might imagine. Wanted to know what the hell was going on. Have you noticed, by the way, that the PM's getting a great deal more touchy these days. Peevish, really. It's something that's happened over the last year or so; suddenly become very snappy, even sarcastic. Not nice. Shouldn't let the voters see that side of the character, as old Harold used to say. It makes them think you're getting rattled, tired – worn out.'

Archie Miller loved a good talk. It had been suggested to him that for many politicians the compelling motive for entering the trade had nothing to do with any craving for power or hunger for change. It was more the simple desire to lecture other people rigid; they wanted the world to grant them a hearing and, better still, to listen respectfully to their words, however inane.

The vilest tyrant probably started out wishing to be heard and turning nasty only when people took no notice. Still, the chief whip remarked to himself, say what you like about tyrants, at least they're seldom boring. Who was the chap in Rome who made his favourite horse a member of the college of priests and a consul? Poor Maurice was in no condition to provide an answer to this or any other question.

'Where was I? Yes, the prime minister was getting a little browned off – tetchy is the word – about the lack of action from our departing friend. Called me in and asked me what was up. Where was the letter expressing infinite regret, pleading for more time with the family, wishing the boss every success, urging the party to fulfil its sacred . . .'

Sir Archie stopped abruptly. The comatose form on the bed had given a perceptible twitch. An eyelid had made a nervous flicker; an eyebrow had jerked. What had he said? Which remark had struck a chord with his unconscious colleague? Not merely a colleague, but a friend – a friend who, apart from anything else, and thanks to a malign fate, represented the sum total of the government's margin of majority in the House of Commons: a single seat.

Come on. What had he said? What was the trigger? Archie Miller tried to trawl back over his words.

'Prime Minister,' he said. The figure on the bed remained utterly still.

'Rattled.' There was no sign.

'Letter.' Nothing.

'Let me see, now. Regret.' Silence.

'Tetchy.' Perfect silence.

'Family.' Maurice was sunk in a trough of immobility.

'Spend more time with the . . .' It was useless. Archie Miller decided that he must have imagined the tiny convulsion which had animated poor Maurice for a fragment of a second. He was not an unduly sensitive man; his wife insisted he was capable of conducting entire conversations without registering a single fact – age, sex, nationality, choice of clothing – about the person he was addressing. Mrs Miller claimed that once or twice he had spoken to her at length apparently without noticing that she was, in fact, his own wife. Never mind. Thank the Lord he hadn't made some grossly improper suggestion, as he said to her at the time. Not that he ever would these days, of course.

'So, as I was saying, the boss was absolutely hopping . . .'

Maurice Lovelace's eyebrows rose once, twice in little flutters. It was the contrast with his previously impenetrable stillness that lent the movement its full dramatic force.

'Boss,' Sir Archie repeated.

Andrew Moncur

There was another – what was it? Another small wince.
'The boss. Of course.'
Maurice actually made the faintest of whimpers.
The chief whip stood up and smacked his right palm on to his left leg. It was a very Bavarian, lederhosen-slapping sort of gesture. A look of pleasure, even boyish delight crossed his long face. What a relief. What a signal of hope.

So long as old Maurice retained some vital signs, the government's Commons majority remained intact. There was no prospect of a wretched by-election with the ever-present possibility of disaster haunting the party, this time in the Walsingham seat.

Maurice Lovelace knew the game and he would know the score. He must have been in the Commons since – when would it have been, now? Probably since 1983. That's right. He was one of the June '83 intake. Never mind his vegetative state, or whatever the medics called it; if push came to shove he would have to be wheeled across to the Commons and taken through the division lobby on a stretcher. As long as the doctors could find a trace of life in the old carcass, duty demanded that he should come – all right, be brought – to the aid of the party. Lovelace would have expected nothing less. He had seen older colleagues dragged around the place on trolleys, still voting in divisions when, from a medical point of view at least, all hope was lost. In one or two cases members had swung important votes at the very last or even, arguably, beyond; they had reached that point where it would have amounted to gross flattery to suggest they had just the one foot in the grave.

Sometimes, when tension eased off, the parties would agree it was sufficient in order that a vote should count only to bring the sick member within the precinct of the Palace of Westminster; they were usually left lying in an ambulance parked in Star Chamber Court. But when feelings ran high, as at the present time, the rival whips would insist on honourable members being hauled inside, however poorly they might be. In the dog days of James Callaghan's government the Tories even demanded proof that one Labour MP, lying deathly still on a trolley brought into the House, was still alive. A colleague had to twang the poor patient's life-support wiring until he could make a vaguely convincing flicker appear on the monitor screen.

Maurice Lovelace had never had a near-death experience; in fact, he used to complain to his secretary that after a couple of years in the House of Commons any reasonable man would fancy a near-life experience.

Now, had it been possible for him to process the information, he would have been touched to know that at least one other person cared whether or not he lived. That the individual concerned was the chief whip, motivated by low political considerations, would not have troubled him in the slightest.

Across the river at Westminster, in a cramped office shared by lobby and gallery staff from the *Daily Telegraph*, a young reporter was flicking through the latest green-covered issue of the Commons *Hansard* report. A written reply from the Transport Secretary caught her eye. The minister was responding to a question tabled by Constance Verity, MP.

'Motorway of life,' she read. '*The Secretary of State is pleased to note the hon. member's remarks about signs of economic recovery as evidenced by traffic volumes and general improvements in the national road network achieved by HM Government. There are no proposals under immediate discussion for any change in regulations governing use of the motorway hard-shoulder.*'

The reporter yawned. She twirled a length of hair around her right index finger. 'Constance Verity?' she said aloud. Familiar name – but she could not for the moment call to mind Miss Verity's parliamentary seat.

She made a mental note to check *Dod's Parliamentary Companion*; then she yawned once more and turned another page of *Hansard*. It was very nearly too late to catch the third edition deadline anyway.

In his garage, under the white light of the long neon tubes, Harry Green loaded the striped surveying poles into his Land Rover. He wanted to make an early start tomorrow.

'A merry joust, my good sirs,' he said, waving a pole in the air. In actual fact he would be taking levels in that ten-acre field overlooking the western side of Little Walsingham, across there on the far side of the old railway yard and the road where the line used to run.

His scheme was a good one. It could make his fortune. It would not require a miracle for its success; merely a large amount of hard work and, in the first place, the right sort of publicity.

Harry turned out the light and stepped into the yard. The vast sky was a silent, unfathomable ocean pin-pricked with starlight. From somewhere in the night, across the fields towards the tower of St Peter's Church, came a short scream of real terror. A vixen? A weasel at work in the rabbit warren over by Gerald Beavis's land?

The night was still again. There was only the faintest rustle, as though made by some small animal doggedly creeping forward and back in pursuit of its prey: a steady, rhythmical sound stealing through the darkness. Then, at last, Harry Green stopped scratching the seat of his pants and turned to walk inside the house.

Chapter Seventeen

Rosie Maguire left the building at eight forty-four p.m. Her taxi cab had by that time been waiting for an hour and a quarter at the kerbside near the main door, at a point where the shrubbery planted at the base of the tower appeared to have been torn up by particularly active vandals or wild animals.

'The Surprise, please,' she said, settling her light frame in the corner and pretending to fasten the seat belt.

'I know that place,' said the cab driver, glancing up at his interior mirror. 'And I know the prices. Not so much the Surprise. Shock, more like.'

'Driver,' said Rosie Maguire, leaning forward a fraction. 'Would you mind doing me a very great favour?'

'What's that?'

'Will you just go and boil your head for me, please. Thank you so very much.'

And with that she closed the sliding partition with a snap. The driver, who had already clocked a handsome fare while sitting at the kerb doing nothing, gave her a nod and a wink through the glass.

Reggie Lightsome was alone at the table, tapping his glass with a white finger. He was a little man. As the editor crossed the floor towards him she observed that sitting just so, straight backed, his feet actually failed to touch the ground. The soles of his little boots were parallel with but about half an inch above the carpet.

'Hey! Rosie. Delightful. Good, good. Great,' he said, half rising and gathering from his lap a handful of dangling tablecloth which he screwed into a tight wad and tucked absent-mindedly into the waistband of his trousers. 'Terrific to see you.'

'Reg,' said Rosie. 'Where's Gwen, then?'

'Held up, I'm afraid. She'll be joining us.'

'When, roughly?' Rosie Maguire pulled up her chair.

Andrew Moncur

'Oh, you know. Soon. Soonish.'

'When you and I have finished talking about the vulgar business side of things?'

'Let me get you a drink,' said Reggie, with a gingery sort of smile. At last she placed him. With his reddish colouring, neat little frame and understated pugnacity he reminded Rosie of a border terrier.

They had been discussing terms for almost half an hour before they were interrupted. Roughly three minutes had been occupied by the matter of money; the remainder of the time was spent on questions of office accommodation – Gwen Lightsome would need to have her own en suite bathroom adjoining her office, as well as a window giving a view of the River Thames – and details of the level of secretarial support suitable for a writer of her level of celebrity. Mrs Lightsome would require the services of a personal assistant as well as a secretary. There was barely a quibble about the type of company car she would receive as part of her employment package at *Home & Beauty*. It would be of the same German manufacture as the one she had been given by *Woman's Week*, the magazine she was now preparing to depart.

'Only it will have to be this year's model with the fuel injection and the power steering. Gwen is very, very particular about the power steering,' said Reggie emphatically.

'Reg,' said Rosie Maguire, looking at him in a frank way. 'Reg, your Gwen absolutely cannot drive. I doubt if she can ride a bicycle. Why on earth should she give a toss about power steering?'

There was a stir throughout the restaurant as Gwen Lightsome approached the table at the centre of a moving knot of waiters, led by a dark-haired man who was walking backwards across the dining room like a functionary of some medieval court. There was something about his progress which suggested he should be bearing a sword of state or a gilded mace, while he was in fact carrying only a menu in a mock leather binding.

'Plis, plis,' he said, 'Plis to seat here, lady.'

'Yes, yes. Never seen such a fuss! God, why do people have to make such a bloody performance?' Gwen boomed across the crowded room. Other diners, swivelling to stare at the new arrival, might have failed to gather immediately that Gwen Lightsome

110

positively demanded this sort of attention from those who served her. It was practically a condition when she agreed to patronise a restaurant.

'Hello, Dickie,' she cooed, waving towards a group seated in the window. Three men at three separate tables more or less in her line of sight each raised a hand in tentative salute.

The head waiter fussed around, taking her shawl and her brief-case and easing her broad hips into a dining chair which seemed miraculously to rise to receive her.

'Good evening, Gwen. And congratulations,' said Rosie Maguire as the flap of waiters around the far side of the table slowly sub-sided.

'Congratulations?'

'Yes. For driving such a hard bargain.'

'My dear,' said Gwen Lightsome with a dazzling smile. 'I can't be bothering with all these details, this – how do you say? – yes, this minutiae. My responsibility is to my dear friends out there . . .' She gestured wildly with a large, jewelled hand at the far end of a white arm. 'The people who need what little help I can offer. That's what matters. Poor people. Good people. Ordinary people. Such problems, such problems.'

'Oh, absolutely . . .' Rosie started to say.

'Do we get the office on the river side of the building?' snapped Gwen. 'With the shower and loo?'

Her husband leaned across and, smiling, touched her arm. 'It's all agreed. All arranged. And that includes the 528i with the alloy wheels, six speaker hi-fi and power-steering.'

It is one of the many curious aspects of a career in journalism that certain rewards are only handed out to employees when they have ceased to be appropriate. So, for instance, a young reporter struggling to build a reputation and ceaselessly travelling the country from end to end will definitely not be provided with a company car or, come to that, any other means of transport.

On the other hand, an established writer who never leaves the office except to buy a sandwich will be issued with the keys to an unexciting but thoroughly reliable vehicle, maintained at the employer's expense.

Andrew Moncur

A real star, a household name, will be provided with a large and even glamorous company car although by this stage it is clear to all concerned that there's no real chance the limousine will ever, for one minute, be used on the company's business. It may well be that the person concerned hasn't the remotest clue how to drive or what, exactly, makes cars go.

It doesn't matter. Journalism needs winners more than it needs a sensible transport policy.

'You know why we need you on board with us at *Home & Beauty*, Gwen?' Rosie asked. 'It's because we want you there caring for people. We want your warmth and care . . .'

The head waiter, with two assistants, was hovering at the edge of the pool of light thrown by the table lamp. He was waiting to take a dinner order from the three guests; they all ignored him.

'We think you can give us all some spiritual values,' said Rosie.

'I shall want the suite decorated by a designer of my choice. Perhaps Ollie Kinkel. He did those fabulous silk swatches for Polly Marshall.'

'Of course,' murmured Rosie.

'And is it true that you're giving the old heave-ho to poor, dear Constance Verity?' Gwen Lightsome leaned across the table. Her eyes were bright with ill-concealed pleasure and malice.

'Let's say Constance is unwell. There was a terrible road accident and the prospects for recovery are not good,' said Rosie Maguire, looking away into the darkest corner of the restaurant. 'Ah, good. There's the wine waiter. Shall we order?'

Gwen had taken her husband by the wrist and was shaking his arm with an awful, vigorous force.

'Reggie! Reggie! I've left my phone in the briefcase. Be an angel and run and fetch it for me . . .'

Reg Lightsome had taken barely two or three paces before the white linen cloth, still tucked into his trousers, was dragged off the table in a cascade of flying glass, silver, candle wax and cut flowers.

'You stupid, stupid man!' Gwen Lightsome snapped venomously at the head waiter who was by then kneeling at her feet, picking up knives from the carpet.

* * *

The Harlot's Prerogative

Mrs Veronica Legg bent over the kitchen sink, rinsing her right-foot wellington boot under the cold tap. There was an odd shade of pink in the drain as the water swirled away.

The clockwork timer on the side table gave a preliminary ping and, without a moment's hesitation, she reached across to stifle its familiar bleating. Then she put aside the boot, wiped her hands on her apron and opened the door of the roasting oven of the Aga. She removed the toasted cheese and, juggling with the hot plate, hurried over to the kitchen table.

After she had eaten, Mrs Legg placed the plates in the dishwasher and rinsed her knife and fork. She was looking forward to adding another chapter to her planned book, *The Full English Breakfast*? It was in her mind's eye already being hailed as the encyclopaedia of good bed-and-breakfast practice. She could see the reviews: Veronica Legg, the Mrs Beeton of the British guest-house trade . . .

'Children,' she wrote at the top of a fresh page. 'And parents,' she added. 'Parents of young children operate on a different time scale to the rest of us, which is probably what Albert Einstein had in mind when he arrived at his theories about relativity and the space-time continuum, knocking Newtonian mechanics on the head,' she wrote.

He will have noticed that parents are not so bothered as other folk about mess in bathrooms, untidy bedrooms and grubby fingermarks on paintwork on stairways and halls. Not to mention breakages in the china and glassware departments. It is all to do with time.

Parents can tell themselves that at some point in the future – five, ten or even twenty years hence – their children will be grown up. Mother and father will once again have a nice house where everything will be in a clean, satisfactory and unbroken condition, what we in the bed-and-breakfast business call hunky-dory.

It is difficult for parents to turn their minds to a way of thinking that the house must be smart, clean and free of grimy fingerprints not in twenty years' time, not tomorrow, but – yes – today. Such is the case, as we know, for the B&B landlady.

Andrew Moncur

It can cause friction when a bed-and-breakfast host has to tell a parent that while his or her child may well grow up to be a respectable solicitor or bank manager in another two or three decades, it is not, meanwhile, acceptable to go scribbling with a crayon on the lounge wallpaper or tearing down the shower curtains. Or, for that matter, running up and down stairs shouting and screaming and demanding to know why the guest house does not possess a video recorder especially for the use of visiting children. These things are, shall we say, not on.

One has one's responsibilities to one's other guests however much one would like to play a constructive part in the decent upbringing of young persons. The adult guests must come first. They have to be treated with care. This is merely a matter or respect for those who have, with the passage of years, gained that right. Besides, they expect to pay full price.

It is a painful conclusion but one I have arrived at after much careful consideration. Children: no, it is best not to . . .

Mrs Legg was suddenly alert. There had been the faint sound of a key in the lock and a creaking of stairs. That young woman had returned to the house and had now gone upstairs to the Rose Room. Veronica Legg was convinced that, whatever she might say to the contrary, Miss Bright was really and truly a pilgrim. She sensed some problem in the love life, possibly a failed romance; or maybe she had come to Walsingham to seek help before having an operation. Yes, that was probably the answer: a surgical operation of some delicacy.

A cock pheasant's sore-throated cry cut across the impenetrable darkness of the garden.

Clive Wilson's bicycle was found lying half hidden under the hedge outside the Bull just before closing time. The front wheel had been badly buckled and several spokes were broken. There was also blood on the paving stones nearby, which prompted the finders – a Roman Catholic priest and a teetotal Methodist plumber from Fakenham – to look around a little more carefully.

The Harlot's Prerogative

They discovered Clive on the far side of the hedge. His nose was broken and there was a great deal of blood in his beard. The poor man was confused and badly shaken.

He was unable to explain what, exactly, had happened. He could remember leaving choir practice at the Oddfellows' Hall. He had spoken to one or two tenors and to Elsie, the pianist, at the door.

Then he set off to cycle home to Great Snoring, meaning to post a letter first at the Shirehall. He thought he had carried out this task. Everything after that was a blur. He could dimly remember lights and a high-pitched noise he described as 'like an aircraft engine'. Beyond that, nothing.

Clive was driven to hospital in King's Lynn where his nose was set, slightly imperfectly. From that night onwards he would be a terribly noisy sleeper, fighting for breath and developing a frightening range of mouth and palate noises; it was unfair really, given his home address.

Chapter Eighteen

Mrs Canty sat at the bedside, facing the window and the view of the rain-smoothed Thames. Maurice Lovelace lay motionless, a clear plastic tube emerging from his nostril. His hair had been neatly brushed, which seemed incongruous given his present state.

'And I found five separate socks, all odd, which I should say you had hid, up there behind the lagged tank in the bathroom cupboard. Well, I've washed them – and I don't care if they are odd either,' said Mrs Canty.

What was it Constance Verity had said in that book she had at Christmas? *In life's great airing cupboard there's many a mismatched pair thrown together in a muddle. But who worries about little differences when we're lying side-by-side together in the warm and the dark?*

She rose and crossed the room to adjust a painting, an insipid watercolour of Windsor Castle. It was one of Mrs Canty's few failings that she could never let a picture alone; she always left them hanging more crookedly than she found them.

'What else to tell you? Yes, we've been looking at your history book – that's me and Mr Canty. He thinks it's very interesting although it's full of what he calls religious nonsense. Lord, he said to me last night, the way they carried on in King Henry's day you'd have thought religion was a matter of life and death. And those burnings. Didn't we laugh.' She stood back and squinted at the picture frame, now sagging markedly to the right.

Maurice remained utterly silent. His face was as pale as the pillow and as untroubled.

It was generous to describe his notes as any sort of history of Walsingham, a place he had known for the best part of twenty years. He had been astonished by the village on first sight, which had been on that day when he gained selection for the parliamentary seat almost by mistake. He had become more profoundly attached

116

to and more ambivalent in his feelings about the place with the passage of time.

He had set it all out in the handwritten manuscript found by Mrs Canty:

On the ups and downs of life's switchback, the sixteenth-century citizen had what was by any standards a hard ride.

The destruction of the holy house at Walsingham was a significant part, but only a part, of the great, cruel and bloody religious upheavals of the age.

The course for collision was set when Henry VIII decided that his marriage with Catherine of Aragon must be nullified, insisting that the death in infancy of all their children – except for the future Queen Mary – was the judgement of heaven on an unnatural alliance. Catherine had first been married, when they were both only fifteen years old, to Henry's older brother, Arthur, who died the following year, probably from plague.

Catherine always swore that the earlier marriage had not been consummated. Henry came to believe otherwise. He concluded, after seventeen years of marriage, that he was in breach of Old Testament law forbidding the union of a man and his brother's wife.

Henry quarrelled with Pope Clement VII who, having at first shown signs of accommodating his wishes, finally rejected the king's case for divorce. Henry started to apply pressure upon the religious orders in his realm, compelling them to recognise him as protector and supreme head of the church and clergy in England. From that moment it was inevitable that he would be the instrument of their destruction although he was, in fact, a conservative in doctrinal terms. He was no protestant and certainly no follower of Martin Luther, the reformer who railed against the iniquitous sale of indulgences for the forgiveness of sin, a shameless method of raising cash for the Church of Rome.

The title of Defender of the Faith – still borne by British monarchs – had been granted to Henry by the pope because of the way the English king disputed with Luther. Henry continued to insist on the fundamental doctrines of the Church of Rome even when he had dissolved the great Catholic religious houses of England. He maintained that his fight was with the pope, not the church.

Henry and his henchmen brought about the destruction of the great priories and friaries and obliterated all the most revered shrines in England, including one of the most famous of all in Walsingham.

But before ever he raised a finger, there was a climate of critical opinion running through Europe about the state of the church. In England there were outspoken attacks on 'idle abbey-lubbers which are apt to do nothing but to eat and to drink'. Henry's officials were able to throw together evidence of laxity, sexual incontinence, superstition and credulousness in religious houses. If only a fraction of it were true, then the clergy, the monks and nuns would still have had explaining to do.

The king's examiners were able to make much of the dubious or spurious relics they found displayed in churches and the miracles and cures claimed for them. The milk of the Virgin Mary was surprisingly abundant, enjoying a place of honour at various sites apart from Walsingham. At one rival place of pilgrimage in north Norfolk, the Priory of Bromholm, they claimed to have not only a hand-wide piece of the true cross but also the milk of St Mary and her girdle. It was claimed that thirty-nine dead people had been raised to life by the supposed wood from the cross.

The king's visitors reported an endless list of improbable relics. The Cluniac priory at Castle Acre, in Norfolk, attracted pilgrims who came to venerate the arm of St Philip – although by the mid-sixteenth century its drawing power was much reduced; it was bringing in an annual income of only ten shillings. The king's men found, at various houses, the coals on which St Lawrence was toasted; the nail clippings of St Edmund, who died by being shot full of arrows by Danes; a jawbone of St Ethelwold; the penknife and boots of St Thomas à Becket, the Canterbury martyr; and no fewer than two heads of St Ursula. There must be room for a plea of mistaken identity in this case since the saint, supposedly the daughter of a British king, was reputedly slain in Germany along with 11,000 other virgins by extremely energetic and bloodthirsty huns.

That improbable figure almost certainly arises because of a mistaken reading of Latin numerals in the tenth century (it's likely there were only eleven virgin-martyrs). However, the legend of the massed ranks of virgins really took off in 1155 when they dug up a heap of bones in Cologne. Regardless of the fact that they most likely came from a forgotten burial ground, and certainly included remains of men and children, they were immediately identified as the bones of St Ursula and her army of virgins – and soon flooded the world relic market.

There had been a lively international trade in relics for centuries. Who could resist the chance to acquire the water pots which Jesus miraculously filled with wine, to the surprise of guests at a wedding in Cana; or the stones used to pelt to death poor St Stephen, the first Christian martyr. The sellers did not always find a ready market. For instance, the piece of cross which ended up at Bromholm had previously been rejected by the monks at St Albans – although they did buy two of St Margaret's fingers instead.

These most probably belonged to St Margaret of Antioch, a popular saint in England, as opposed to St Margaret of Cortona, who was really only popular in Cortona. And then only as popular as a woman can be when she's been wearing a hair shirt for twenty-nine years.

Such relics were not invariably bought and sold on the legitimate market. The monks at Ely had the remains of two sisters, both saints, one of which they had stolen in a carefully planned raid on her original resting place and shrine at Dereham, in Norfolk. The townspeople there still commemorate St Withburga, at whose graveside miracles were reputed to have occurred. Then along came the Abbot of Ely and snatched her bones, having first got the locals helplessly drunk.

119

Andrew Moncur

Twenty years before Henry set in train the course of events which would bring down the monasteries, Walsingham had already suffered scandal. The prior himself was found to have had a hand in the till or, rather, in the riches of the holy house.

The Bishop of Norwich held an inquiry in 1514. He found that 'the Prior oftentimes goeth alone in the dusk to the Chapel of Our Lady; and without the knowledge of any of the brethren he dealeth at will with the money and jewels there received.'

Some of the canons were out hawking by day and revelling by night; the rest were merely idle, miserable and quarrelsome. They had a pair of high-living servants who grew rich on the priory's proceeds and, to cap all, the wife of one of these men was the prior's mistress.

The bishop, in the finest traditions, ordered instant dismissals – but only of the two servants.

Mrs Legg had risen early, fed her indoor plants and combed the cat before sitting with cup of tea and a garibaldi biscuit to enjoy the view from her kitchen window. The grass was drenched in a quicksilver dew; the border plants beyond the lawn were bowing under its weight.

She liked to be up with the sun, thinking about the day and its uses long before the first of her guests stepped into the bathroom, reached for the lever on the pale green, low-flush toilet and then made a violent, twisting, pumping motion which might yield a flood of water – or, equally, leave half the moving parts of a ball-cock valve in their surprised hand.

She liked the birdsong early in the year. The blackbirds and the wagtails were already at work on the grass in the morning's brilliant sunlight. There was a distant glimpse of orange as her tomcat, Rolf, flitted between the lavender clumps on the far side of the lawn.

Veronica Legg was deeply attached to her house and its garden, her home for twenty-three years. More critical eyes might have dwelt on the random mixture of architectural styles: the original, perhaps eighteenth-century cottage in Norfolk brick and flint, uncomfortably overshadowed by the Victorian Gothic porch and the post-war extension, in fifties new-town municipal style. The

120

metal-framed windows had now been replaced with white plastic.

Both the Leggs had moved into the house – it was known at that time as Henry Hall – when they came to north Norfolk from London. Mr Legg had been unwell even then, his life made miserable by a series of ill-defined pains and headaches. His condition was not regarded as serious, or even noteworthy, by the local doctor who prescribed aspirins and an open bedroom window at night and wondered, privately, how a self-employed brass band musical instrument maker hoped to make a living in rural Norfolk.

It was only later, when Mr Legg mentioned that his tweed hat was no longer big enough for his head – and pointed out how, extraordinarily, he needed a larger size – that the doctor finally reached a diagnosis. The most likely cause was, he said, Paget's disease, *osteitis deformans*. This is a condition, rare in middle-aged men, in which the bones become enlarged and softened. The doctor's view was confirmed when Mr Legg began to suffer deafness, a classic symptom arising when nerves are trapped by the thickening of the skull. It was a patent disaster for a man in his line of business. Within five weeks he had died of heart failure.

Mrs Legg was left with the house, a small sum of life insurance money and eight French horns in varying stages of construction.

Her first act as a widow was to burn her late husband's hat on a fire she built for the purpose in their as yet still largely untamed garden. She looked over the same plot now, sipping her tea.

There was a thud and a little muted scream from the flower bed.

'Cleaning the dining room after feeding,' read the new heading in Mrs Legg's black ledger.

The bed and breakfast hostess should note the undoubted fact that the majority of people throw their food to the left, sprinkling the floor on that side with debris.

The explanation for this tendency seems obvious: most people, even now, are right-handed and therefore convey food to the mouth in a right-to-left direction. From time to time they do so, and miss.

*   *   *

121

Andrew Moncur

'Reggie,' said Gwen Lightsome, raising herself on her white elbow and turning to her husband's side of their enormously wide, super king-sized bed. 'Reggie? Where are you?' By now she was peering beneath the duvet, actively looking for him.

Reg screamed quietly. The sound came from behind her ample back; he had spent the better part of the night on his wife's side of the bed. It was not unusual for Reg to wake in panic.

'I think I've got it . . .'

'Huungh?' Reg sat bolt upright, his eyes wide with alarm.

'The big idea to take to *Home & Beauty*. What d'you think?'

'Sorry?' said Reg, struggling to pull himself to the surface of wakefulness. 'I was dreaming about cars. Four-wheel drive.'

'Mother Of the Year. Supermum. A giant-sized competition. Is Your Mum The World's Best? Fabulous prizes. What do you reckon? Huge promotion; everyone will want to be in on it. Great pull for radio and our friends on TV . . .'

'Great. Super. Love it.'

'It'll have to be a really mumsie mum who wins. The kind everyone loves. You know: stacks of kids, lovely husband; she stays at home, cooks pies, does part-time degree course, darns socks, makes love, blows noses. Lovely, bright, good, kind, sexy and, above all, a real homebody.'

'Hmm,' said Reg.

'We'll need to take on a couple of red hot researchers to do it. Know what I mean? I'll want a really high-powered pair of girls – work all hours, no commitments, no sick kids, no bloody whinging about getting home to make bloody supper.'

'Huuhh.'

'Oh, Reggie.'

'Hey! That hurts . . .'

'And this?'

'Hey!'

'And what if I do this?'

'Oh, God . . .'

'And this. And this. And this. And this . . .'

'Do you believe in miracles, Mrs Legg?' asked Ellen Bright, looking up from the pale green plate, a rubbery egg white and two rashers of streaky bacon.

Veronica Legg took a deep breath and waited for the inevitable outpouring of private problems, longings and forlorn hopes. She made a mental note to pick up vegetable oil at the supermarket in Fakenham later that morning.

'I ask because you must see a great many pilgrims coming to Walsingham. I mean, people must come here hoping for miraculous cures or special prayers to be answered.' Ellen smiled at the land-lady, who was leaning over a table near the dining-room door.

'Some do,' said Mrs Legg, cautiously.

'And have you ever been convinced? Do you know if their prayers are ever granted?'

Here we go, said Mrs Legg to herself. She had been polishing table mats and gingering up her little vases of flowers in a desultory way, and now turned and stared thoughtfully at the younger woman. 'I've seen some sad and unnecessary things happen here,' she said.

'No miracles?'

'We had some very lucky people staying here just the other day,' said Mrs Legg. 'They were in a car crash, or very nearly. Right in Walsingham next to the shrine church itself. You know?'

'And what happened to them?' Ellen Bright had the feeling she was being steered away from the point of her inquiry.

'They were staying here at the Gideon's Well, in the lilac room. It's a very nice twin room next to the bridal suite which has the four-poster. You must remind me to show you the four-poster. You're not married yourself, dear?'

Ellen shook her head. She pushed a forkful of bacon around the plate and attempted to hide it under a slice of toast.

'As I say, they're a nice couple – an older couple, not too well – and they were in the lilac room, yes. They'd been to the shrine in the afternoon for the sprinkling. Have you been sprinkled at all, dear? I don't know whether you go in for that sort of thing.' Mrs Legg regarded her guest carefully.

'You should leave the bacon, dear. If you've had enough. You young people, always on diets and worrying about being slim. It's not surprising you hear these terrible cases with girls going aerobic. Where was I?'

'You were telling me about the people and the crash,' said Ellen, gratefully pushing her plate aside. The bacon had been strangely salty.

'Yes. Mr and Mrs What's-their-name . . . yes, the Wades. She's Hilary. Big woman. Bad legs. Anyway, they'd been to the shrine for the afternoon business at the holy well. They were just leaving and this car came tearing down by the Knight's Gate – you know, where the road's so narrow and the wall's so high? And, wallop, right in front of them. They said the car was completely out of control. Absolute write-off. They couldn't believe their eyes. It was a young man, of course, and you know what a danger they are. The trouble is, they don't just kill themselves. No, it's the other people they take with them. That's what I always say.'

'Was he killed then?' Ellen had a picture in her mind's eye of Maurice Lovelace lying on the pavement in London.

'No. They said it was a miracle. The car was wrecked but the driver wasn't badly hurt at all. Mr and Mrs Wade were terribly shaken up. Mr Wade looked quite ill. Will you be wanting any more toast, dear? I could ask Chef – although, strictly speaking, he's finished breakfasts now. But, as it's you I'm sure he wouldn't . . .'

'No, no. Please don't worry. I've had quite enough, thank you.' She was suddenly anxious to be out of the house.

Mrs Legg was already clearing the table.

'There's just one other thing,' said Ellen, gathering her bag from beside the chair. 'Does the name Martha mean anything?'

'Martha? Martha who?'

'I don't know. Someone with a bit of land. A field, perhaps. It's just something somebody said. I thought maybe it had some connection with Walsingham.'

'My mother had a cat called Martha. That was many, many years ago. Heavens, she was a wild one.'

'The cat?'

'No. My mother.'

Chapter Nineteen

The truth was, Sister Sigebert Buckley wished she had signed up as discalced Carmelite, going barefoot, preferably in some appallingly gritty desert. She had a longing for thorns.

The Mildredine Little Sisters were soft, soft as cod's roe; they were soft all the way through. There wasn't a hair shirt in the place. Even their cocoa was really sweetened drinking chocolate.

Pounding along the old railway track, her skirts tucked up and her black boots kicking dust, Sister Sigebert felt power and strength coursing through her limbs. Her breath was coming with a whoosh, like a piston alive with great driving force. She was lean. She was hot. Her face was flushed and the sweat was running freely beneath her habit.

Later she would work out with the weights in the old garage. She would do her sit-ups and squat presses. If Sister Thomas Figge made another remark about muscular Christianity, she would smash up her biscuits.

Sister Sigebert was a very nice person in herself, the Mother Superior had once said. Only she's just too full of energy.

'Hello,' called a deep voice somewhere off to the left. 'Hail, sister, and well met. A fair morning for girding ye olde loins, if you'll pardon my quoth.'

A man in overalls and wellington boots was standing on the far side of a patch of brambles, on the very edge of a field bordering the abandoned railway line. He had a white-painted stake in one hand and a heavy hammer in the other.

'Get lost, creep,' hissed Sister Sigebert, very nearly under her breath. 'Bless you, and the same to you,' she sang out, running on the spot for a moment but not losing her momentum, 'with bloody brass knobs on.'

'Want a job, sister?'

'What?'

'If you ever tire of toiling in the old vineyard, sister, we'll have a job for you here,' said the man.

'What do you mean?' shouted Sister Sigebert, dancing on her toes, keeping up her guard and throwing heavy left and right combinations at an imaginary punchbag. Jab, jab, jab. Wallop. 'What do you mean, a job?'

'At the theme park,' said the man, hitting his stake a shrewd blow.

'Eh? What park?' She kneed an imagined sparring partner in the groin then followed through with a scything left hook and a right hand peppering to the face and neck.

'The new Walsingham theme park and leisure centre,' he shouted across the track bed. 'Opening here shortly, if not sooner.'

'And what's the theme? Of the park?' She hadn't meant to show any curiosity but her natural sense of aggressive inquiry had gained the upper hand.

'God,' said Harry Green, hitting the stake again. 'The God Park. It's got to be a winner in Walsingham.'

'A God theme park?'

'That's it, sister. A goodly idea? Yea or nay?'

'Oh, get lost, arsehole.' Sister Sigebert made an impatient gesture with her black-robed sleeve and danced off down the track, shadow boxing with an awful intensity as her boots crumbled ribs of sun-hardened mud.

'Sorry?' shouted Harry Green.

'God bless my soul,' sang the distant black and white figure.

Mr Tatham, the Conservative agent, tapped the glass of the baro-meter beside the window. Down in the narrow street, a Coca-Cola truck was unloading outside the corner shop. A little queue of three cars was held up while a woman in a blue coat pushed a child in a wheelchair across the road.

'You have to understand that Maurice Lovelace is an extremely popular and well-respected man in this part of Norfolk. It's a great sadness. Very sad indeed,' he said. Mr Tatham pushed a thumb into the pocket of his waistcoat; he was wearing a tweed suit in lovat green. His shoes were highly polished.

'Yes, it must be very upsetting,' said Ellen Bright, leaning back in

126

the chair drawn up to the desk. 'Have you got an up-to-date bulletin on his medical condition?'

'Whose condition?' George Tatham looked completely blank.

'Maurice Lovelace. Your Member of Parliament.'

'Oh, yes. Still in a coma, I'm afraid. You have to understand that Maurice is extremely popular and well-respected, not just in Walsingham itself but among the farmers and the village people round and about.'

'Well, he's been a public figure here for years.'

'Who has?' He turned to stare at Ellen as though completely surprised to find her sitting there.

'Maurice Lovelace. When was he first selected as the Conservative candidate for the Walsingham seat?'

'Maurice? Oh, he's very well-respected around here. You must understand that. He first came on the scene when old Barton Seagrave announced his retirement back in – let's see – yes, in eighty two. There was quite a scramble. Safe seat, *comprenez*? Extraordinarily safe. Majority of 23,000-odd at that time, with a general election coming up and Margaret Thatcher riding on the crest of a wave after the Falklands show. Just imagine. Maurice was very much the dark horse, a real hundred-to-one outsider.'

'So how did he come to be selected?'

'Who?'

'Mr Lovelace. How did he come to be selected by your constituency party?'

'Ah, Maurice. He's extremely popular around here, you understand. Let's say he came up the middle. People had very strong attachments one way or the other. Between you and me, there were two camps, hopelessly divided. Some wanted what we might call Candidate A but the rest wouldn't touch him with a bargepole. They very much wanted Candidate B; but the other lot would sooner have chosen a bandicoot. Maurice was young, only in his mid-twenties at the time, personable, no axe to grind. He got it by a single vote when it came to counting heads – then they all fell in behind him as a compromise. I always told him: it was the ladies who made the difference as far as you were concerned, dear boy.'

'And what did he say?' This time Ellen leapt in immediately,

Andrew Moncur

adding: 'That's Maurice Lovelace, I mean.'

'Of course it is. Who else?' said Mr Tatham, staring at her as if she had taken leave of her senses. 'Maurice always said, darkly, it was just one woman who made the difference.'

Ellen leaned forward: 'Who?'

'Maurice Lovelace, of course. Dear me, you really must pay attention. I was telling you about his selection. It fell just right for the landslide of June, 1983. It was a great shame that he never caught Mrs Thatcher's eye, you know. Good material. Ministerial. Yes. Yes, indeed.' Mr Tatham looked out of the window again, glancing across the rooftops of Little Walsingham towards the dark bulk of the old Bridewell, the House of Correction.

'And since then I suppose he's come to represent the spiritual values of this community?' said Ellen.

'Spiritual values? We're Conservatives,' said Mr Tatham, squinting at the sky. 'We don't have to worry about that sort of thing.'

'But surely Walsingham's a spiritual sort of place. The shrine and all the pilgrims and so on.'

'Well, they reckon about half a million people come here each year – and that's big business. But we have to think about the sugar beet as well and the carrots and the barley.'

'And who should I speak to? To get a picture of the man?'

'What man?' snapped Mr Tatham, as though stung.

Ellen started to rise. The interview did not seem to be yielding quite the insights she had hoped to gain.

'Maurice Lovelace. Does he have any special friends here?' She adjusted her spectacles and pushed the hair out of her eyes.

'You have to understand that he's an extremely popular and well respected man around this part of Norfolk. I think that you might find it worth your while to take tea in Miss Marks's shop in High Street.' He looked into her face with a shaft of keen intelligence in his eyes.

'What's your name again, young lady? Did you say you were coming to live in the constituency?'

'It's Ellen Bright. And, no, I said I was a journalist – working for *Home & Beauty* magazine. As I explained, I'm here for work reasons.'

128

The Harlot's Prerogative

'Oh, dear. A journalist,' said Mr Tatham. 'Well, I don't think I've said anything which would give you a story.'

'You've been extremely helpful,' said Ellen, holding out her hand.

Mrs Canty was privately and silently worried. It was now ten days since Maurice Lovelace had been admitted to St Wilfrid's in a coma and his condition had not improved or altered by one degree in that time.

'What do you think, Sir Archie?' she had asked the previous evening, meeting the chief whip in the lavishly-carpeted foyer of the medical centre. 'Is there anything more we could be doing for him? I hate to see him lying there like that, lost to the world.'

'Don't worry, dear lady,' said Archie Miller. 'While there's life, there's a government majority.'

'But what about his health? What are the doctors doing? Nobody says anything except wait and see. Fat lot of use.'

'The doctors know exactly what they're doing, dear heart. Best in the business, believe me. World class. We must have faith, my dear.' A neutral observer might have felt that Sir Archie was a particularly affectionate man, to judge by his use of warm endearments.

His wife, on the other hand, would have known immediately that he had simply failed to remember Mrs Canty's name.

It had been gratifying for Mrs Canty, on arriving at her employer's private room, to find that a member of the hospital staff was bending over Mr Lovelace's bed, examining his horizontal form with evident care.

'Oh, excuse me, doctor,' she said, noting the neatly pressed white overall coat and the clipboard with its sheaf of official-looking papers lying close to hand at the bottom of the bed.

'No, no. That's no trouble,' he had said, looking up in surprise. 'I just keep an eye on him.'

'And what's your opinion, doctor? Sorry. Is it doctor? Or should it be mister?' Mrs Canty knew that there was some important distinction about the use of titles in medical circles but she was not quite sure what it was. One way, or the other, meant that a doctor was a surgeon. Or possibly the reverse.

Andrew Moncur

'It's mister. Mister Hopkin,' said Mr Evangeltine Hopkin, the late-duty porter from the Nightingale Wing of St Wilfrid's Medical Centre, who had taken a close interest in the case of the injured MP since the day of his admission. 'He is still showing no reaction to stimuli. Let me demonstrate the absence of plantar reflex.'

At this point he held up Maurice Lovelace's dazzlingly white right foot and scratched the sole with his ballpoint pen.

'Nothing,' he said, smiling thinly.

'Oh, dear,' said Mrs Canty.

'Don't distress yourself, madam.'

'No. It's just that you've drawn a blue line down his foot.'

Mr Hopkin put down the foot and clicked his pen to retract the ball point. He slipped it into his breast pocket and then, leaning across the bed, pulled down Mr Lovelace's lower eyelid.

'What do you see?' asked Mrs Canty, engrossed in the investigation.

'I see his eyeball,' said Mr Hopkin.

'Oh, good,' said Mrs Canty. 'Is that good?'

'It's very much what I expected.'

'And what do you think about his head?'

'It's up the top end, here.'

'I see.'

'Yes, it's something we always look for when assessing a patient.'

Mrs Canty nodded, her lips pursed in concentration. 'Is it all – you know – as it should be?'

'Well, the head bone's connected to the neck bone.'

'Oh, good,' said Mrs Canty.

'And the hip bone's connected to the thigh bone.' He took a toffee hammer from the breast pocket of his white coat and tapped the patient's knee in a rhythmical way.

'Will you have to do more tests?' she asked.

'The routine ones: pleural effusions, uterus, placenta, scapula. Cartilage, of course. Tibia and fibula. Diuretics. Evening primrose. That sort of thing.' Mr Hopkin sketched a few lines in the air above the inert body.

'It's a relief to know that you're on the case.'

'I'll be keeping a close watch on him. Don't you worry. He's in good hands here. Carpals. Metacarpals. We're all doing our very level best for him.'

'That's a great comfort. Thank you so much, Mister...'

'Mr Hopkin,' he said.

'Thank you, Mr Hopkin,' said Mrs Canty. That evening she told her husband, Norman, that it was the first time in well over a week that she had felt confident that poor Mr Lovelace was, at last, being properly treated by medical staff who really knew what they were doing.

Father Bugloss was watching with some dismay as the Sea Cadets marched once again from the side door of the Anglican shrine to the pavement at the main entrance. It was something about the way the first boy on the left moved his arms.

He wasn't swinging them from the shoulder, backwards and forwards on either side of his body in the traditional British way. No, he was rotating his arms across his front; almost throwing them to left and right.

Father Bugloss was trying to put his finger on it, so to speak. He wanted to be able to describe it just so; then he might explain to the boy what was wrong with his marching technique.

If the great annual procession during the national pilgrimage was to be a success – and pray heaven that it should be – then every detail had to be given proper attention. And that included the marching skills of the Sea Cadets who formed Our Lady's guard of honour.

They would flank the image of Our Lady of Walsingham as, decorated with a crown and cope, she was carried aloft through the streets. She would be borne head-high to the ancient priory grounds, to be greeted with the words: 'Joy to thee, Queen! For once again thy fame is noised abroad and spoken of in England ...' There would then be fanfares and a pilgrimage mass.

Father Bugloss watched the boys approach for the third time. They were going to keep rehearsing until it was right; just so. Suddenly he snapped his hairy-backed fingers and held up his hand. He had it. He recognised that swagger.

The front-marker, the cadet on the left, was marching in that horribly hearty way – arms swinging from side to side, almost shoulder-high – which hand-picked Young Communists always used to use when approaching the microphone to start bawling slogans at party rallies. The chosen youth always had a neck scarf, a clean-cut, earnest face and a horrible little quiff.

'Ben,' said the priest. 'Ben, I wonder. Could I have a little word about a small matter of detail.'

'Oh, Jesus,' murmured Ben out of the side of his mouth.

Ellen Bright bought a postcard from one of the gift shops in the centre of Walsingham. The sickly-sweet picture showed a nun with the appealing looks of a spaniel; she seemed to be in the process of being struck between the eyes by a bolt of lightning.

'First successful trial of the humane system of martyrdom,' Ellen wrote on the card. 'As approved by the Vatican and the Sacred College of Cardinals.'

She addressed it to Daphne Chapman at *Home & Beauty* and placed it in the post box in High Street. Then she looked up and found herself face to face with a real, flesh and blood nun who was staring at her.

'Elly?' said the nun, screwing up her eyes and peering more closely.

'Ye-e-s,' said Ellen, wishing that she had chosen a different postcard.

'Elly Bright?' The nun showed four front teeth in a smile of greeting.

Ellen gave a desperate shrug in return. 'I'm sorry,' she said, 'but who . . .?'

'You don't remember me, do you?' The large pale face was crestfallen. The nun took a bite at her lower lip. There was something about that expression . . .

'I do, you know,' said Ellen, trawling furiously. 'Of course I know you. It's Nicky, isn't it? Nicky Angel.'

Oh, Christ, she said to herself. Nichola Angel's become a nun. I don't believe it. Nobody from school would believe it. My mum wouldn't believe it. God Himself wouldn't believe it. Nicky bloody Angel. The nun beamed radiantly; her cheeks glowed pink.

Ellen suddenly covered her mouth and muffled a little shriek. 'Oh, I see! I get it. Sorry, Nicky . . .'

The Harlot's Prerogative

'What?' The nun's broad face clouded again.

'I thought for one terrible moment that you were a real nun! Would you believe it? It's a great costume, really it is. What are you? Don't tell me you're a strippergram. Come on. That's it, isn't it?'

'No. No, it isn't. Really. I am a nun.'

There was an awful silence.

'I'm terribly sorry, Nicky,' said Ellen. 'It *is* Nichola, isn't it? Nichola Angel?'

'It's Sigebert, actually, these days.'

'Sigebert? Oh, then you're married?' Ellen had spoken the words before she was able to stop herself. 'I'm sorry. That's really...'

'Not at all. I'm now called Sigebert Buckley. Sister Sigebert Buckley. I'm named for Father Buckley, the last Westminster Benedictine, you know. From the time of the dissolution? England's apostasy and all that? Right, well. OK. Never mind.'

'But you were always going to do Phys. Ed. You were always so good at games, Nicky. I thought you were going to do sports science at, what's it, Loughborough. I remember you in goal – I remember you knocking over that umpire's chair at Beckenham. Do you remember that trip to Wimbledon?'

'That dirty old man who fell over the hedge!'

'Fell? I thought you hit him.'

'Oh, dear.' Sister Sigebert rehearsed a left jab and a right hook. 'Lord. The time. What's the time? I've got to get back.'

'Where's that? Where do you live now?'

'Right here, in Walsingham. It's the Mildredine hospice, just round the corner by the pub. It's the smallest in Walsingham. Only half a dozen beds. Soft as hell.'

'I'll drop in and see you,' said Ellen, in a sudden excess of friendliness. 'Are you allowed visitors? When can I call?'

'Any time,' shouted the sister as she turned away. 'Any time except for the canonical hours – lauds through to compline – and mucking out time, of course. And feeding time. And quiet reflection time. And ... Oh, just turn up.'

Having by then reached the street corner, she picked up the skirts of her ankle-length habit and sprinted away.

Chapter Twenty

Sonia Marks had laughed when she first heard about the God theme park, thinking it must be one of Harry Green's little jokes.

'I laughed,' she said. 'I laughed and laughed. How I laughed. I was fairly amused. Then I saw he had applied for planning permission and I thought, hold on, maybe this isn't so funny after all.'

Her aunt Elsie, the pianist, organist and sometime cattle man, nodded and sipped her tea. 'They say he's going to build Noah's ark up there, according to the original dimensions,' she said in her light voice. 'Whatever they might be.'

'One minute,' said Sonia. She was gone for about four minutes, thumping about in her bedroom upstairs.

'This is the relevant passage, I think,' she said, returning to the tea room. Then she read from *Genesis*, Chapter 6, verse 13:

And God said unto Noah, The end of all flesh is come before me; for the flesh is filled with violence through them; and, behold, I will destroy them with the earth.

Make thee an ark of gopher wood; rooms shalt thou make in the ark, and shalt pitch it within and without with pitch.

And this is the fashion which thou shalt make it of: The length of the ark shall be three hundred cubits, the breadth of it fifty cubits, and the height of it thirty cubits.

A window shalt thou make to the ark, and in a cubit shalt thou finish it above; and the door of the ark shalt thou set in the side thereof; with lower, second and third stories shalt thou make it.

And behold I, even I, do bring a flood of waters upon the earth, to destroy all flesh, wherein is the breath of life, from under heaven; and every thing that is in the earth shall die.

But with thee will I establish my covenant; and thou shalt

come into the ark, thou, and thy sons, and thy wife, and thy sons' wives with thee.

And of every living thing of all flesh, two of every sort shalt thou bring into the ark, to keep them alive with thee; they shall be male and female.

Of fowls after their kind, and of cattle after their kind, of every creeping thing of the earth after his kind, two of every sort shall come unto thee, to keep them alive.

Aunt Elsie took another sip of her tea. 'What's a cubit?' she asked eventually.

'Hang on,' said Sonia, turning to run upstairs again. She was back with a dictionary in less than a minute.

'It says here,' she mumbled, for one moment holding the middle knuckle of her forefinger between her teeth. 'It says a cubit is an ancient measure of length, approximately equal to the length of a forearm.'

Elsie took a morsel of biscuit and dipped it into her cup. 'How long's a forearm?' she asked, raising the soggy biscuit to her lips.

'Don't move an inch,' said Sonia Marks. This time she climbed the stairs a little more slowly; she was back in about two and a half minutes, holding a pink tape measure.

'Give us your arm,' she said and reeled out the tape. Aunt Elsie's forearm, including her hand and fingers, was seventeen inches long.

'So how big's the ark?' asked Elsie.

'Let's see,' said Sonia. 'One cubit is . . . call it a foot and a half. A foot and a half times – what was it? – 300? Yes. That equals 450 feet long. And, just one moment . . . right, that's seventy-five feet wide. And forty-five feet high, isn't it? That means each floor, or deck, must have had fifteen feet headroom.'

'And how does that compare with Lord Nelson's flagship at the battle of Trafalgar? The *Victory*, I mean.'

'Just a moment,' said Sonia. She walked upstairs and was gone for almost ten minutes.

'HMS *Victory* was only 226 feet six inches long. That means it was only half the size of Noah's ark. Or Noah's ark was twice as big as the *Victory*. It's going to have to be a scale model, isn't it?'

135

Andrew Moncur

'Well,' said Elsie Marks.

'Well what? What do you have to say about that, then?'

Aunt Elsie sat quietly for a couple of minutes. 'What's gopher wood?' she asked in her light way.

'Hold on,' said Sonia Marks. Then, in turning, she finally noticed that a customer was waiting to be served.

Ellen Bright had been standing for several minutes by the counter where the cakes were displayed. She was holding a pile of the day's newspapers under her arm, to a depth of roughly one cubit.

Peace reigned in the editor in chief's suite of offices at *Home & Beauty*. Muriel Oliver was organising a collection.

'Right, Juliet. I want you to go straight back to the subs' room and tell them that sixty-five pence will not do. It's insulting, cheap and demeaning. Sixty-five pence! Between seven of them? I've never heard anything so disgraceful in my life. And, believe me, I've heard some fairly shameful things in my . . .'

Juliet Neckles, her assistant, rocked forward on her chair and bit her lower lip. She was trying to find a way of telling Muriel that fifty pence of that sum had, in fact, been contributed by Troy from the post room.

Miss Oliver had organised the collection to buy flowers for Constance Verity, the long-serving contributor whose work had become such a feature over the years.

The trouble was, as Juliet saw it, nobody on *Home & Beauty*'s staff had ever met Miss Verity. She never came anywhere near the office. No one would recognise her if they bumped into her on the street. It wasn't unkindness. There was simply no sense of friend-ship and personal loyalty towards her.

It was like asking people to chip in to buy a bunch of flowers for the President of the Board of Trade. It was all too distant and impersonal to draw a response.

Juliet was also searching for a way to break the news to Miss Oliver that she had been offered a new job elsewhere on the *Home & Beauty* editorial floor. It was a tempting prospect. She would be secretary to Gwen Lightsome, the personal advice columnist, and answerable directly to Mrs Lightsome's personal assistant. There

The Harlot's Prerogative

would be an increase in Juliet's salary of £610 per annum. Her mother, who read Gwen Lightsome's agony column, would be delighted and so very proud.

But, yet. Somehow Juliet felt an intense sense of loyalty to Muriel. She had been a fair and kind boss who was only really rude to other people. And she was ferociously efficient . . .

'I hear you've accepted the new job with Gwen Lightsome, then,' said Miss Oliver, looking into her assistant's face with open-eyed frankness.

'Well, you know . . .'

'Of course I do,' said Muriel. 'You would be mad to refuse. It's a wonderful opportunity for you and well deserved. Really it is.'

'Oh, Muriel . . .' Juliet felt a great sob rising in her throat. 'I don't, I don't know how to . . . how to thank . . .'

'Tosh. Piffle. Absolute mush,' Muriel snorted, tossing her head like a pony which has been startled by a sudden noise or by a child's rush of smothering affection. 'Now what about this collection? So far we seem to have raised – let's see – yes, £2 and the odd three-pence. It won't do, if you ask me. Which you won't, of course, as I know from long and bitter experience. Oh, no. Nobody ever asks me anything. Not a thing.'

'Anyway, isn't Miss Verity supposed to be a man?' said Juliet.

'Please,' said Muriel in her cross voice. 'Not you, too. Don't you start asking daft questions about all that nonsense.'

Mrs Canty had spent the morning cleaning out the kitchen cup-boards, the cabinet in the bathroom and the chest of drawers in the main bedroom. She had not touched the bundle of letters, tied with green gardening string, which she discovered in Mr Lovelace's sock drawer. It would have been a bloody nerve, she felt, although she did pause long enough to decipher the Norfolk postmark on the top envelope.

Mrs Canty came three mornings a week by bus to the flat in what estate agents call the division bell area of Westminster. Mrs Canty and her husband, on the other hand, called it something else. So far as they were concerned, London consisted of Lewisham, where they lived, the East End and the Other End.

137

Andrew Moncur

It was thanks to her hard work that in the flat, Up The Other End, the furniture shone and the rooms were warm with the scent of wax polish. The bath, the kitchen cooker and the sink were as bright as, well, the buckles on the fatal carriage harness, also up there, in the Royal Mews only ten minutes' walk from Maurice Lovelace's front door.

They had never reached the point of familiarity where they would call one another anything but Mr Lovelace and Mrs Canty. They had discovered, within minutes of first meeting, that they shared a birthday, 10 January – although Mrs Canty would always point out, usually quite unnecessarily, that she was the older by seventeen years. He had made it a ritual to take her out to lunch on their shared day, when they would sit in a pub off Artillery Row and drink a toast to Capricorns. Mrs Canty would say that she was not a political animal.

'You have to live and let live,' she said. Then she sat down and read Mr Lovelace's account of the deaths of ten Carthusians, monks of an austere contemplative order, who were starved to death in chains at Newgate through the summer months of 1537. They came from the London Charterhouse at Smithfield and had refused to renounce the authority of the pope in Rome and accept the supremacy of King Henry.

'By then,' Maurice had written:

Sir Thomas More, the king's former chancellor, and John Fisher, who had been made a cardinal by the pope, had both been put to death on charges of treason for rejecting royal supremacy. Their executions had caused revulsion throughout Europe – or, at least, among its scholarly conservative churchmen. Thomas More had, incidentally, spent four years as a young man at the London Charterhouse.

There was to be bloodshed, too, at Walsingham in the course of the upheaval which surrounded the king's final break with Rome and the subsequent dissolution of the monasteries. Walsingham was to have its own so-called rebellion, which would be put down with the sort of grotesque butchery which characterised the judicial process of Tudor England.

The Harlot's Prerogative

Overall, though, it has to be said that the suppression of the monasteries and religious houses took place with an extra-ordinary lack of resistance on the part of those most closely concerned. The surrender of the priory and holy house at Walsingham was no exception.

The process was piecemeal. They were, it was said, first deflowered that they might be devoured.

The king, pursuing the great matter of his desire to end his first marriage and make Anne Boleyn his queen, backed the clergy into a series of tight corners, first extracting their submission in terms of legislative rights and taxation. Next, starting with the preaching friars and moving on to those in monasteries and other foundations, came a demand that they swear on oath to accept the king as supreme head of the church. They were also required to repudiate the pope and to deny his jurisdiction over England.

Few monks, when put to it, declined to do as they were asked.

Those who did make a stand could expect, at best, to be expelled or imprisoned. At worst they might face torture and death. The executions took place in public at first, but later those who opposed the king's power, like some of the London Carthusians, suffered in obscurity. Seats of resistance were broken up and destroyed in this way.

At the same time Henry's minister, Thomas Cromwell, was preparing to reform the church in the most drastic way. He set out to dissolve first the smaller and often much-diminished monasteries and convents, confiscating their possessions and revenue for the crown. The monks and nuns would be offered pensions. The larger houses were then to be similarly treated. By the time their turn came, it was too late for any sort of realistic opposition.

Cromwell sent out his agents, royal commissioners, to examine all individual religious houses. Their tasks were numerous: to issue severe new regulations controlling the behaviour of the monks, perhaps intending to drive them to capitulation – or, alternatively, to provide grounds for

139

suppressing houses which disobeyed the rules. They also had to check on the assets of the monasteries – which had already been the subject of a countrywide audit – and prevent the dispersal of this wealth; to find evidence of wrongdoing, which might be used against the religious. They were also required to act against superstition and the display of relics for 'increase of lucre'.

There were about 800 religious houses in England at the outset. Within five years they were all but rubbed out, fundamentally changing the religious and social life of the nation and, into the bargain, its patterns of wealth and land ownership.

The commissioners were soon active in Walsingham, which they visited in 1536. Half a dozen canons were declared guilty of 'notorious incontinency' and grave superstition and much forgery was detected in 'feigned, pretended miracles and relics'.

The crystal reliquary of Our Lady's milk attracted particular attention. The commissioners also claimed to have found a hidden workshop used for purposes of alchemy. Cromwell received a report that his men 'did there find a secret privy place within the house . . . in which there were instruments, pots, bellows, flies of such strange colours as the like none of us had seen, with poisons and other things to sort and divide gold and silver, nothing there wanting that should belong to the art of multiplying'.

Defenders of the Walsingham shrine have always insisted that the commission had, in fact, stumbled across a metalsmith's workshop making the medals which pilgrims bought to commemorate their visits to the holy house.

A year later Walsingham, by then on the brink of its surrender and dissolution, would witness what can only be regarded as an act of bloody, calculated brutality, designed to crush any resistance to the crown's overarching purpose.

Mrs Canty, who liked a bloody murder, set the folder aside with every sign of reluctance.

Chapter Twenty-One

'Gwen, my dear,' said Rosie Maguire, fixing a pale eye on her newly acquired agony aunt. 'Gwen, there's something I have to tell you. It's necessary.'

Gwen Lightsome sipped her coffee and, all but closing her eyes, took a private view of her editor – or, rather, her editor soon to be; she had yet to take up her new appointment. She peered over the rim of her cup and through the heavily-blackened fringe of her own eyelashes.

'It's the picture byline, isn't it?' Gwen's voice was rigid with suspicion. 'That's it, isn't it? You won't have it, will you? Despite our agreement. Despite the promises. You're going back on everything you . . .'

'Shut up,' said Rosie, in a horribly chilly way. Then she smiled, which was far more menacing. 'What I have to say has nothing to do with arrangements for your byline. Your picture will appear alongside your name on everything you write for the magazine. It's all covered in the personal contract you signed yesterday. This is a different matter. Altogether different.'

Gwen Lightsome shifted her weight from one buttock to the other and regarded the editor again. 'Then it's the view. It's my windows,' she snapped. 'I knew it. I told Reggie. Reggie, I said, she's going to renege on the office deal. And that's what you're doing, isn't it? You've decided I can't have a room on the river side?'

Rosie Maguire pushed back her chair and walked towards the window. The editor's office gave a squint-angled view of roughly a thirty-second part of the Victoria Tower of the House of Lords, glimpsed beyond a tangle of air-conditioning ducts.

'Gwen, dear,' she said, at last. 'Will you belt up, please. I simply want to tell you about the – well, about the true nature, let us say, of poor Constance Verity.

'We've kept quiet about this. But since you're joining the family and as you're the sort of person we can all, you know, confide in – well, I feel it's important that you should be told the truth about her.'

Gwen gave a light wave and brushed a strand of hair from her prominently rounded forehead. Her eyes had widened with greedy interest. 'Rosie, Rosie,' she boomed. 'As Constance herself would say: a secret shared is a problem halved and a price far above rubies.'

The editor looked at her for several moments in silence.

'It's something to do with sex, isn't it? I can always tell,' Gwen Lightsome crashed on, unstoppable and, indeed, in some ways unreachable. 'As soon as you mentioned dear Constance and I thought to myself, Gwen, my dear, there's sex at the bottom of this. We get used to it on our side of the business, you see. Yes, that'll be it. I knew it, instantly. I said to myself, it's some sort of a messy secret involving sex.'

'Well, that's true – in a way,' said the editor. Then she told Mrs Lightsome all that she knew of the real identity of *Home & Beauty's* long-serving and much-loved contributor.

As Constance Verity had in actual fact once written: '*You think that nobody's interested in you? Then try keeping a personal secret. Soon your private affairs will be making the news on the great Internet of life.*'

Ellen Bright was waiting in the car park. She was idly scuffing her shoes, kicking pebbles and, at the same time, trying to make sense of a partly obliterated sign attached to the fence. As far as she could make out, it said something about biting horses. Ellen took this to be a warning of peril rather than a request that people should refrain from doing it.

She had been practically pushed out of the tea shop, round the corner in High Street. Sonia Marks had told her that she wanted, please, to talk privately. Could they meet in ten minutes over in the car park? Her aunt would look after the shop. 'Of course,' Ellen had said. 'See you in a little . . .'

And the street door had been shut in her face.

She glanced at her watch, then took another turn across the width of the parking place. It was uncomfortably cold when she walked in the shade. The shadow was cast by the tall building which loomed up at the town end of the open lot. It looked blind, as if its eyes had been put out. At some stage boards had been used to blank out the high rows of windows in the front face of the gaunt, red-brick – what was it? A warehouse? Some sort of Victorian factory? There was a tall brick chimney at one end of the block.

Ellen didn't exactly shudder. An animal would have raised its hackles. It was one of those moments when an involuntary shiver, a little internal tremor, makes a person draw breath and say: 'Someone stepped on my grave.' Ellen had been thinking just then of dark, satanic mills.

'Someone just walked over my grave,' she said to herself, crossing back into the sun, 'which is strange, since I actually want to be cremated.' She stared up again at the featureless windows in the tall building overlooking the car park.

They would once have been covered with iron bars. Inside this block, in its days, there had been a great mill where prisoners toiled like caged mice, endlessly turning a treadwheel. The shadowy building, although she did not know this at the time, was the old House of Correction. It had been built as the local prison, on a site occupied in an earlier age by a leper hospital.

The treadmill, the hand-turned crank and the silent system were all used in Walsingham's corrective prison. The regime imposed on this jail, in the progressive spirit of the mid-nineteenth century, meant that turnkeys and taskmasters would use all their powers to keep the prisoners not only hard at work, but also isolated from one another and in fear of punishment for uttering any sound.

They did not take the system quite to the lengths imposed at the new model prison which opened at Pentonville, London, in 1844. There, each inmate was deliberately stripped of his identity; he was made to wear a face mask and answer only to a number.

The rule of strict silence was meant to prevent prisoners sharing information of a possibly criminal nature; it was also supposed to provide the opportunity for reflection and moral improvement. Convicts were made to attend daily worship so as to be exposed to the improving influence of prayer and scripture readings. Religious books were made available for the same purpose. Then, so spiritually refreshed, the prisoners were put back to their hard labour.

Walsingham's Bridewell was relatively small – although as many as ninety-seven prisoners were locked up there on any one day in 1840 and more than 460 men and women were committed in that single year, a considerable number for a local prison. This wholesale supply of convicts speaks eloquently not so much about the number of miscreants in nineteenth-century rural England but more about the severity of the system of criminal law and punishment at that time.

Most of these people were farm labourers. They were in jail for poaching, for fighting, for leaving their jobs and abandoning their families as a burden on the parish. Frequently they were locked up for vagrancy. From time to time the jail would hold convicted smugglers or prisoners sentenced to transportation to the colonies for farm machine-breaking.

The prison regime was intended to ensure that the inmates suffered in silence. The internal disciplinary record for the House of Correction at Walsingham shows that punishments were meted out to serving prisoners typically – indeed, virtually without exception – for offences of making noise.

The prisoner caught talking could expect his bread ration to be stopped. For the offence of whistling, the inmate would be confined in the dark cell. For the serious and seditious crime of singing there was a double penalty: incarceration in the dark cell and loss of bread ration for two or three days. That left water on the menu.

'I hail with much satisfaction the increased facility in prospect for a better separation of the prisoners,' the prison chaplain reported in 1841:

The silent system has done much, since its introduction, to prevent communication and to diminish the number of reports for misconduct.

The reports now are, with very few exceptions, for infraction of rules of silence; and when better arrangements shall be made for every prisoner to have a separate sleeping cell, there will be little cause for reporting at all and consequently little

144

or no punishment in the prison. This of itself will be highly advantageous, and we may hope will be an additional means of producing in prisoners reflection and resolutions of amendment.

The dark cell still strikes a chill. The treadmill has gone now. It was a model of its type with five bays where prisoners, secured behind gratings and forbidden to speak or look away from their work, would pass their days at the ceaseless task of tramping – or climbing – up the treads of the great wheel.

The treadmill had another purpose: grinding corn. It made money for the House of Correction. In 1840 its recorded earnings were £42 and some odd shillings. Just to give some idea of relative values, this compares with the pay of a turnkey at that time of £26 a year.

The jailers of the day were also responsible for putting prisoners to work at the most futile task of all: turning a crank by hand. The warders could make the job lighter or more strenuous, requiring more or less back-breaking effort, by adjusting a screw – so earning themselves a contemptuous name-tag which persists to this day.

'It was a prison, you know. It still looks creepy.'

Sonia had approached silently, taking Ellen by surprise. 'Do you know why prisoner officers are called screws?'

'Sorry?' Ellen had been staring at the clouds, lying low to the north-west. She was unable for the moment to make out in any detail the features of Sonia's face.

'Screws. You know?'

'No, I don't. Although given enough time I have a feeling I could dredge something up from the memory banks. Someone once said to me that journalists know a good deal, but only for a very, very short time.'

'I had you down as another pilgrim.' Sonia was watching her carefully.

'Well, that's usually the case here . . .' Ellen started to say.

'Myself, I don't think of it as pilgrimage. Between you and me, I call it religio-tourism. It's what this place is all about. All the gifts. All those statues and paintings with eyes like labradors'. It's really

Andrew Moncur

---

a holiday resort. There ought to be Walsingham rock on sale with Our Lady running right through the middle.'

'Isn't it good business for tea shops, too?' Ellen asked.

'Of course it is. But I'm not selling them anything else into the bargain. I'm not offering miracles. Only tea. And rock cakes.'

There was a short silence. They had reached the boundary wall of the car park. 'You wanted to know about Maurice, didn't you? Will you tell me something first?'

Ellen nodded.

'What sort of journalist are you? Are you digging dirt for the tabloids? Or what? Are you hounding Maurice Lovelace? Would you tell me if you were?'

Ellen Bright was a painfully honest sort of journalist, in actual fact, but was hardly likely to say so. Instead she spoke about witnessing the accident and feeling that there might be a special interest in the case of the injured politician. She talked of those who triumph over tragedy and Walsingham's place in the hearts of people who believed that good could come out of disaster. She mentioned *Home & Beauty* magazine and its award-winning record, its commitment to decent values and its sense of service towards its family of devoted readers. She touched briefly on her own feelings about accuracy in reporting and the need for a certain sensitivity when writing about matters of life and death and those who hovered between the two after suffering terrible injury or illness. She made one or two remarks about the place of a free and responsible press in the political processes of a liberal democracy and the need for women, in particular, to have a voice which could be heard in the life of the nation.

'I see,' said Sonia, eventually. 'So what it boils down to is this: you want to know how me and Maurice Lovelace ended up in bed together?'

'Good grief,' said Ellen. 'Is there something you want to tell me?'

Muriel Oliver peered with exaggerated caution around the door of Room 309 in the Nightingale Wing of St Wilfrid's Hospital. There were a good deal fewer than 309 bedrooms in the block: the number indicated, rather, that it was the ninth room on the third floor of the

146

building – which, incidentally, had started its life as a margarine factory and warehouse. The margarine workers, long since laid off and forgotten by the huge vegetable oils conglomerate which owned the site, would not have recognised their slippery old workplace beside the river.

It was about as plushy as a hospital could be. There was no sense here of the financial shortfall, the peeling paint and the wearying queues that betrayed the average National Health Service hospital. Instead it hummed with efficiency and the confidence which comes with assured cash-flow. The prices levelled for bed and breakfast alone would have shaken rigid most guest-house landladies, the billing system amazing them with its sheer creative dash. The rooms were handsomely decorated; the carpets were a superior quality Wilton.

'Hello,' Muriel cooed. 'Hellooo. Is anybody here? Cooee. May I come in?'

Silence lay across the room like snow in a winter field.

'Miss Verity? Hello,' sang Muriel, still clinging to the door as a weightless astronaut might hang on to the roof rack of his orbiting shuttle, whirling through the pitiless vacuum of space.

There was a tiny glow from a lit monitor on the far side of the bed. The rest of the room was cast in a golden half-light, with the window blinds pulled down to shut out the day.

She finally advanced into the room, closing the door behind her and creeping forward with the sort of elaborate care normally seen among aboriginal tribesmen hunting with blowpipes in the Amazonian rain forest. She was carrying a large bouquet of brightly coloured carnations wrapped in crackly cellophane.

The greater part of the florist's charge had been paid by Miss Oliver herself, although the card attached to the flowers claimed that they came with love and warmest good wishes from the editor and entire staff of *Home & Beauty* magazine. Muriel believed it was the job of the editor's secretary to see that these things were done properly and, if absolutely necessary, hang the expense. Or, at least, offset it against the petty cash box containing the senior staff's coffee money.

The editor had not been involved at all. She was away from

the magazine for a couple of days, investigating collaborative arrangements with similar publications in Europe – which meant she had slipped off to Paris with her mother.

Muriel Oliver had taken it upon herself to arrange the presentation of flowers to the injured Constance Verity. She had copied the address of the hospital and the number of the private room from the editor's desk pad. There had been a note scribbled alongside, and heavily underlined: 'Constance Verity – fax him the chop.'

Muriel could not make much sense of these words and so ignored them.

Now she approached the bed on tiptoe, trying to stop the flower wrappings from making too much of a din.

'Miss Verity?' she said, craning forward and peering over the side of the bed. She was looking into the abandoned, vacant face of the patient. It was all she could do to stop herself recoiling with a little cry of dismay.

Constance Verity was badly in need of a shave. Worse, there was a tuft of black hair bursting from the open neck of the pyjama jacket where her cleavage ought to have been.

'Oh, my giddy aunt,' said Muriel Oliver in a low voice. 'No wonder she's steered clear of the office. Her complexion's almost as bad as poor Sarah's in the beauty department.'

She laid the bouquet on the foot of the bed. Then, flapping her hands in sudden alarm, she ran to the door to check that she had entered the right room.

She ran back and snatched up the flowers once more. Something made her stop and walk to the foot of the bed, bend and squint at the chart and file cards tucked into a box on the frame. She noted the name displayed there. Muriel straightened and, returning to the bedside and putting down the flowers once more, she leaned over and checked the plastic wrist band.

'Can I help you at all?'

Muriel came bolt upright and performed her impression of a horse being frightened by an erupting volcano, with full range of facial expressions and elaborate flailing of hands.

'Is there anything I can do, at all?' The man looking round the door was holding up a medical instrument in dull silvery metal; it looked absurdly like a toffee hammer. He had an impressive row of pens peeking from the breast pocket of his white coat.

'No, no. Thank you, doctor. I'm just leaving some flowers for Miss . . . for Mr Lovelace. There's a vase here,' she said, indicating a plastic measuring jug on the bedside cabinet.

'Give me the flowers. I'll take care of them,' he said, using both hands to signal her to advance. He did so in the manner of the ground control crew at an airport guiding a jumbo jet across the tarmac.

'Flipping heck!' Miss Oliver said to herself. 'Crikey Moses. That's private medicine for you. Doctor offers to look for a flower vase! In the health service you're supposed to feel grateful if they agree to go looking for your blooming appendix.'

And she took another long look at the unconscious man stretched out on the far side of the shaded room.

So, Daphne Chapman had been right all along. Daphne, typically, had got hold of the right end of the stick; everyone in the office had worked it out. They had all known the score. Somehow Muriel was always the last to know.

Constance Verity and Maurice Lovelace were right there in bed together – in as much as they were, indeed, one and the same person.

Mrs Legg kicked and turned, pushing herself through the water with the thrust of her powerful white legs. She swam a strong and stately breast-stroke, causing a bow wave to bubble up to her lips, nose and the white goggles she wore in the pool.

Her games teacher at school had told her – she could only have been aged fourteen or fifteen at the time – that she was his picture of the Corinthian ideal. The young Veronica had thought vaguely that he was speaking of some concept, some vision, of noble sporting perfection.

It had been painful to overhear him later the same afternoon explaining to the pool attendant that he had, in fact, been talking about her legs. They reminded him of classical Corinthian columns: sturdy, fluted and ending in what looked suspiciously like a riot of acanthus leaves.

Andrew Moncur

The teacher concerned had been badly hurt in a cycling accident at the end of that term. He was at the time riding one of those fold-up bicycles with little wheels. Unfortunately, it folded up underneath him just as he was pulling out of the school gate and moving at some speed into a line of traffic.

Nobody ever established what had caused the locking bolts in the bicycle frame to give way so disastrously.

Mrs Legg ploughed steadily on her course the length of the pool. Nobody got in her way.

Chapter Twenty-Two

May was a big month for Father Bugloss in the sweet-scented, candle-softened, incense-sharpened, statue-haunted, genuflecting, bead-counting, water-sprinkling Anglo-Catholic stronghold of Walsingham. These were always busy times for the Anglican shrine and its College of Guardians, for the Priest Administrator, for the Priests Associate of the Holy House and for the Community of Sisters whose convent lies within the confines of the shrine. Their agenda was as packed as could be. It seemed that no sooner was Easter out of the way than events piled one upon another. There was Ascension Day, with its concelebrated mass, the vigil of Pentecost, then observance of Whit Sunday itself with night prayer and benediction. This was to be followed by the Anglican national pilgrimage to the shrine with its great annual procession of Our Lady's image through the village before an open-air mass in the Abbey grounds among the surviving fragments of the Augustinian Priory. It would be celebrated by an archbishop and, as Father Bugloss always put it, by more bishops than you could shake a stick at. There would be priests almost beyond number.

They could all expect to be roundly abused from the sidelines by protestants from the low and pentecostal end of the spectrum who loathe and deplore these Anglo-Catholic baubles, graven images, dolls, smoking censers, fancy rituals and other abominations in the eye and nostrils of a wrathful, plain-speaking God. These dissenters know that idols and images are offensive to God because He told us so, in an exclusive interview with Moses.

These protestors make their own pilgrimage in order to have a few words – at the tops of their voices – with those who revere Our Lady of Walsingham. They seek to remind their brethren that protestant martyrs went to their deaths in cruel and horrible circumstances in the belief that England should have a reformed church, free of superstition and over-powerful priests.

Andrew Moncur

May was *the* month. Church festivals and the big national gathering would bring the world to Walsingham. Then, apart from these major public events, there would be the now traditional pilgrimage by peers and members of parliament. They came each year to ask for blessing on their work at the Palace of Westminster and – in the case of those fortunate enough to enjoy such a thing – their responsibilities in government.

Neil Bugloss had a modest enough part to play in all this activity but that aside he had given himself two further tasks. He was anxious to find out what, precisely, was meant by these pervasive rumours about a theme park planned for Walsingham.

And he was eager to find from scripture a successful system of numbers. He could not as yet say what form it might take – but he would know it when he found it.

Reggie Lightsome was thrashing backwards and forwards. His little legs looked hot and sticky; he was flushed strawberry pink around the knees.

'Eighty-seven, eighty-eight, eighty-nine . . .' One stroke with each of his whistling exhalations. His shorts had rucked up in his groin which made him feel uncomfortable, fretful and helplessly victimised.

Gwen was lying in the bath. If he glanced up he could see the top of her head in the white and yellow shower cap, just visible through the linking door from his dressing room. He watched her raise her arm and squeeze the sponge, sending a cascade of water pouring over her own semi-submerged form.

'Eighty, eighty-one . . .' he puffed. 'Oh, shit.'

He had lost count again. He cranked himself back and forth on his stainless steel rowing machine for a further half-dozen pulls, imagining he was coasting to the finishing line on the tideway. For some reason he always pictured himself as stroke in the victorious Cambridge boat. Reg had never been to Cambridge; he had not been at university at all. His early career had been in newspapers. Delivering them. He had left school at the earliest opportunity, which had been roughly two years before school-leaving age.

He leaned on his knees, drawing breath, feeling a flicker of compassion for the once-again-defeated Oxford eight. His thigh and stomach muscles forwarded messages to the brain which recorded a satisfactory level of ache before switching circuits to deal with more pressing signals coming in from another source.

'Of course, it's obviously an embarrassment for the government,' said Gwen, speaking into the steamy air which lingered over the bath. 'Difficult to square with the leader's much bleated-about values.'

'What's that?' Reggie was struggling to ease the wrinkles out of the gusset of his shiny shorts.

'A Conservative backbench MP passing himself off as one of Britain's best-loved women. It's a bit much, Reggie.'

'It seems to me,' said Reggie, sitting up and kneading the small of his back, 'It seems to me that Maurice Lovelace, in the part of Constance Verity, has upheld values that any political party would be pleased to call its own. She's been – he's been – an absolute paradox of virtue.'

'A paradox?'

'What do I mean? A parameter? A parable?'

'A paragon, Reg?'

'That's what I think, anyway.'

'Sometimes you're so naive, Reggie. Credulous, I should say. Can't you see what the tabloids would make of it? Think of the headlines: Top Tory's Sex-Swap Secret: He's Connie, The Magazine Queen.'

Reg Lightsome climbed gingerly from his apparatus and walked into the bathroom. His wife, without looking at him, held the sponge in the air. When he took it she lurched forward in the bath, revealing the wetly shining pink expanse of her back and sending a tidal wave surging towards the taps.

'Anyway,' he said, soaping the sponge, 'nobody need know. Why should Lovelace's name ever come into it? Constance Verity simply goes into a well-deserved retirement. She could be run over by a bus, if you like. They'd probably give her a memorial service at St Whatsit's in Fleet Street. I'm sure you and Rosie and the rest of them at *Home & Beauty* would all . . .'

'Reggie. Reggie. Would you please shut up a minute. I'm having a bright idea.'

'Oh, right. Don't mind me. I'll just go and put my head in the bidet,' said Reggie, drawing a childishly rude shape in the soap on his wife's back.

'That's it. That's the story for us. Don't you see? We should be arranging a miracle for Maurice Lovelace.'

'Sorry?'

'Reginald,' said Gwen, tugging off her shower hat and looking up at him in about as serious a way as a soapy, naked woman ever can look at anybody. 'Restoring somebody's life – bringing them back to life again after they've been run over by a royal carriage – could be seen as the pinnacle of achievement for an agony aunt. It's the ultimate problem sorted, isn't it? It's almost, well, it seems almost biblical to me.'

Sonia Marks first met her local Member of Parliament at his weekly surgery held in the Conservative club. She had made an appointment and called there one Saturday morning in June. She could remember the date easily enough. It had been her birthday: the seventh.

'What an amazing coincidence,' Maurice Lovelace had said, taking her hand and shaking it warmly for what seemed a long time. 'So it's our day. We really should make this a double celebration – drink a glass of something together. What a good idea.'

And having said that he left the committee room. He returned in a few minutes with two glasses of champagne. 'Here's to us. Here's to birthdays,' he said, raising his glass. 'Many happy returns!' He had laughed out loud.

'It was a surprise to discover – it was almost a year later – that his birthday wasn't in June at all. It was in January,' Sonia had explained to Ellen Bright. 'He didn't tell a lie. He didn't actually tell me anything at all, really. Somehow he'd implied that June the seventh was his birthday as well. And it wasn't. It isn't, I mean. It was just his way of making you feel special. He was good at that. He *is* good at it. God, I must stop talking about him as if he's dead.'

In the first place, she had come to see Mr Lovelace at the MP's advice surgery to ask for his support to help a charity working with fat children. Next thing, she was drinking good champagne. Very soon Mr Lovelace was wandering off to find the bottle. One glass was never enough, he declared over his shoulder.

During their second glass Maurice had asked about her work, her family, her home: all the main features of her life. Somehow they got round to the topic of painting and to Thomas Gainsborough and an unfortunate portrait, dashed off in haste, of some gallant eighteenth-century soldier. Through an oversight the sitter had ended up being portrayed in possession of two hats: one clamped on his head at a jaunty angle, the other held aloft in his outstretched hand, raised high in triumph.

Then there was Johann Zoffany who painted a group portrait of his family in which his daughter, Claudina, appeared twice – once on the extreme left, once on the far right. Every bit as well balanced as the Mitfords, said Maurice.

The bottle had gone down remarkably quickly.

Eventually the club steward had arrived to find out why Mr Lovelace had seen only one of his callers when he ought by rights to have seen half a dozen. One woman had given up and was seen leaving the waiting room, heading for her home in Little Snoring. She was about as happy as a cod on a fishmonger's slab, said the steward. Sonia had noticed Harry Green sitting in the queue, looking bored.

She had departed in a slight daze, having accepted an invitation to join Maurice for dinner that same evening. They had dined overlooking the quay at Blakeney, watching the small boat sailors putting to sea to catch the late tide. The sky was like watered silk, shot with rose pink, crimson lake and grey; for a while the waters of the tidal inlet and the anchorage were mother-of-pearl. The colours grew more beautifully far-fetched as the long dusk wore on.

'What does it call to mind?' Sonia nodded towards the fading sunset.

'Oh, I don't know. School dinners perhaps,' said Maurice.

'I see.'

'I mean, it's the colour of jam mixed up with one of those puddings. Semolina, I think.'

'You're saying it has all the romance of a milk pudding?'

155

'Yes. I'm very moved by it.'

It had grown cool by then. Sonia was glad of her cotton sweater.

They had spoken about politics for only one brief moment. 'If you could call it politics,' said Sonia. 'He told me that he was disappointed with life at Westminster. Didn't think he'd done anybody any good by being there.'

'And what did you say?' Ellen asked.

'I asked what gave him the right to think he could do good in the first place.'

They had returned from Blakeney by taxi; the driver did not appreciate the idea of companionable silence. Recognising Maurice, he filled the dark miles with complaints about poultry breeders and their sharp dealings. Sonia and Maurice sat side by side in the back, not merely a captive but also a belted-in audience, washed over by accounts of fowl pest and compensation, European subsidies, financial strokes and mass graves filled only with turkey feathers.

It was warm in the car. She thought for a while that Maurice Lovelace was absorbed in the stories or lost in thought; then she realised that he was struggling not to laugh. 'It wasn't what you'd call statesmanlike,' she said.

Back in Walsingham he had taken her hand again and held it for a little longer than is entirely usual while bidding someone good night. He had strong hands which were warm enough to have been in the airing cupboard. Sonia had remained on the step for a moment watching him walk away.

He had only taken about a dozen paces when he turned and walked quickly back to her door. 'Will you meet me in London? Some place away from here?' He was trying to see her eyes but her face must have been virtually invisible against the light from the hall.

'Yes. Yes, of course. Somewhere,' she had said.

'Good.' He had smiled. 'People round here have limited vision – but they see so damned much.'

This time he walked almost to the corner before stopping and then retracing his steps to her door.

'Can I tell you something for nothing?' he said.

'All right.'

'Romance isn't necessarily confined to puddings.'

The Harlot's Prerogative

'Thank you, Maurice,' she had said. It was the first time that she had called him by his first name or, indeed, called him anything at all.

This time he had left without looking back.

Just then the night stillness was broken by a hollow hooting. A large tawny owl was visible for a moment, gliding along the centre of High Street. He turned his head, eyes left, and observed Sonia steadily as he drifted by, unblinking.

A report on the theme park proposals appeared on the front page of the Snorings and Creakes edition of the *North Norfolk Weekly Chronicle*. It wasn't the splash story. The page one lead was given over instead to a piece about increased car parking charges in Fakenham on market days.

Nobody at the *Chronicle* genuinely believed that a five-penny rise in pay-and-display parking charges made a better news story or a more interesting topic than the arrival of a Judaeo-Christian religious multi-media theme park at Walsingham, in the centre of the circulation area. Not even the editor thought so.

He was, however, a cautious and careworn twenty-nine-year-old who had once been described in public by the group chief executive as 'daring' and 'editorially innovative'.

These amounted to serious charges in the enclosed world of the East Anglian *Chronicle* series and the editor, badly scarred, had no intention of ever allowing that sort of career-blighting abuse to be heaped on his head again.

His reporting staff was cast into gloom when it became known that the Walsingham story was being slashed and gutted. It was cut to a two paragraph brief at the foot of the front page, with a cross-reference to page nineteen where the remainder of the item was tucked away so as to be virtually invisible.

'It pisses me off, Roger,' said Kate Scantlebury, the chief reporter. 'I can't tell you how much it off-pisses me when a good tale gets wasted.'

'Me, too,' said Roger Matthews, her reporting staff. 'They cut out the best bit.'

'Which bit was that, Roger?'

Andrew Moncur

'The bit about the fornicators.'

'Fornicators, Roger?'

'Well, adulterators. It's been chopped.'

'I should think so too, Roger,' said Ms Scantlebury.

The outline proposals put forward for the theme park included a number of hands-on, interactive displays where visitors would, for instance, be invited to cast the first stone at a woman taken in adultery; knock down Goliath with a sling shot; or, perhaps, arm-wrestle with Samson.

The twenty-eight-acre site, to the west of the disused railway line on the edge of Walsingham, would feature an Inside The Whale multi-media show and what was described as the Exodus Thriller Ride, featuring the Parting of the Red Sea water chute.

The *Chronicle* newsroom had been puzzled by a small building described on the plan as 'Daniel's Den'. Roger Matthews had been able to establish that it was in actual fact a lion's den, where there would be daily performances by big cats. At other times they would be taking part in the Christians versus Lions arena show.

Other features of the park included the Garden of Eden Experience (with associated plant nursery), a replica Noah's Ark, with animals in pairs, and some life-like tableaux depicting the plagues of Egypt and scenes from the heyday of the Holy Office of the Inquisition. There would be a New Testament Miracle Pavilion, with wave-making equipment, as well as something called the Baby in the Bulrushes Creche and a Loaves and Fishes Diner.

The vision of Lady Richeldis, the destruction of the shrine and the horrible executions of the Walsingham Conspirators would be key features of the theme park. There would be a shopping mall and parking for 500 vehicles.

'A 60-bedroom Pilgrims' Lodge Hotel is also proposed by the developers, Jericho Properties. A company spokesman said the theme park would create up to 250 jobs. He said the project had the enthusiastic backing of Walsingham's Conservative MP, Mr Maurice Lovelace,' the *Weekly Chronicle* reported.

'Mr Lovelace, who was injured in a recent road accident, is still being treated in London's St Wilfrid's Hospital where his condition yesterday was said to be poorly but stable.'

The Harlot's Prerogative

* * *

'. . . *is still being treated in London's St Wilfrid's Hospital where his condition yesterday was said to be poorly but stable,*' Mrs Canty read aloud from the newspaper laid across the side of the bed.

'Stable? Makes you sound like a horse,' she said to Maurice Lovelace's inert form. 'Sorry. Sorry. I didn't mean to mention horses. Not when they've given you so much grief.'

She folded the copy of the *North Norfolk Weekly Chronicle* which she had brought to read to her comatose employer at his hospital bedside. It had become a routine. She sat at his side, most evenings, delivering news and gossip. Mrs Canty chose to believe that somehow the sound of her voice could strike a chord in his poor, bruised brain.

She liked to read out their horoscope and the football reports from the London *Evening Standard*. After that she picked out highlights from the readers' letters page in *Mother's Own* or perhaps Fiona's Society Diary in *Hiya!* The *Weekly Chronicle* was delivered to Mr Lovelace's London flat and Mrs Canty had lighted upon it as a means of keeping him abreast of events in his constituency; she read out those reports which mentioned either Maurice himself or any person with an improbable name. She was easily drawn to anybody called Gotobed in Great Snoring or the Raspberry family of Wood Norton.

'Now,' said Mrs Canty. 'There are one or two things about this theme park business which I need to have explained to me. Why do these developer people say they've got your support? Why would you want to have anything to do with lions and frogs?

'It all sounds dodgy. What's their game? That's my feeling at any rate. You'll be able to put me straight about all this just as soon as you're better.

'And, yes, my sister's boy – that's Russell, the one with the business in office stationery and the ankles. You remember the day he fell off his bike? And you signed his passport forms when he was going to America with that girl, Lesley – what was her name? But they never went in the end. Remember? Because of her mother's goitre. And then it was all over. Well, anyway, you'll be surprised to hear that Russell's getting married at last. He's been living with her long enough. That's Claudia, with the hair. You probably think of her as the one with the photocopier because when you saw her – on that Sunday with the van – she didn't have the hair. That was later. It seems they finally decided to go ahead after the operation on Russell's cat. Claudia's cat, really. We don't know why they want to make it kosher at this stage, unless it's children, of course . . .'

Mrs Canty had at last noticed that the man she regarded as being in charge of Maurice Lovelace's case had slipped into the room. He was holding the detached nozzle of an industrial size vacuum cleaner and showing close interest in her one-sided conversation.

'Hello, Mr Hopkin,' she said, waving a corner of the newspaper. 'Here's Mr Hopkin to do some more tests on you, judging by the look of that instrument. It looks horribly like part of a Hoover. Oops. What will the doctor think of me? I must let him get on. Mr Hopkin has been very good to you, you know.'

She patted the visible hand of the figure lying motionless on the bed. There was not the faintest hint of a reaction.

'No, no. Please. Just you carry on,' said Evangeltine Hopkin, describing a generous circle in the air with his nozzle.

'Don't let me hold you up, doctor,' said Mrs Canty, half rising from her chair and reaching for her basket. 'I know how busy you are, doing your best for all these poor people.'

Chapter Twenty-Three

Mrs Canty was acquainted with the facts of the Walsingham Conspiracy having read about it in Maurice Lovelace's history of the pilgrim village.

She had started to mention the grisly affair to her husband, Norman, during a Sunday afternoon drive, pausing only to point out that they were passing the gates and perimeter fence of the Metropolitan Police dog training establishment at Keston, in the country fringes of south London. A forlorn-looking man at the gate half raised a hand in greeting then let it drop, seeming to lose confidence in the possibility of human contact as they passed by.

Mr Canty was interested in dog-handlers having once in his youth been bitten by one. It happened during a football match against an RAF Regiment XI when Norman Canty, then in the Royal Corps of Signals, had clashed with the opposition goalkeeper. He was compelled to restrain the goalie by taking his head in an arm lock. Norman had been astonished, and pained, to find the Air Force policeman sinking his teeth into the ball of his thumb. The marks, little purple half-moons, had remained for several weeks.

'There was some unrest in Lincolnshire and the North of England after King Henry started to close down the monasteries,' said Mrs Canty. 'Mr Lovelace reckons it was stirred up not only by the religious thing but also by social change and worries about land ownership.'

'Never,' said Mr Canty, slowing down for temporary traffic lights at road works.

'They called it the Pilgrimage of Grace which, thinking about it, is a funny thing to call an uprising. They were fobbed off by the king with promises and pardons. Then he had a few of them strung up and the whole rising collapsed.' Mrs Canty cocked her head and watched a black and white bird with a long tail bounding along the grass verge in a series of great two-footed hops.

161

Andrew Moncur

'I remember,' said Mr Canty.

'You remember?'

'Yes. I shouted at the ref: Ref! Ref! He's bitten me! And the ref takes me aside and asks was he – that's the goalie – was he foaming at the mouth at all? If so, he says, you'll probably get rabies. Then he gives us both a yellow card. He asks the keeper: What's your name? Gnasher? And the bloke looks totally blank and says: No, that's my dog.' Norman Canty shook his head, bared his front teeth and made a little coughing noise.

'Yes, yes,' said Mrs Canty, who had heard the story probably no more than 300 times before.

She had for a moment been lost in the sixteenth century. She could have told her husband that while King Henry, through his ministers, at first responded in a conciliatory way to the northern malcontents, he had, in contrast, come down like a ton of bricks on the first, smallest sign of dissent in Norfolk the following year. The alleged conspirators at Walsingham had been treated with the utmost savagery.

As Maurice Lovelace's manuscript put it:

The maxim that careless talk costs lives was never more true than in the Norfolk of 1537. Unguarded murmurings of discontent – among, for the most part, simple and leaderless country people – led to convictions for treason and executions of a kind calculated to strike fear in the hearts of their neighbours. Poignantly, they had set out, like their fellows in the north, not to overthrow the king's rule but trusting that all would be set right if only they could lay their case before good, bluff King Hal.

Their trust was horribly misplaced. The so-called Walsingham Conspiracy was put down with a vengeance, having been unearthed and prosecuted with great zeal by the local gentry. They eagerly enforced the king's law with at least a hint of collaboration from, of all places, within the confines of Walsingham's sacred places – the place of pilgrimage the conspirators sought, to at least some extent, to preserve.

Catholic historians have repeatedly pointed the finger at

The Harlot's Prerogative

Richard Vowell, the nineteenth and last prior of Walsingham's Augustinian Priory of the Annunciation of the Blessed Virgin Mary. Their evidence is largely circumstantial. Let us say he still has questions to answer under cross-examination at the bar of history's judgement. Or he would stand so arraigned were he not, of course, dead.

Remember, the so-called Walsingham Rebellion took place more than a full year before the actual suppression of the shrine and the priory which served it. The writing was on the wall by then, of course, but the image of Our Lady still remained in place and wax tapers continued to burn in the holy house.

Prior Vowell had already gone along with the demand that he should acknowledge the king as supreme head of the church in England, in place of the pope. Vowell's name still attracts odium today because it heads the list of twenty-one canons at the priory who signed the Act of Supremacy in 1534. In fact, there was nothing the least bit out of the ordinary about that. Virtually all other clerics and monks yielded in the same way; the superiors of the rest of England's religious houses signed up in precisely the same manner. Only a handful of individuals stood out – and they would soon be forced into an impossible corner.

They were caught in a fork whose sharp tines cannot but be admired by those familiar with the process of law-making at Westminster.

'Yes,' Mrs Canty said to herself, setting aside the manuscript. 'But you have to admit that Vowell *sounds* a downright suspicious sort of name.' She sniffed and returned to the text.

First of all an Act was passed making it an offence of treason to say or do anything to deprive the king of any dignity, title or name attaching to his royal estate. Then, just days before that law came into force, Henry adopted the additional style of Head of the English Church. Previously, denying the king's supremacy might have meant falling from favour or even languishing behind bars; now, suddenly, it became a capital offence.

Shortly the religious houses of England would be subjected, one by one, to scrutiny by officials acting on behalf of the king. As we know, this visitation had a multiple purpose. It was carried out in order to compile an up-to-date record of the wealth of the abbeys and friaries – to remember all the jewels of all the monasteries in England, as the king's first minister put it – and, more urgently, to prevent their riches and lands being dispersed or hidden away. This liquidation process was already known to have started as the more far-sighted superiors saw the shape of things to come.

It is my belief that in the case of the fabulously wealthy shrine at Walsingham the king's mission failed. At least, his agents failed to close all the routes by which gold and treasure might be spirited away. In my view a hoard of great value was hidden away in the pilgrim village.

When trouble stirred in Walsingham and the surrounding villages it seems to have started with a fateful discussion between friends. One, Ralph Rogerson, had a special interest in the future of the sacred places; he was a singing man employed at the priory as well as being a small landowner in his own right. He voiced his anxieties to George Guisborough, a farmer.

They were worried about the likelihood of the priory and other monasteries in the area being dissolved – although there's no very compelling reason to believe that they were troubled solely on religious grounds. Rather, they feared that if the shrine closed pilgrimages would cease and trade would suffer. At the same time the already land-rich gentry could be expected to take over the monastic estates, and they would hardly prove to be better landlords for the common people.

The two sounded out other neighbours and held meetings, including one at an archery contest in the nearby village of Binham. Their aim was to tell the king of their worries. The conspirators, perhaps thirty of them in all, planned to gather in May, 1537. They included a handful of clergy and friars.

The Harlot's Prerogative

Their scheme grew more ambitious as the numbers increased: soon they were talking of severing the road link with London and marching to join the northern rebels – whose uprising had, in fact, already been subdued.

Then the inevitable happened. The plotters, seeking more recruits for their cause, approached a man in the village of Letheringsett who betrayed their trust.

William Guisborough and his son, George, were arrested in Walsingham and taken to London to be examined. George, being questioned, said 'he thought it very ill done, the suppressing of so many religious houses where God was so well served' and admitted calling for 'an insurrection of the commons who were oppressed by the gentlemen'.

Others were soon rounded up, including Ralph Rogerson and, most significantly, the sub-prior at Walsingham's ancient priory, Nicholas Mileham. In all more than two dozen men implicated in the plot were imprisoned in Norwich Castle. Of the entire bunch, it is Mileham, the canon, whose case has the strangest ring to it, still audible across the centuries.

The reason is the curious role performed by the prior of Walsingham, Richard Vowell. He suddenly comes under scrutiny because of two transactions which are hard to explain.

First, out of the blue he wrote to Thomas Cromwell, the king's powerful minister, offering thanks for favours shown both to him and to a relative. He also enclosed a gift: the then considerable sum of £100. What possible motive could there be for a monk, chief guardian of one of the holy places of England, to make such a cash payment to the very man who posed the greatest threat to the future existence of his priory and its shrine?

Simple, Mrs Canty had thought. It must have been what we call, in the world of professional football, a bung. It was either a big pay-off – or a promise of special treatment in time to come. 'This sort of thing is completely unknown in politics, of course,' she said to herself.

She returned to the manuscript.

165

Andrew Moncur

'Secondly,' it said:

Vowell was later named as playing a significant part in exposing one of the so-called traitors. We know this because of a letter which survives from the period. It was written to Thomas Cromwell by one of the king's officials in Walsingham; in it he praises Vowell for his part in the whole affair. It says the prior had been the 'taker of one of the most rank traitors privy to the Walsingham Conspiracy'.

Historians have not hesitated to draw conclusions: they accuse the prior of betraying Nicholas Mileham, his fellow canon in Walsingham, and sending that unfortunate man to his death.

Prior Vowell was prepared to go to extreme lengths to ingratiate himself with the powers in London. The reason can only be a matter for supposition. It is my view that such men are at their most dangerous – most ready to sacrifice honour and, if necessary, the lives of their friends – when they believe their cause is noble. Or even godly.

The 'rank traitors' did not pose any sort of threat to the king; as rebels go, they were almost pathetically unfrightening. Even the landowner who first acted against the plotters described them as 'very beggars' and stated that their arrest gave rise to no risk of commotion. But Henry was in no mood to let off lightly any opponents, however feeble.

On May 25, 1537 – five days after Prior Vowell had written his curious letter – the conspirators were tried in Norwich. Twelve were sentenced to death (although only eleven were executed), three were given life imprisonment; another eight were pardoned. Two local priests were left to lie in jail untried.

The executions were carefully calculated to achieve the greatest impact on the ordinary people of Norfolk. Five of the plotters, including Ralph Rogerson, were put to death in the castle ditch at Norwich on the day of the fair; another pair met their end in Yarmouth. William Guisborough and another friend were despatched at King's Lynn.

Nicholas Mileham and George Guisborough were brought

166

back to Walsingham itself. They were held in the cellar of a house which still stands in High Street, opposite the gatehouse of the priory which they must have known so well. On the morning of May 30, 1537, they were taken to a field on the western edge of the village. There, where a shallow bowl on the hillside forms a natural amphitheatre, both men suffered a pitiless execution.

It had been decided that the half dozen deemed the principal plotters should die in the most brutal manner. They were drawn, hanged, beheaded and quartered. The other five were granted the mercy of death by hanging. It was arranged that the crowd at each place of execution would be treated to at least one demonstration of the full price extracted from traitors by the industrious Tudor headsman.

Chapter Twenty-Four

Gwen Lightsome came through the door like a tugboat. The editor bobbed along in her wake.

'. . . fine by me,' Rosie Maguire was saying. 'You should set that up and then we'll see about getting some heartrending pictures.'

In the outer office, where the potted palm, the Swiss-cheese plants and the calamondin orange climbed over each other in their exuberance, Muriel Oliver half rose from her revolving chair at the desk.

'Mrs Lightsome,' she said, holding out her hand. 'I wanted to welcome you on behalf of all the secretarial staff at *Home & Beauty* and say what a pleasure it . . .'

Gwen Lightsome, the newly appointed associate editor and columnist with the caring brief, did not deviate from her path or spare a glance for the editor's secretary as she swept by.

'We really must have lunch, Rosie,' she called over her shoulder to the editor. And then she sailed on, turned to the left and was gone.

'Ah, righty-ho,' said Miss Oliver after a moment. 'Righty-bloody-ho. Fine, fine.' She remained in the same half-upright position with her bottom sticking out ridiculously in mid-air.

Rigor mortis had set in for the pork sausage, which would have enabled a Home Office pathologist to estimate the probable time of its death. Ellen Bright pushed it round her plate again. She had tried once or twice to stab it but the prongs of her fork were reluctant to puncture its sheath-like skin. It was the sort of plastic film they used in hardware stores to seal packs of nails or brass hinges.

The chips were flaccid and pale. They lacked backbone. The smell of cooking oil seemed to hang at picture-rail height across the entire bar room of the Muckspreaders' Arms.

Sonia Marks, across the table, had taken a single bite from the

168

shockingly white sandwich which now lay back on its laurels – or, rather, on the undergrowth of shredded lettuce, detached collars of raw onion and cubes of watery, mutilated radish which obscured her plate. Sonia had been chewing this mouthful for what was already an unnaturally long time.

'Everything all right?' said the balding barman, who had walked round to lift two dripping glasses from a pool of tomato juice – or, possibly, arterial blood – on the far end of the table. He was looking over their heads towards the street door.

'No, frankly, it isn't,' said Ellen. 'Tastes like diesel fuel.' She shunted the oval plate away. The whorls of her thumbprint formed instantly in colourless grease.

'Murrff,' said Sonia Marks, still chewing in a dense kind of way.

'Good, fine, great,' said the barman. 'Hello, padre.'

A priest was in the act of insinuating himself into the pub; his pale features and conspicuously hairy ears and nostrils were immediately familiar to Ellen Bright. He gave a nervous wave to Sonia as he made his way to the bar, approaching it in a strange side-on fashion as he crossed the room.

Ellen was struck by his passing resemblance to a hieroglyph on the wall of an Egyptian tomb.

'Afternoon, father,' said Sonia, at last. The clergyman raised a hand again and pursed his lips as though a spot of lemon juice had touched his tongue.

The two women had come away from Walsingham although possibly not far enough. If they had stopped to look back from the pub car park the sharp spire of the parish church of St Mary and All the Saints was still visible, rising distantly from the canopy of trees to one side of the village.

Its needle-point marks one of the curiosities of Walsingham. The Anglican parish church has a fine peal of bells. They must have been inspiring because a former vicar, George Ratcliffe Woodward, was sufficiently moved to compose the carol 'Ding dong merrily on high.'

Oddly enough, at that time the six bells could scarcely be allowed to make themselves heard.

'If they'd given them a real ding dong the tower might have

169

collapsed on their heads. It was unsafe. The whole thing needed to be strengthened; in his day the best they could hope to do was sway the bells gently. And that's what they did.' Sonia picked up her sandwich, looked at it thoughtfully and then returned it to the plate.

'It's funny, but Maurice didn't – sorry, I mean to say Maurice doesn't . . . I've got to stop talking about him as though he's dead and gone.'

'It's all right,' said Ellen. 'He'd probably find it amusing.'

Sonia Marks dropped her chin for a moment. 'It was all over between us anyway. For quite some time,' she said. 'I was trying to tell you how he really didn't – doesn't – trouble about the religious side of life in Walsingham at all. I don't mean he ignores it. How could he possibly ignore it?

'But if you asked me about his faith I would have to say he believes in the Church of England more than he believes in God. Were you to tell him there was going to be a second coming tomorrow, with trumpets and choirs of angels, he'd be horrified.

'Who wants God to come along and wrap the whole thing up, once and for all anyway? Nobody really longs for that moment, surely? If you went out and talked to people in the street and told them God's kingdom has come and He'll be here first thing in the morning to judge the quick and the dead, then those people – ordinary men and women – would just about throw a fit. Say to them: that's it, here's your harp, get on with a little worshipping – well, they'd sooner be dead.

'The things they hope for, live for, are the daughter's wedding next year or the birth of a new baby or the chance of falling in love. They might want to get into bed with someone – or get a job done properly or win a big game. In every case, it's a matter of looking forward; it's the only way people can work. Nobody wants it to end, do they?

'Maurice Lovelace is the same. He doesn't pray for the Almighty's winged chariot to come down; he doesn't look to the dreadful day of judgement. Full stop. He's C of E, for Christ's sake.

'I can tell you he isn't devout; he certainly doesn't throw himself into it in the way they do at their shrine. But I'm certain he took a

170

decision right from the start that if the place would have him, with all his flaws, then he would take the place. He would have it just as it stood, however quaint or downright strange it might seem. And, of course, the real place isn't necessarily what you see.'

She paused and looked at her plate again.

'Bloody sandwich,' she said.

'Bloody pub,' said Ellen Bright.

'Everything all right, then?' said the barman, arriving at her elbow and picking up the sausage plate.

'The E-coli contamination was delicious,' said Ellen.

'Super, super,' said the barman, scooping up a squashed sachet of tomato ketchup. Father Neil Bugloss was sitting on a tall stool, bending over a small pile of printed papers on the bar. A glass of fruit juice stood untouched at his elbow.

'Do you know that Maurice sent rejection letters signed by Constance Verity to every single member of the government, declining to publish their poetry. He thought it was very funny,' said Sonia.

'The only trouble with Maurice is that he has too many birthdays every year,' she sighed. 'About half a dozen too many, I guess.'

After more than ten years in women's magazines Muriel Oliver was not easily shocked. She had been made to confront forms of depravity and squalor which are, sadly, all part of the daily fare in the world of current affairs. And that was just in the reporters' room.

It would not be an exaggeration to say that she was shaken to what she would describe as her lower abdominal regions by the task the editor had now asked her to perform.

It was, Muriel said to herself, kicking a man when he was down. Or, in this case, while he was in a coma.

Veronica Legg did not encourage activities of a sexual nature among her bed-and-breakfast clients. In fact, in so far as it was possible for her to influence the behaviour of guests and harness their instinctive drives, she sought to prevent sex ever raising its head on the premises.

'Sex,' she wrote in her ledger, underlining the heading three times. Mrs Legg then stood up, took a turn around her kitchen table and sat down again heavily.

> Sex is all too often a messy and embarrassing business – and not only for those most intimately concerned. The hostess, her domestic staff and other guests can all be discommoded by the actions of those under its distressing influence.
>
> Guests who are more interested in bed than they are in breakfast can quickly start to display antisocial patterns of behaviour. They are likely to create disturbing noises. They will be late for meals. They tend to leave strange things down the bed, leading to difficult moments for staff who know little of the world.

Veronica Legg had quickly discovered the value of the pre-emptive strike. Couples staying at the Gideon's Well Guest House who wandered upstairs to their bedrooms during the afternoon were allowed roughly six minutes' grace before Mrs Legg, using her pass key, burst into the room with a vacuum cleaner and an outsize aerosol can of furniture polish.

Guests who retired early and in a significant manner would soon be startled by a terrible hammering on the bedroom door.

'Hello! Hell-oo!' Mrs Legg would call. 'This is an emergency. We have mislaid Rolf the cat who needs his worming pill. Could you please search your room . . .'

Those who lingered in bed in the morning might find their peace shattered by inquiries about fish for breakfast or Chef's special black pudding. They might be brought up short by Mrs Legg's cooee, signalling delivery to the bedroom door of promised extracts from the bus timetable or details of National Trust opening times.

Healthy young people could emerge from a stay at Gideon's Well with the weary, shadowed-eye look normally associated with a weekend of sexual excess. They were sometimes unusually snappy and bad tempered.

'What's this, then?' Miss Oliver stuck her forefinger into the wire tray and flipped the first of the piled sheets of paper.

The Harlot's Prerogative

'It's from Miss Lightsome,' said Troy from the post room, who had just delivered the filing tray to her desk.

'You mean Mrs Lightsome, Troy.'

'Yes. Well, she wants you to do some typing for her. At least, her personal assistant said to tell you so. That's Miss Buffy.'

'Miss Duffy, Troy.'

'Right. She said you should type it for her – and make it snappy.'

Muriel Oliver's friends would have become alert at this point to the fact that her temper was being stretched and might at any moment snap.

'Oh, dear,' she said, just then. 'I seem to have knocked that heap of waste paper all over the floor ... No, no. Don't worry about collecting it all up, Troy. The cleaners will do it later.'

Chapter Twenty-Five

Ellen Bright waited until the pony had passed, pulling at a smart clip a governess cart driven by a dark-haired man in a panama hat. He tipped his brim and smiled and Ellen raised a hand in reply before pulling across the lane and into the driveway.

The doors of the garage were wide open; it was empty, apart from a red lawnmower tractor, and no vehicle was in sight on the gravel in front of the house. She guessed the building was only three or four years old. The garden was still raw. It looked exceptionally neat inside the garage. Some black and white striped poles were leaning against the wall. A dog barked from the far side of the house.

Ellen turned off the engine and sat for a moment or two, waiting to see whether the dog would tear out to meet her. All was quiet again – until, suddenly, the awful, mournful cry of a peacock echoed across the valley. Then a diesel engine came into earshot.

She stepped out of the car and was starting to make her way towards the house when a Land Rover swung into the gateway behind her.

'Can I help you, fair lady?' The man at the wheel had a gingery moustache and a face full of freckles. She had a terrible desire to smack him round his pink and white ear.

'Mr Green? Harry Green?' Ellen walked toward the driver's-side door. 'My name's Ellen Bright. I'm a journalist. I hoped . . .'

'Get lost.' He roared the engine and leaned away from her, reaching across to the passenger seat.

'You lot have done enough bloody harm already,' he snapped. The newspaper he pushed towards her was the *Mirror*. The front page headline said: 'For God's sake! It's the holy roller-coaster.'

'Yes?' The woman was strikingly pale, her face as smoothly polished as a Japanese Noh mask. Her mouth seemed to open and close

174

without disturbing the unlined skin of her cheeks and chin.

Ellen tried to guess her age. Mid-sixties? Perhaps seventies. Her hair was so beautifully dressed, her make-up so carefully applied, a silk scarf so perfectly knotted at her throat that she appeared to defy mere chronology. Her rings and earrings, the quadruple string of pearls, were only a stop short of vulgar. She remained remarkably still.

Her pleated skirt, her shirt and cardigan were neat in the way that speaks of clothes folded away between sheets of tissue paper in lavender-scented drawers. She was wearing black stockings and perfectly polished court shoes.

'Bunty Westlake?' Ellen asked, tucking a strand of hair behind the arm of her spectacles.

'Mrs Westlake, yes.' The woman's eyes were pale blue and piercingly cold.

'My name's Ellen Bright. I was hoping . . .'

'Is it the loose covers?'

'No, I'm afraid not.'

A tiny glimmer of irritation showed in the older woman's chilly eyes.

'I was anxious,' said Ellen. 'That's to say, I wanted to speak to you in your position as – I hope I'm correct – chairman of the Conservative Association. That's the Walsingham and Snorings constituency . . .'

'Couldn't you have called first?' Mrs Westlake gave an un-mistakable signal of impatience, changing the weight on her feet and shifting her hand on the door jamb. It was clear that she wanted to close the front door in her young caller's face.

She looked away over Ellen's shoulder, across the wide lawn and beyond the copper beech towards the curving drive and the distant white gates where thickets of the darkest green holly shielded the house from the Snoring road. Somewhere in the house a clock started to chime.

The light of the hall seemed to cast a silver halo around her head. The white paintwork had been newly glossed; the heavy brass handles and the bell push had been worked to a brilliant shine. Ellen could smell the metallic tang of brass polish. A pop-eyed miniature spaniel trotted down the corridor and took shelter behind Mrs Westlake's feet; it had a blaze of white running up the bridge of its nose and between its eyes. Ellen had time to register with surprise that there was a tiny spot of red in the centre of its forehead, like the caste mark of a Hindu.

'I'm a journalist, Mrs Westlake. I'm here researching a piece about your poor MP, Maurice . . .'

'How dare you?' The older woman practically spat. The anger contrasted alarmingly with the strange immobility of her face. The little dog, as though sensing her mood, made a couple of gargling barks. Then it retreated, darting into the corridor.

Ellen Bright recoiled. She couldn't help it; she had never found a way to cope with sudden outbursts of anger. It only took a shout or a few venomous words to make her eyes smart, partly with frustration at being so easily reduced to stupid tears.

'You people. You come here, to the house, like vultures, digging and hounding – you should be taught a lesson. You should be shown what decent people – how decent people – how they hate this intrusion of hateful – this invasion of privacy.'

She's enjoying herself. She actually likes this, Ellen noted in the part of her mind which was dispassionately recording the scene.

'I'm sorry,' she said aloud. 'I don't know why you're reacting in this way. I'm making perfectly proper . . .'

'Go away. Get away from here. You expect me – me? – to speak to you? That poor, injured – that poor young man. How dare you come sneaking about here, trying to wheedle your way in.' Mrs Westlake, far from closing the door on her unwanted caller had opened it another foot, the better to drive home her attack.

'Look, this is just way over the . . .' Ellen raised her hands and let them drop in a gesture of disbelief.

'You'll hear more of this. I won't let this pass. I shall take this up in the very highest quarters. I am a personal friend of the chairman of the Press Complaints Commission. You and your editor will . . .'

'Bunty? What's all this? What's up?' An elderly man was approaching from the far end of the hall, behind Mrs Westlake's outflung arm. His chin was tucked down on his chest and he tilted his head to keep one bright eye on whatever lay ahead.

The Harlot's Prerogative

'It's nobody,' said Mrs Westlake and shut the front door with a juddering smack.

Ellen Bright stood there for perhaps half a minute, closely examining the woodwork. So that's what they mean when they talk about showing you the door, she told herself. A woodpecker started work somewhere off over her left shoulder among the ash and horse chestnut trees on the far side of the drive.

'Oh, I do love a woman with lavender-scented drawers,' said Daphne Chapman, reclining in her swivel chair and resting both feet on the cardboard box full of rejected poetry under her desk.

'She was the second person to chuck me out in less than an hour. You've no idea. I've been given the bum's rush today by some of the most influential people around here. The absolute bloody cream.' Ellen moved the telephone to her other ear and held it there by will-power, hitching up her shoulder to wedge it in place – in exactly the way that healthy-living features in magazines insisted was inadvisable and a menace to health and safety.

Still, Ellen knew several magazine journalists who had done themselves serious injury while actually researching and writing healthy-living features.

Standing there beside a little triangular green, with only a sheep pasture, a bank of trees, a stream, a little white-painted footbridge, a brick and flint barn and a couple of cottages in view – tethered to the competitive world by the merest telephone and a ripple of electromagnetic waves – Ellen Bright experienced an undeniably strong emotion welling through her size-twelve frame.

'God,' she said to herself. 'God, I wish I was in a crowd in a noisy part of London with somebody who knows how to make me laugh.'

'Listen. I don't know how to tell you this without making your lousy day a good deal worse,' said Daphne Chapman, speaking from the walk-in cupboard which passed as an office for the features editor at *Home & Beauty*. 'Basically, there's big news at this end. And it has implications for you, I'm afraid.'

'Oh, bloody hell,' said Ellen. 'I knew I should have stopped in bed.'

'For a start, we're dumping dear old Constance Verity, lying there in her, so to speak, hospital bed.'

'Never.'

'Oh, yes we are. Our beloved editor put round a memo this morning, praising Constance for her sterling work and giving her the old heave-ho. You know the sort of thing. Pathetic. Now – and this is the really big one – I want you to guess who we've taken on as an associate editor, staff writer and superstar. She's already moved in.'

'I don't know. Give me a clue.'

'It's somebody you would probably like to have stuffed and mounted in a glass case.'

'Mother Teresa? Cliff Richard?'

'Worse. It's Gwen Lightsome.'

'Oh, God . . .'

'Who, as you appreciate, is someone we all love and admire. The really bad news is that the first thing she wants to write for the features pages involves your friend Maurice Lovelace, of all people.'

'Where does that leave me?' Ellen's asked, immediately accepting the inevitable: her work was going to be superseded and she, personally, was about to be walked all over by the Lightsome caravan. All she could do was argue for the best possible terms.

'I'm already here,' Ellen said. 'I've put in a good deal of time on this, as you . . .'

'Look, don't worry. She's coming in to talk to me about it tomorrow afternoon – what day's that? Yes, Wednesday. I'll make sure you don't lose out at all.'

The features editor was conciliatory in a way born of long experience of treating and seeing people treated disgracefully.

'What shall I do? Am I supposed to pack up here, then? Should I come back to London?' Ellen's tone remained admirably neutral.

'Stay there for the moment, at least until we know what's planned,' said Daphne. 'It might be useful to have someone on the spot who's already upset all the most influential people in the whole damned town.'

Chapter Twenty-Six

Evangeltine Hopkin parked the stainless-steel trolley in the corridor. It was the sort of businesslike hospital trolley familiar to a world audience from a thousand episodes of TV medical drama. It lacked only a body hovering artfully close to death.

In fact, it was altogether wanting in terms of dramatic impact. Mr Hopkin could not even enjoy the consolation of wheeling a delivery of life-saving drugs or the essential parts of an iron lung around the Nightingale Wing.

His trolley was heaped instead with little plastic pots of long-life milk, paper envelopes of sugar, prettily packaged bars of soap, cartons of tissue paper, sachets of coffee, tea bags, shower caps and faintly perfumed antiseptic wipes whose major clinical function was the removal of make-up. Guests – they tried not to speak about patients – guests in private hospitals like St Wilfrid's expected to be treated in the manner to which international hotels and club-class travel had made them accustomed.

'Ah-ha. There you are,' said Mr Hopkin, sliding round the edge of the door and entering Maurice Lovelace's private room. 'Been hoping to see you.'

'Gracious. You made me jump, Mr Hopkin.' Mrs Canty, sitting at the bedside in her raincoat, had been digging about in her shopping bag, trying to find the new tape she had brought in for Mr Lovelace. 'Would you like an orange?'

'No, thank you. There's something important – really important – I've got to tell you about our patient here. Sit yourself down now. Sit yourself down.'

Mrs Canty was already sitting down but didn't like to say so. Her chin came up and her mouth steadied itself, waiting to hear the worst. Her fingers tightened on the carrying handles of her bag. 'Go on. Tell me, doctor,' she said in a small, firm voice.

Andrew Moncur

'Do you know they're going to take him away? They're coming for him on Thursday night.'

Mrs Canty's hand flew to her throat. 'What? You mean . . . You mean, it's all over? What do you mean?'

Mr Hopkin hurried across the room and patted her shoulder in a clumsy, gentle way.

'There, there,' he said. 'It's all right. There's no need to go upsetting yourself. You'll be giving yourself what we call, medically speaking, a bit of a nasty turn.'

'Yes, but what about Mr Lovelace? What are you telling me about him? Please, what's happening?'

'Don't alarm yourself. There's no change from the medical point of view. He's no better, no worse; he's just lying there, on the drip. It's a funny thing, but I reckon myself that he has the occasional dream. You can see a sort of fluttering. His eyes start to go like . . .'

'Mr Hopkin. Please, Mr Hopkin.' Mrs Canty had brought her palms together.

'No, no,' he said quickly. 'This isn't nothing medical. Lord, no. This is politics. They're coming to collect him in the evening and taking him over the river – to vote in the House of Commons.'

'I don't believe it!' Mrs Canty's jaw had absolutely, and gratifyingly, dropped.

'It's true. Management called us in to tell us all about it. I've got to get Mr Lovelace ready for loading by nine o'clock. I'm booking the ambulance and tea for the crew – in a medical capacity, you understand. They're taking him to Westminster and then, after its all over, they're supposed to get him back here by half past midnight.'

'The bastards,' said Mrs Canty. 'They're going to wheel him into the House of Commons – that poor man – just to get his wretched vote. In his state.'

She patted Maurice's hand, lying apparently lifeless on the bed covers.

'Can they do that? I mean, can they move a patient in this condition?' She had never really thought of the possibility.

'Course. We move him all the time,' said Mr Hopkin. 'We sit him up in the chair there sometimes or walk him around in a wheelchair.

It's good for his circulation. We have to be careful with his eyes, you understand, because he can't blink.'

'But what about his tubes? What about his drip thing – that plastic bag?'

'Easy,' said Mr Hopkin. 'That's his high protein liquid feed, going in through that nasal gastric tube. It just comes with him, if he's going away for any length of time. It can be connected up more or less anywhere. For a short trip you probably wouldn't bother. He's not going to starve, is he.'

Mrs Canty hesitated for a delicate one-twentieth of a second.

'And what about, you know, the other end?' she asked.

'Simple. There's another tube and another bag collecting. We have to make sure we use sterile bags, of course, but otherwise it's no fuss.'

'So he can be carted about more or less anywhere?'

'Makes no difference to him, does it?' said Mr Hopkin. 'We've been put on standby to do it again, taking him to parliament maybe once, maybe twice, next week. He's needed over there. It's the government, see. So no-one can't do nothing about it.'

'Can't they, indeed? We shall see about that,' said Mrs Canty. And then she picked up her shopping bag in much the way that Queen Boadicea might have gathered the reins of her war chariot.

There had been an unfortunate scene involving a blue, two-drawer filing cabinet. Muriel Oliver had noticed two or three weeks earlier that it was standing unused in the L-shaped alcove where the photocopier lived. She had immediately labelled it: '*Do not remove. Editor's Secretary.*' Miss Oliver took it as her right, in her capacity as senior secretary on *Home & Beauty*, to control the movement of all office furniture. She spent a good deal of her free evenings and weekends worrying about how some spare desk or redundant stationery cupboard might best be used back at the office.

It is surprising how quickly time flies when you have something worthwhile to think about.

Then, one Monday morning, she went to photocopy the note she had written to the head of security about the state of the waste-bin area on the Plume Street side of the tower block, which was a disgrace. And suddenly she noticed that the two-drawer cabinet had gone.

Muriel had been pretty cross. She immediately made an un-obtrusive, low-key tour of inspection of the most likely areas of suspicion on the editorial floor – travelling incognito, as she described it to herself. Several members of staff were startled to find the editor's secretary leering around room dividers, rolling her eyes at items of furniture buried in coats and old newspapers, while whistling out of tune.

In the end, she met her former assistant, Juliet Neckles, at the coffee machine and took the opportunity to outline the bare facts of the mystery.

'A little blue filing cabinet?' asked Juliet.

'Two-drawer,' said Muriel.

'Yes, we've got that. Hilary had Troy from the post room carry it down to our suite.' Juliet pressed the drinking chocolate button.

'Hilary? Hilary? Hilary told Troy?' Muriel looked stunned.

Hilary Duffy was personal assistant to Gwen Lightsome, agony aunt and associate editor. Like her boss, she was newly installed in an office on the river side of Mameluke Tower.

She was speaking on the telephone when Muriel Oliver bowled into the room. Muriel's nostrils were flared and her breath was coming in snorts like a cavalry charger. Miss Duffy continued her conversation. She was conspicuously failing to notice the arrival of the editor's secretary, who was by now conducting an inventory.

'I'm sorry,' Miss Duffy said at last, replacing the receiver. 'Have you come to do a little cleaning?'

'I beg your pardon?' Muriel straightened her back.

'You seemed to be poking about the furniture. I assumed you were looking for dust.'

'I'm looking for an item of furniture which I fear may have been purloined. Do you know anything about it?'

'I'm afraid I have very little time to devote to domestic services.' Miss Duffy started to rearrange some papers on her already per-fectly neat desk.

'It's a blue filing cabinet which has been removed from . . .'

'I'm sorry,' said Miss Duffy, 'but this sounds like a matter to be sorted out at secretary level. We personal assistants do not have the opportunity, pleasant though it might be, to concern ourselves with time-wasting questions about furnishings, nilly-willy.'

'Nilly-willy?'

'Nilly-willy, yes.'

'You mean willy-nilly.' Muriel did not hide the note of scorn in her voice.

'I mean what I say: nilly-willy.'

'Nilly-willy! Hah!'

'You'll have to excuse me now, Miss . . . Miss Thingy. I'm sure you have some secretarial duties to perform.'

'Hah!'

Personally, I am involved in very delicate negotiations on behalf of Miss Lightsome,' said Miss Duffy with a malevolent light in her eye. 'It is a most important mission. I'm arranging for a politician in a coma to be taken to Walsingham. I don't expect a shorthand typist like yourself to know that Walsingham is a place of pilgrimage and healing. A religious place.'

Muriel placed both hands flat on the other woman's desk and leaned over until their noses were perhaps six inches apart.

'Thank you so much, Miss Duffy, for explaining that point of detail,' she said.

'Think nothing of it.'

'I won't. Let's just hope that your travel arrangements go every bit as smoothly as St Ursula's.'

'St Ursula?'

'Look her up. I think you'll find she was a virgin who had her head chopped off.'

On the lane to Little Snoring Ellen found herself driving beside a sparrow hawk which was effortlessly cruising the wide grass verge, heading in the same direction as the car. They travelled side-by-side for four or five hundred yards before it turned its head and regarded her for a second or two.

She decided to clock the bird in return. It was, she discovered, flying at a speed of precisely thirty-two miles an hour.

Chapter Twenty-Seven

Father Neil Bugloss was buying soluble aspirin in the mini-super-market. His head always gave him trouble for a week or two before the Whitsun bank holiday and the arrival of thousands making the great national pilgrimage to Walsingham. He put it down to the onset of the pollen season; it seemed never to occur to him that stress or exhaustion might account for the headaches.

He turned from the checkout, holding the little blue and white packet and struggling to drop a handful of coins into the gaping mouth of his leather purse.

'Whoops. There you go, kind sir,' said Harry Green as the priest's lightweight frame cannoned into his own more substantial shoulder.

'So very sorry,' said Father Bugloss, looking up at last. 'Mr Green. Ah-ha. I've been wanting to have a serious word with you.'

'Oh, yes, vicar?' He steered the priest away from the cash till and towards a shelf unit stacked with breakfast cereals. 'What canst I be a'doing of for you then?'

'I believe,' said the reverend Father, giving him a penetrating look, 'that you're proposing to open here in Walsingham some sort of theme park devoted to almighty God.'

'That's right, yes.'

'But that's monstrous. This is a holy place.'

'The end came to the holy house at Walsingham not with a bang but a bureaucratic whimper. Such is the way the world ends,' Mrs Canty read from Maurice Lovelace's manuscript setting out the thousand-year history of the North Norfolk pilgrim village.

He has a nice turn of phrase, she reflected. Not with a bang but a whimper. Yes. The sentence wasn't that bad. Not brilliant, of course. But not bad. She glanced out of the bus window; there were another half-dozen stops yet before her own.

'Scarcely a year after the bloody executions in Walsingham the

184

The Harlot's Prerogative

king's commissioners arrived, full of purpose, in the midsummer of 1538,' she read. 'They came to perform the final stock-taking and form-filling, the last acts in the story of that holy house which had, over five centuries, become the premier shrine to the Virgin Mary in all England.'

The king's men came to lay hold of the treasures of the chapel and, most significantly of all, to seize the image of Our Lady of Walsingham. The ancient effigy of the Virgin with the infant Christ on her lap stood flanked by statues of St Margaret and St Catharine, the patron saint of pilgrims. They could offer no protection now.

They took away the image and 'such gold and silver things as were in the chapel'.

Similar scenes were being enacted all over the realm. At Canterbury the shrine of St Thomas à Becket was stripped of cartloads of gold, silver and jewels. The shrine of St Edmund at Bury St Edmunds yielded lashings of gemstones and precious metals worth 5,000 marks. They also went to work at Westminster Abbey, the church of a great Benedictine monastery which had by then occupied that Thames-side site for nearly 600 years. They plundered the marble, mosaic and golden shrine of St Edward the Confessor, its steps worn away by the knees of pilgrims, its base set with recesses in which the sick were left overnight to be cured by the saint. The tomb was decorated with gold statues, including one depicting St Peter trampling on the Emperor Nero, and with jewels and cameos.

Relics were swept away. At Westminster Abbey alone they scattered, buried or destroyed the following: the Virgin Mary's girdle, a stone marked with a print of Christ's foot at the Ascension, His blood in a crystal vase; a piece of the true cross set in jewels and the skull of St Benedict, founder of the order which created the abbey – and now, in our own day, the patron saint of all Europe.

So it was for the carved Virgin in Walsingham. Bishop Hugh Latimer, who was later himself to suffer at the stake as a protestant martyr under Bloody Mary, had urged that the image be burned in public. 'Our great sibyll the doll at Islington with her older syster of Walsyngham . . . would make a jolly mustere in Smythfield. They would not be all day burnyinge,' he wrote.

And so it came to pass, only the destruction was to take place not at Smithfield, a traditional place of execution in London, but at Chelsea instead.

The fate of the statue was recorded: 'It was in the moneth of July, the images of Our Lady of Wallsingham and Ipswich were brought up to London with all the jewelles that honge about them, at the Kinges commaundement, and divers other images, both in England and Wales, that were used for common pilgrimages, because the people should use noe more idolatrye unto them, and they were burnt at Chelsey by my Lord Privie Seal'.

The Priory itself was surrendered to the Crown in August. Richard Vowell, the prior, is further damned by the fact that he received the notably generous pension of £100 a year for the rest of his days (a figure of £6 per annum was the top rate paid to the other canons).

The pilgrim trade must have died overnight, ruining some of Walsingham's landlords, who may not have been greatly mourned. They had a reputation for rapacity.

Local landowners did, indeed, benefit from the sale of monastery lands. The site of the priory was sold to the governor of the leper hospital for £90. Of the great church, 244 ft long, which had loomed up beside the chapel of the holy house, only ruins would remain. Once the lead had been stripped from its roof, local people felt free to use it as a ready-made quarry for building stone. Houses all over the area have visible courses of dressed stone in their otherwise modest walls of brick and flint. Today the gaunt towers of its east end stand alone to testify to its lost grandeur.

The holy house itself was so obliterated that over the years even the knowledge of its exact whereabouts was lost.

And yet, is it really to be believed that Walsingham

The Harlot's Prerogative

surrendered so supinely? Did it yield up its entire wealth so easily? Many have clung to a belief that the image itself may have been miraculously preserved. Others, more temporal, speculate about gold and the riches of the church.

It was certainly not unknown for treasures, of one sort or another, to be spirited away from the king's grasp by monks. At Glastonbury the abbot was found to have hidden a number of precious objects; a search was organised and hiding places were discovered in 'walls, vaults and other secret places' where treasure was unearthed 'as would have sufficed for a new abbey'. The abbot went to his execution refusing to say a word about any other hoard.

At Westminster Abbey, although the rich shrine of the Confessor was mutilated, they managed to smuggle the saint's body away and secrete it in an obscure place of safety. Imagine the black monks slipping through the night, bearing the remains of the king – dead since 1066. Picture the body: well preserved, with yellow beard, a circlet of gold still around the temples and a cross and chain at the throat. The remains were eventually brought out of hiding twenty years later near the end of Queen Mary's reign. The remains were restored with great ceremony, the scene lit by a hundred lights.

And, let it be remembered, Walsingham was unusually wealthy. Before the suppression the shrine had received an income in offerings of just over £250 annually – a considerable sum compared with, for instance, the £36 given at the shrine of St Thomas of Canterbury. And . . .

Mrs Canty made a muffled squeak. Lowering the sheaf of typescript, she had recognised the road junction and the traffic lights. She had overshot her bus stop.

Hilary Duffy sat before her computer screen and tapped out an internal memorandum. It read as follows: *'For attention of Dept heads. Copy to M. Oliver, editorial (typists): Please note that arrangements are in hand for* Home & Beauty *to convey a VIP to Walsingham, Norfolk, for therapy. No assistance will be needed from staff or freelance journalists outside this immediate section and any person so engaged should be stood down with immediate effect. H. Duffy, personal assistant, per pro Gwen Lightsome, senior associate editor.'*

Muriel Oliver placed the sample sachet of Wrinkle Lift gel in an internal envelope. She addressed it to *'Hilary Duffy, Personal Problems (Embarrassing) Section,* Home & Beauty' and popped it in the mail out-tray beside her office door.

Chapter Twenty-Eight

Ellen met Veronica Legg in the front hall at the Gideon's Well, beside the bench that the landlady called the monk's seat. Mrs Legg was carrying a brightly-polished French horn; it had a chequered tea towel wedged in its bell. She had wrapped another cloth, of a similar pattern, round her head.

'You've been asking questions about our Member, Maurice Lovelace,' she said in a tone part suspicious, part accusing. 'Word gets about, you know, Miss Bright.'

'I'm sure it does, Mrs Legg.' Ellen was desperately tired; her limbs suddenly felt as though they had been wading through rivers of porridge.

'I want you to know that I won't say a word about him. Not to you. Not to anyone else.'

'I see.' Even her voice sounded weary.

'What we had was in the past. And it's nobody else's business. Nobody else's at all.'

'Oh, I see,' said Ellen, suddenly wide awake.

'These days it's strictly a matter between me and my journal. I don't want to rake up old memories. Private, deeply personal, emotional memories. Not for one moment.'

'No. Right.'

'Life can be lonely for a widow, you know. Alone. With no-one to care. No tenderness . . . But, believe me, I have no intention of saying a thing about those days. And those nights. And that man. Is that clear?'

'Well, that's all right then,' said Ellen, backing against the wall near the foor of the staircase.

'It's no use you trying to talk me into it,' snapped Mrs Legg. 'And if you've heard anything about any photographs I would advise you to pay no attention whatsoever. I hope I make myself understood.'

Andrew Moncur

'Photographs?' Ellen was unable to keep the surprise out of her voice. 'Photographs?'

'Don't you start dragging photographs into this. I'm amazed you should even think about such a thing. It's frankly, well, distasteful.'

'Tell me, Mrs Legg,' said Ellen. 'Do you by any chance share a birth date with Maurice Lovelace?'

'I do. February the ninth. How did you know that?'

'It was just guesswork,' said Ellen.

Mrs Legg looked closely at the younger woman. 'Have you decided yet when you're leaving? I'll need to make up the bill.'

'No, I haven't. I mean, I'm waiting to hear from my office about, you know, the way things are shaping up. I should be here a little longer, probably. If that's all right.'

Mrs Legg had already hitched the brass instrument on to her hip and was swinging away down the corridor towards the kitchen area at the back of the house.

Above the front lawn a skylark pumped himself up into the thin, high air, twittering as he climbed on his long liquid song flight.

Muriel Oliver chose a mushroom omelette and a green salad. She would normally have ordered a crispy bread roll and a portion of chips – the Mameluke Magazines canteen did a very good chip, if she was any judge – but the zip on her good lavender skirt had absolutely refused to close all the way up that morning.

'You realise what's happening, don't you?' said Daphne Chapman, leaning her elbows on the table.

For the moment Muriel was lost. She had been thinking of waistbands and pale flesh.

'One more disastrous set of circulation figures and your boss, our esteemed editor, will be on her way to the job centre,' said Daphne. 'And we can all see who's in line to take over.'

Muriel's fork hovered in mid-air, trailing a strip of mushroom and a dribble of egg.

'Gwen Lightsome's a big name, a real operator. A couple of big spreads and she'll make the world think she *is Home & Beauty*. Once she takes over where will we all be? She'll want to bring in her own people – certainly a new features editor, very probably a new secretary . . .' Daphne crushed the plastic water cup in her fist.

Miss Oliver laid down her fork, pushed back her chair, walked to the counter in a dreamlike state and ordered some chips.

Sonia Marks had not, she explained, expected things to progress quite so quickly or in remotely the way they did.

As it happened, she did not have to travel far from Walsingham to meet Maurice Lovelace again. It was an early summer afternoon and North Norfolk seemed utterly deserted; one of those days when a tractor in a distant field is the only sign of human life and the world belongs to the birds, the droning insects and the skittish hare.

They had walked on the beach at Holkham, a great plain of sand whipped into little dervish swirls by the wind coming in over the sea from the north-west. Zephyrs, said Sonia as though solving a crossword clue. Lovelace of Arabia, he said, sliding his eyes from horizon to horizon like Rudolph Valentino in *Blood and Sand*. Or possibly it was Valentino's camel, Sonia had said. Or was it a horse?

Later they had driven inland a couple of miles, parking in a patch of shade near the start of a greenway track; it was sheltered from the wind there and extraordinarily quiet.

They had walked through a stand of ancient oaks. They had trunks of massive girth, rising in their own shade; it had been blinkingly bright by contrast out in the sunlight on the grass path. It cut across a newly-ploughed field like a green ribbon, running at right angles to the road. The sun was warm. The air was sweet. Maurice Lovelace had suddenly stopped still, holding out an arm.

'Look!' In the long grass on the edge of the path there had been three fledging birds. They were long-tailed tits, not long out of their nest made of spider's web and scraps of moss; they were extremely small and already moulting their black and white feathers.

The next minute he had turned and taken her in his arms, sliding his hands under her jacket and drawing her close. 'Yes?'

'Yes,' she said. 'Yes. Now.'

A jet fighter had appeared low on the skyline. It suddenly changed its profile, showing the geometrical outline of its wings as it pulled into a tight turn. It was only at that moment that they heard its roar. Maurice had led the way.

191

Andrew Moncur

'It was as simple as that,' said Sonia, pausing to sip her tea. Ellen Bright nodded and kept her mouth shut. It was quiet there in the gallery where the two women had agreed to meet to talk.

Sonia could recall the whole picture: the trees, the sunshine, the sudden wash of desire. There was a doorway close by. It was a simple building with thick whitewashed walls and a heavy wooden door which swung shut behind them. It was dark and cool inside; there was a good smell. It was the faint scent of moist, newly-turned earth. A shaft of light from old, pale green glass illuminated the bare timbers of the roof.

There was no electricity and no light. They had no need for lighting anyway. They could soon see perfectly well in the deep shade. There was a red velvet cushion running the length of the bench.

It seemed just a little shocking, looking back, that Sonia Marks and Maurice Lovelace should have made love for the first time in a box pew in the nave of a tiny country church dedicated, as it happened, to All Saints.

Lots of churches in England celebrate those, known and un-known, who are redeemed and gone to heaven. All Saints was always the second most popular dedication for churches, out-stripped only by those named for the Blessed Virgin Mary.

The afternoon really hadn't been planned that way, said Sonia. They had been coming to the church, certainly, but for quite another purpose: in the first place they had wanted to see the Saxon win-dows and the Norman door arches built on earlier pillars. It was an unusual building, one of those sufficiently remote to have escaped the attentions of restorers and improvers.

'Well, it's original,' said Ellen. 'In future I shall always say to myself that I'm experiencing an overwhelming desire to take a look at some Saxon windows . . .'

Maurice had made a point of signing the visitors' book at the back of the church when they left some little while later.

'The fledglings had disappeared by then,' said Sonia.

'I'm not at all surprised,' said Ellen.

Both front doors, side by side, were painted the same shiny black.

The Harlot's Prerogative

The one on the left bore a china plaque, a modern thing shaped like a fat comma or a tadpole: it was the figure of a woman in a blue cloak holding a baby. She was crowned by a halo in a rather sickly yellow.

The door on the right had a polished brass plate with finely engraved lettering. *'Magis mutus quam piscis,'* it read.

Well, thought Ellen, and which door shall I try? The one with the brass looked the more businesslike of the two. It also had a slightly larger knocker.

'Ah-ha, yes,' said the plump young nun who appeared, smiling brightly, to answer the door. She held out a dimpled hand. 'Blairlogie?'

'Sorry?' Ellen was for the moment completely lost. She must have worn an expression of utter blankness.

'Oh! Golly! My. Mistake,' bellowed the nun, making exaggerated lip and tongue movements. 'You. Are. Welcome. Here.'

She was bobbing and curtseying in the most extravagant way, throwing out her arms in great sweeping arcs.

Oh, God, it isn't only a convent, Ellen told herself. It's obviously a home for nuns who've gone round the twist.

'I'm so sorry,' Ellen murmured, trying to smile in an encouraging way.

'No! No! No! Not. At. All!' roared the nun, her hands flapping in agitation, her face turning a terrible purply plum colour. 'You. Have. Come. A. Long. Way. From. Scotland. Yes?'

'Eh?' said Ellen.

'Scotland? Yes?' There were veins throbbing on either side of the nun's nose from the effort of shouting. The volume was terrific. On the far side of the market square a party of schoolchildren stopped, open-mouthed, crisp packets in hand, and stared across at the scene on the doorstep. Above their heads a cat froze in mid-stride on a garden wall. A flight of pigeons erupted from a tree beside the Roman Catholic church.

'Scotland?' Ellen felt as though she was losing her grip on the whole encounter. 'I don't . . .'

'Where. Is. Your. Party?' the nun bawled. She shielded her eyes and stared around in a pantomime gesture used by Hollywood Red Indians and cavalry scouts.

'My what?' Dear, goodness, thought Ellen. This poor young woman is completely barking.

'Wait!' screamed the nun. 'I will. Get. Sister. Augustine. She. Knows. The. Language.'

And with that she turned and fled down the corridor, leaving Ellen Bright leaning against the door frame feeling slightly dizzy.

The nun came flying back again almost immediately.

'Sorry!' she roared, gesturing madly. 'Come. In. Wait. Here. I. Fetch. Help.'

Then she was gone again. Ellen stepped into the flagged passage and swung the door almost, but not quite, shut behind her.

'Elly! Hello.' Sister Sigebert Buckley had come wandering into view. She was supporting by the elbow a frail elderly woman and, at the same time, holding a rumpled heap of bedlinen in the bearlike embrace of her other arm. She guided the old woman to a chair at the foot of the stairs then dumped the sheets on the hall floor and hurried to the front door.

'Lovely to see . . . Is everything all right? I could hear a frightful row.'

'I've just been talking to a rather strange nun,' said Ellen. 'Youngish. Full figure. She was absolutely yelling at the top of her voice. She screamed something about fetching Sister Augustine.'

'The tubby one will be Sister Christopher Bagshawe. She's quite harmless, really. We're expecting a group of deaf pilgrims from Scotland – somewhere around Stirling – so she's probably got confused. It would explain the screaming and shouting. She'll have wanted to find Sister Augustine Bradshaw because she does a little signing, you see.'

There was a faint crump by the stairs. The elderly lady had toppled off her chair and come to rest lying lightly on the pile of linen.

'Just coming, Mrs Dalrymple,' called Sister Sigebert, hurrying down the corridor. 'Why don't you come up to the day room, Elly? I'll make us all a cup of tea.'

The nun picked up Mrs Dalrymple with one powerful fist and stroked her gently, smoothing her hair and straightening her dressing gown. The old lady remained silent and unblinking. 'Come

194

on, team,' Sigebert cried with the voice of a born rugby pack-leader as she stamped upstairs, the silent, immobile Mrs Dalrymple clamped to her side.

'Nicky,' said Ellen, following behind. 'That Latin script on the front door. What does it mean?'

'It means as silent as the grave, which is what this place is supposed to be. Literally, it's "quieter than a fish".'

The modern-day shrine of Our Lady of Walsingham is a tiny rectangular structure within the shrine church itself, an unexciting building which dates from 1938.

Father Neil Bugloss did not see the church in terms of design or building materials or its setting or its passing resemblance to a Spanish restaurant combined with a village hall. He saw it as a place of devotion and stillness and prayer.

He was kneeling now in the Chapel of St Helena and St Hilary, where, rearing up behind the stone and flint altar, there is an extravagantly baroque reredos – a multitude of cherubic faces surrounding a doll-like child. This striking piece was given to the guardians of the shrine by the good people of Milwaukee Cathedral, USA.

Father Bugloss was there, head bowed, asking for guidance and assistance in bringing about his great scheme.

If it came to pass then the Chapel of St Helena, the entire Anglican shrine church and, indeed, even Milwaukee Cathedral would be left in the shade.

The wheelchair was surprisingly comfortable. Ellen found that she could propel it along the corridor at speed and turn it on a sixpence.

'Since you've lived here, Nicky, have you ever heard of anyone called Martha? Possibly Martha's Field? Anything like that?' she asked, climbing out of the chair and putting it back in the alcove beside the bathroom.

'I knew a Marcia once,' said Sister Sigebert. 'She was in my class at junior school. We used to go swimming together. I broke her mother's sewing machine. It was an accident.'

'Thank you,' said Ellen. 'That's absolutely no use to me at all.'

Andrew Moncur

* * *

Juliet Neckles was in tears. The skin around her mouth and chin was pulled into strange puddly circles of grief and her nose was running inconsolably.

'She's given mm-me the chop, Mm-Muriel,' she sobbed.

'The chop?' said Muriel Oliver, not very helpfully.

'She says I don't have the right caring im-image.'

'Caring image? You couldn't care more!'

'Mm-Mrs Lightsome wants what she calls caring-with-style.'

'What?'

'And she says I haven't got it.'

'The unmitigated cow.'

Miss Neckles stared at Muriel in complete surprise. She had never before heard her say anything with quite such force.

On her way to the chemist's shop in Little Walsingham that evening Ellen Bright stepped off the pavement and came within a quarter of an inch of being run over by a car. She felt the rush of air as it passed. It seemed hot and gritty. Her heart took an awful leap and she caught and held her breath for what seemed an impossibly long time.

She felt so stupid afterwards. She had absolutely failed to see the driver, note the make of the car or even take notice of its colour. She thought it might have been grey or a dull blue. Or possibly silver.

An elderly woman on the far side of the road stood gaping at her. 'That was close!' the woman shrilled, when Ellen eventually gathered herself and crossed over. 'It looked as though she took a deliberate run at you.'

'Who? Who was it?' Ellen asked. 'Did you see?'

'I'm a stranger here, dear.' The woman patted her arm.

The perfect end to a perfect day, Ellen told herself.

Chapter Twenty-Nine

She had been left hanging on the telephone for at least three or four minutes. It's a good long time for anybody to be made to stew by the switchboard staff, Mrs Canty remarked inwardly, wondering whether the hospital went in for any of that charter nonsense.

'Hello? Are you there, caller?' The operator had one of those sing-song voices which sound insincere without trying.

'Yes, of course. Where else would I be?' said Mrs Canty, snappily.

'I have Dr English for you, caller. Trying to connect you.'

There was another extended pause. Mrs Canty had decided to take the bull by the horns and speak to the hospital's duty doctor directly to protest about the shipment of poor Maurice Lovelace to the House of Commons.

'. . . be seeing them at dinner tomorrow, Angie,' said a man's voice. He was clearly too busy and important to conduct only one conversation at a time. 'Hello? Yes? Who is this?' This time he was speaking into the telephone mouthpiece.

'Is that Dr English?' Mrs Canty asked in her small and polite voice.

'Yes. Hello?'

'I wanted to have a word about Mr Maurice Lovelace, who is a patient there. Now, I'm very worried about them taking him . . .'

'Are you a relative?'

'No. I don't think he has any relatives. I'm somebody who . . .'

'Are you his common law wife, then?' The doctor sounded impatient.

'Certainly not,' said Mrs Canty. 'I'm a married woman, thank you very . . .'

'I'm sorry, madam, but we can't involve ourselves in complications like that. Unless you have some relationship with Mister – with the patient – then we really can't discuss his individual case with you.'

'But he's being dragged halfway across London in a state which anyone can see is . . .'

'Please. We have the very highest standards of patient care at St Wilfrid's and you may rest assured that he's in excellent hands.'

'Well, I've had a conversation with your Mr Hopkin, the consultant, and he's not at all . . .'

'Hopkin? You say Hopkin?' The note of hostility hardened in the doctor's voice. 'We have no consultant of that name at St Wilfrid's.'

'But I know him very . . .'

'I repeat, madam, there is nobody of that name on the medical staff.' He sounded pleased with himself.

'Oh, bollocks,' said Mrs Canty and put down the phone. 'Pardon my French.'

Daphne Chapman was as sympathetic as it was possible for her to be, coming on the phone with further difficult news to break.

'Sorry and all that, my dear,' she said. 'But you're off the case altogether in Walsingham. Our friend Mrs Lightsome is taking care of him all by herself and absolutely refuses all help from freelances.'

'I see,' said Ellen Bright.

'Don't worry. I'll find something else for you to do. Why not take a little break? Drop in and see me at the beginning of next week.'

'Well, there's a big parade here at the weekend. I would quite like to see it.'

'Right. Only stay clear of Big Gwen. She's coming to Walsingham as well. She'll run right over anyone who gets in her way.'

'Oh, bollocks,' said Ellen.

Gwen Lightsome was speaking to a partner in the Rich, Balfour, Rafferty consultancy which had the contract to handle public relations for St Wilfrid's Medical Centre. The tone was so friendly, so full of banter that any casual observer would have assumed they were friends from way back, picking up threads. They had, of course, never spoken to one another before.

'Hey, Gwen, I must say this. You were terrific on Jerry's show,' said the PR man.

'Wasn't lovely Ruby a scream?' said Gwen.

The Harlot's Prerogative

'Beautiful. Just beautiful. You know, I can't imagine why, but I don't think you've ever been down to the polo with us . . .'

'Never, I'm ashamed to say.'

'Well, we'll soon put that right. A car down to Windsor. A little lunch by the river. Then an afternoon in the Great Park. Some champagne . . .'

'Hmmm. Sounds good to me. But first, a small business matter . . .'

In no time at all Gwen had made the necessary arrangements for a private ambulance and medical staff to call at St Wilfrid's Hospital to take a certain party, as she put it, for two days' alternative treatment in East Anglia. The patient concerned had no close family; there was nobody who needed to be consulted.

Yes, the name and logo of St Wilfrid's Medical Centre would figure prominently in the magazine feature which would result from this expedition – a sort of caring, touching, triumph-over-tragedy piece.

No, the hospital wouldn't raise any problem about granting permission to move the patient. In no way would difficulties arise over questions of medical confidentiality or any nonsense of that kind. Not when a personality of Mrs Lightsome's fame was involved, one who was well-known for her good work with those in need.

It was as easy as that.

Mr Hopkin held a protective hand around the mouthpiece. His head was enveloped in the transparent plastic dome of the payphone in the hospital lobby. A nurse hurried by in the high, starched cap, the pink uniform dress and the broad silver-buckled belt which were the symbols of the St Wilfrid's private care package.

'You know they're moving poor Mr Lovelace to vote in parliament tomorrow night,' he hissed down the line.

'Yes, Mr Hopkin, I had taken that on board,' said Mrs Canty.

'Well, we've been told another lot's coming to take him away again – on Friday morning.'

'Never!' said Mrs Canty. 'Are they taking him to Westminster as well?'

Andrew Moncur

'No, they're putting him in a woman's magazine. They're going to have the body for the whole weekend.'

Mrs Canty drew herself up until her back was very straight indeed. She had always known – it was something absorbed over a lifetime spent reading girls' stories and watching the more wholesome sort of film – that sooner or later there came a time when a person had to make a stand. It was that moment of decision. It had arrived.

'Right,' she said at last. 'This is what we are going to do.'

And she told Mr Hopkin, right there on the telephone.

'Are you with me, Mr Hopkin?' she asked.

'I'm with you, Mrs Canty,' he replied.

'What about your hypocritical oath?'

'I'll bring it along.'

Muriel Oliver sat in the bath that night and decided that it was her solemn duty to intervene. She did so not for reasons of self interest, she told herself, but out of a sense of common decency. There was something obscene – wasn't there? – about a sick man being whisked out of his hospital bed and carted around the countryside for the sake of a photo-opportunity with Gwen Lightsome.

It was perfectly proper in the circumstances to put a spanner in the works.

Muriel was not, after all, intending any serious act of sabotage. She merely meant to inform the hospital of what was going on. She would explain the true nature of the proposed jaunt; tell them, from the inside, that it was meant to benefit Gwen Lightsome far more than it would ever help poor Constance Verity or Maurice Lovelace or whatever the name was.

She had met that very approachable doctor on her previous visit to St Wilfrid's, the one who helped with her flowers. She would go and find him again and ask him to intervene on medical grounds.

There would be nothing in writing. Nothing on record. No incoming phone calls logged. But on Thursday night after work she would drop in at the hospital and try to have a brief, private and completely anonymous word in his shell-like ear.

The pink flush which spread across her more visible parts had

The Harlot's Prerogative

little to do with the warmth of the bath water.

Sir Archie Miller, the government chief whip, stretched out his legs and sipped his glass of scotch. It was amazingly quiet up there in the prime minister's flat at 10 Downing Street; difficult to believe that they were sitting close to the heart of one of the world's great cities where – even now, late at night – millions of people were in vigorous motion within a radius of a few miles.

'Can you get us through tomorrow?' asked the PM for the umpteenth time, edging forward on his yellow brocade chair.

'Can you do it?' the PM asked again. 'Like it or not, it's a confidence vote. If we drop this one we're looking into the abyss.'

'Don't worry, Prime Minister. As I was saying earlier, we'll do it.' Sir Archie positively beamed. He was valued by the PM not least because the deeper the crisis, the more cheerful he seemed to become.

'It's all under control. We've done our sums. As you know, it's a damned good thing that dear Maurice Lovelace is reliably – so very reliably – on our side. He'll be there for the big one. And the next. And the one after that.'

The PM raised his glass. He might have to think about something in the honours list for Lovelace. Always assuming the poor chap actually managed to survive the next few weeks – like the government itself, come to that.

Chapter Thirty

The weight of traffic on Westminster Bridge had eased after the homeward rush. Vehicles were still nose-to-tail but they at least remained in motion, crawling between the lights. The crowds had thinned, too.

Muriel Oliver had walked at a gentle pace along the Embankment; in the early summer evening light the entire scene – the water, the riverside buildings, the sky itself – shone with a particularly delicate lustre.

'My God, it makes me feel sick,' said Muriel more or less to herself.

A light was already showing on the clock tower of the House to signal that parliament was sitting; the twenty-three-foot diameter faces of the clock itself looked like full moons.

Thursday was always a busy day at the office. There was the weekly editorial meeting where heads of department tore the latest magazine to shreds and chose the cover-lines for the next issue in hand. They were working six weeks ahead, which always gave the process a certain surreal quality. Muriel had never grown accustomed to that time shift. She always found it especially strange when the Christmas issue was being put together in early November and the office was suddenly warm with the smell of mince pies from the trial kitchens. Then at Christmas the staff were full of talk about the Valentine's day special – and so on through the year.

There was a uniformed commissionaire outside the main doors at St Wilfrid's. Muriel gave him a sweet smile as she approached; like many large women she walked with grace on shiny, tip-tappy shoes which looked all the more delicate for being down there, bearing up. The doorman, a cigarette cupped in his hand, turned to admire her swinging step and generous form.

As she entered the hospital lobby Big Ben sounded the hour.

The Harlot's Prerogative

Muriel was aware of being hungry; her stomach made a little grumbling noise.

The reception area was full of Arabs, as it had been on her previous visit. There were three or four men in long shirts, seated on sofas in attitudes of abandon; they were talking to one another very loudly indeed. The women, perhaps a dozen of them, were sitting quietly in separate little circles. One woman, with a sleeping child sprawled on her lap, was wearing a mask made from some sort of dark leather. Others had their faces covered by what Muriel took to be beaded crochetwork in black yarn.

The woman on the reception desk was tapping a keyboard. She took no notice as Miss Oliver walked confidently by and straight into a waiting lift.

There was a feeling of busyness on the third floor of the Nightingale Wing. It took a moment for Muriel to grasp that it was, of course, a popular visiting time. There was a murmur of conversation. The seats around the reception area were all occupied. It was a strange group. People in their outdoor clothes were side by side with, here and there, someone sitting quite unabashed in pyjamas and dressing gown. One man was walking across the lobby holding his own drip and its plastic feed line.

Nobody took the slightest notice as she crossed the lobby, followed the corridor and, pausing to check the nameplate beside the door, stepped into private bedroom 309.

The small filling station just off the New Kent Road was much favoured by London cab drivers. It was open round-the-clock and managed, miraculously, to keep up an old-fashioned service and keep down its prices.

The camper van bucketed across the forecourt in a series of great hiccuping bounds. It finally stopped so abruptly that it appeared for a fraction of a second to stand up on its nose.

Mrs Canty relaxed her grip on the steering wheel. 'Norman's car is an automatic,' she said to Mr Hopkin, who was pushing both feet so hard against the floor that he had practically launched himself vertically out of the back of the passenger seat.

'It hasn't got so many pedals, of course,' said Mrs Canty. 'But

I'm getting the hang of this one, don't worry.'

'Yuh?' said a youth with yellow hair who had arrived at the side window.

'Fill it up,' said Mr Hopkin in an expansive way.

'Four-star?' asked the youth.

'Make it five-star,' said Mr Hopkin with an imperious wave.

'We only got four-star.'

'No five-star? Hmmm.'

'Or we got unleaded.'

'Oh, no. We'll be having the lead.'

'Or diesel,' said the youth.

'Make it as many stars as you've got, with lead,' said Mr Hopkin, in the way he might have spoken to a dial-a-pizza service. There was a moment's silence while everyone waited in case he wanted to add anything about anchovies or olives.

They had borrowed the van from Mrs Canty's neighbour's son who didn't know anything about the arrangement because he was in Saudi Arabia. 'It'll do it good to have a run,' his mother had remarked, handing over the keys.

'I'm going to clear up Mr Lovelace's cottage in Walsingham,' Mrs Canty had said to her husband, Norman. 'Don't forget to take your malt and cod-liver oil.'

'I'm away on a conference. Got to keep abreast of the latest techniques. Hipposuction, nose-enhancing, penis-straightening. That sort of thing,' Mr Hopkin had told his long-term girlfriend, who immediately knew he was lying. She did not doubt for one moment he was really working double shifts of overtime with his porter's trolley.

The camper van, running a little more smoothly now, crept into the service road at the side of St Wilfrid's Hospital. A figure climbed from the passenger side and flitted around the back of the vehicle. Moments later the same person – a man – returned from the shadows beside a concrete loading ramp and beckoned to the driver to reverse into the darkening space.

The engine coughed into life. Then the van suddenly rocketed backwards and ran him over.

* * *

The Harlot's Prerogative

The gentle snoring from the bed was strangely reassuring. It seemed difficult to imagine that anyone would snore if in any way close to death's door. 'You don't hear of famous last snores, do you?' said Muriel to herself. 'No. Course you don't.'

She was sitting patiently at the bedside, watching the lights come on across the river and the occasional twinkling fairy-lights of a pleasure craft pushing upstream. She had made sure that the figure stretched on the bed was indeed Maurice Lovelace. Somebody obviously came and shaved him regularly and kept his hair neatly trimmed.

It was sad, really. His silk dressing gown was laid over the back of the chair as though they were expecting him at any moment to climb out of bed and walk. The bedside screen was pulled well back as if they wanted him to enjoy the view. Magazines and newspapers were piled on the table. The nursing staff had left a glass tumbler at the bedside and a jug of water protected by one of those lace covers edged with glass beads. Would he ever, she wondered, be able to sip from that cup?

Muriel was willing to wait for the doctor to appear. Somebody had to be told that it was wrong, plain wrong, for a patient in this condition to be dragged around the country for the greater glory of a magazine agony aunt.

She was far away in her thoughts when the rap on the door brought her abruptly back to reality. Muriel was suddenly filled with alarm.

'Sorry!' sang a voice on the far side of the door. 'Was forgettin'. You won't be wantin' no tea. Huh!'

The rattle of the trolley dwindled. Muriel at last drew breath again. What if it had been somebody from *Home & Beauty*, arriving to plan the removal? How would she explain herself?

It might be better to wait out of sight and check the identity of all newcomers before they had a chance to see her. Miss Oliver swiftly moved her chair behind the folding screen. She sat there, straight-backed, with her hands in her lap.

'I'm all right. Only a bruise or two,' hissed Mr Hopkin.

'Terribly, terribly sorry,' said Mrs Canty.

Andrew Moncur

'Look, we've only got about twenty minutes before they come from Westminster to pick him up. We've got to move right along.' He limped ahead of her towards the service lift.

The doors closed behind them with a clash. It was the first time that Mrs Canty had seen St Wilfrid's in this light. This wasn't so much the comfortably plush hospital-cum-hotel: round the back here it was more like a factory on an industrial estate.

'Let me go first,' she whispered, as they reached the third floor. 'They're used to seeing me with Mr Lovelace. No-one will take any notice. I'll make sure the coast's clear and then we'll whip him on to your trolley.'

In a second she was gone. The corridors were quieter now that nearly all the visitors had departed.

Muriel Oliver stiffened. The door to Mr Lovelace's bedroom had opened and closed; somebody was in the room and advancing towards the bed. On tiptoe, for heaven's sake.

Muriel squinted around the edge of the screen, hoping that it might at last be the arrival of her doctor friend. Oh, Lord. Her eyes rolled. It was a woman. There was something overwhelmingly stealthy about her approach.

The stranger craned across the bed and peered down at the snoring form. Muriel held her breath. It wasn't a nurse. Nurses didn't creep. It was nobody she recognised from *Home & Beauty*. Who the flipping heck was it?

At that instant the unknown woman turned and, up on her toes, hurried back to the door. Muriel knew then with complete conviction that the newcomer was up to no good. Further, she guessed that this person – whoever she might be – was acting on behalf of the odious Gwen Lightsome. Could it be they were preparing to move the patient sooner than expected? It was the only possible explanation.

Thank goodness Muriel had kept out of sight.

Waagh. She almost screamed. The door had opened again and this time – oh, no – her friendly doctor was obviously working with the enemy. The woman stood aside while he wheeled in a trolley and brought it smartly alongside the bed.

206

The Harlot's Prerogative

Together they rolled Maurice Lovelace from his bed to the trolley. It took only seconds. Then the rectangle of light appeared again; the woman glanced left and right along the corridor.

And, as quickly as that, they were gone. So was the recumbent patient. They had stolen Maurice Lovelace.

Muriel sat there, dumbfounded. A full minute ticked by, then another. She had achieved nothing. It was so deflating.

At last she stirred herself. It was no use sitting there in the hospital, hiding behind a screen and staring at an empty bed. She was tired and she was hungry and it was time to be on her way. Slowly, she walked towards the . . .

The voice on the far side of the door frame came through to her with astonishing clarity.

'L-O-V-E-L-A-C-E, Lovelace. That's the one. It says so here, Ron. No, no. Over here. Ronnie! I tell you . . .'

Muriel turned and absolutely ran back across the room, holding in her bottom as though she was about to be bitten from behind. She was making a quite involuntary whimpering noise.

She would hide behind the screen again. No, that wouldn't do. The hospital had been robbed of a patient in a coma. They'd turn the whole place upside-down. Hide! Hide! She ran once around the bed, snatching at anything which might provide her with cover. The dressing gown flew in the air.

There was only one thing to do.

They must be given the impression that all was well. Then they would go away and she could escape.

With a great scissor kick Miss Muriel Oliver leapt into the bed left vacant by the absent Maurice Lovelace.

By the time the door opened she had pulled up the covers and started to snore in a most convincing way.

The driver of the ambulance flashed his pass at the uniformed policeman on the kerbside who waved him through, pointing straight ahead between the stone pillars and the elaborate, wrought-iron gates. The driver followed the roadway down and around, coming to rest under the bright lights at the members' entrance.

A second police officer approached, checking the registration number of the vehicle against the clipboard in his hand.

He gave a thumbs-up sign to the ambulanceman and indicated a set of double doors wide enough to take a medical trolley.

The driver slid from his seat, opened the back of the ambulance and with an easy economy of movement helped his crewman to lift their burden to the ground. They rolled the chrome-nickel and black plastic trolley in through the doors where a tall young man with a shock of dark hair and wide-set eyes was waiting to meet them.

'Withers,' he said. 'Whips' office. Have you got him?'

'Lovelace, Maurice. From St Wilfrid's Medical Centre,' said the ambulance driver. 'Delivered, safe and sound.'

'Good grief. He looks bloody awful,' said the junior whip, glancing at the upturned face on the pillow and hurriedly looking away. It was terrible: a colleague only needed to be gone for a little while and you forgot how he looked. Having taken a quick squint at Maurice, he'd almost be prepared to believe they'd slapped a bit of make-up on his poor old cheeks.

The figure emitted a snorty, trumpeting sound.

'Been doing that all the way over,' said the crewman. But Mr Withers had already turned away and was speaking into his portable: 'Biggles to Auntie. Biggles to Auntie. Panda Bear has landed. Repeat, Panda Bear has . . .'

The trolley moved forward at speed. Muriel peered through her eyelashes at the ceiling, rocketing by. She was being wheeled rapidly through endless corridors. There was a brief moment in a lift followed by a glimpse of a high ceiling and a few fleeting faces looking down; then more dim passageways.

As soon as they reached the operating theatre, that would be it. She wouldn't care if they did rumble her. There had to be a limit. She would simply sit up and say: Stop! I am Muriel Oliver. There has been a dreadful mistake. Take me home!

Just then the trolley turned sharp left and came to a halt. She was aware, at the periphery of her squinty-eyed vision, that the men, fore and aft, had stepped away. She heard the word 'smoke'. Their voices faded and then there was the clump of a door closing.

Muriel opened an eye and took in her surroundings. She was in a little room with wood-panelled walls. There was not a sound to be heard. Her empty stomach made a noise like an ancient radiator. The room fell silent again.

It was, she assumed, some sort of ante-room to the operating theatre. If she was to escape, now was the time. Her hand snaked around under the covers and found the items she had secreted there in her first moments of panic.

It was the worst possible timing. She was sitting up on the trolley, with her feet not quite touching the ground, when the door opened again and the same tall young man slipped into the room.

He had, fortunately, all the deep dyed-in-the-fibre instincts of a gentleman; they had been ingrained in him from the age of three or four right through to his hooligan years at Eton College.

When he found himself in the presence of a woman his immediate reaction was to apologise and look at the floor. His next, to explain himself in a stumbling way.

'Withers,' he mumbled. 'So sorry. In charge of, you know, this little operation . . .'

Operation. Oh, God. That word had been the trigger, Muriel realised later. She was propelled by fear. In any event, Panda Bear crossed the room at speed and brought up her knee with surprising force smack in the groin of Biggles.

Mrs Canty moved back into the inside lane. She looked across and smiled at Mr Hopkin. He was rubbing his right knee.

'So far, so good. Not a hitch,' she said. 'Apart, that is, from knocking you down in the loading bay.'

'No problem,' said Mr Hopkin. 'I don't think I dented the back end.'

'Who would have thought it was so easy to help yourself to a Member of Parliament?'

There was a snuffling sound from the mound of bedding lying in the back of the camper van. Then the snoring resumed peacefully.

'I've been meaning to tell you I'm not – well, not completely – a medical man,' said Mr Hopkin.

'I think I've gathered that,' said Mrs Canty. 'You're all right, though, Mr Hopkin. That's all I need to know.'

A signpost loomed up in their headlights. The next turning off the motorway was the A11 for Newmarket and Norwich.

Members were streaming towards the division lobbies. It was one of those nights of high political drama when the atmosphere at Westminster crackles with bloodlust and fear. Those in the governing party worry that they might soon be out on their collective ear; everyone else worries that they might not.

Into this fever-swamp air stepped an individual of a sort rarely, if ever, seen in these particular corridors in the most hallowed part of the House of Commons.

The members knew that the halt and the lame were being dragged in to vote in the night's vital division. They had heard that Maurice Lovelace was arriving in, according to some, a coma. They didn't much like it – but they were expecting to see him nonetheless.

What they did not expect was the appearance, in the middle of the vote, of a palpable Arab woman. The crush of overwhelmingly middle-aged, middle-weight men in middling quality suits fell silent; the crowd parted as she walked with great dignity through their nonplussed ranks.

She had emerged, they agreed later, from the little room normally set aside for terminally-ill MPs who struggle to the House in order to take part, often unwittingly, in important votes.

She was wearing an ankle-length embroidered robe which, as somebody pointed out, might have passed for an old-fashioned man's dressing gown. Over her face – and this is the bit which proved she was Gulf Arab – was a mask which looked like one of those water jug covers with glass beads round the edge.

Nobody challenged her. Not a soul stood in her way as she walked gracefully across the Central Lobby, down the main corridor, through the checkpoint where incoming visitors had to submit to security sniffers and metal detectors, out through the St Stephen's door and away into the night.

It was only later, when the government had fallen after being defeated by a single vote, that anybody thought to ask seriously who the devil she was. By next morning two rumours were current at a by now feverishly excited Westminster.

Withers, the junior whip, had cast his vote against the government.

The Harlot's Prerogative

He had been seen wandering around, doubled-up, before eventually tottering into the opposition lobby. He had still been there – protesting feebly – when the doors were locked. Second, and stranger still, plenty of honourable members were willing to testify that a colleague had risen from his sick bed and fled into the night disguised as a woman.

One thing was known for certain: Maurice Lovelace MP had been altogether mislaid. Only an abandoned trolley remained to show that he had ever been brought to the House of Commons on that fateful night.

Chapter Thirty-One

'You've lost my patient? What do you mean, you've lost my patient? How can you lose a bloody patient?' Gwen Lightsome's voice had in seconds gusted from light breeze to gale force.

The public relations consultant at Rich, Balfour, Rafferty knew of her reputation as a warm, caring, womanly magazine writer. He guessed that she must be worried sick about what had become of the missing MP, Maurice Lovelace.

'A missing MP?' Mrs Lightsome screamed down the phone line. 'What about my missing story, you pathetic, cretinous prat? I've arranged a photographer. I've got a priest lined up, for God's sake. An archdeacon in the Church of bloody England. How can he do a healing, for crying out loud, if no bugger shows up for him to lay his hands on? What use are you? What use is your stupid hospital?'

It was a painful conversation in every way. Even before Mrs Lightsome bounced the phone on to its rest, causing several stress fractures in the plastic, she had decided on her course of action.

'Hilary!' she shouted. 'Hilary! Get me a cripple!'

'Right, Mrs Lightsome,' said her personal assistant. 'Was there any particular type of cripple you were wanting?'

'A photogenic one. We're going to Walsingham. If we can't take our own man we'll find another one instead and have him cured. These sick people all look the same anyway.'

'Very well, Mrs Lightsome,' said Miss Duffy. 'I'll arrange for one to be provided in Norfolk. Nothing visually undesirable. Meanwhile, I'll confirm the hotel, restaurant, car-hire, car-valeting and priest-rental reservations for you and Mr Lightsome immediately.'

The Lovelace history of Walsingham did not flinch from stating its frank suspicion:

It seems to this writer inconceivable – nay, improbable beyond belief – that the riches of the holy house could have been turned over to the Crown in their entirety without some valuables, for whatever reason, going astray.

It might have been a form of resistance, a hiding away of a particularly valued possession, just as the black monks hid the bones of St Edward the Confessor in the hope of better days to come. It could have happened for baser motives – in the pursuit, say, of mere personal gain. My reading, though, convinces me that such a thing took place for more complex reasons.

Consider the circumstances. A system of life was crashing down. It was one which had sustained not only the religious houses but also the village itself, a place which owed its very existence to the pilgrim trade, now doomed. Everything was up for grabs. Lead was being peeled off the rooftops; statues were being pilfered and cemented into the walls of private houses; land was being gobbled up; men were being betrayed and sent to a grisly death; deals were being struck; even the prior himself was implicated in the vilest pursuit of personal gain.

And in the middle of this extraordinary scene stands a great treasure house, stuffed with the wealth of centuries. Is it credible that it was left untouched and handed over entire to the king's men?

Mrs Canty stopped reading aloud at this point, looked over the top of the page at Mr Hopkin and raised her eyebrows. 'Well?' she asked.

'Sounds unlikely to me,' said Mr Hopkin. He took another sip from his coffee mug. The sky to the east, across the salt marsh, was washed with an astonishing flush of pink, red, purple and pearl-grey. The sea was breaking on the distant sand bar. They could see over there the old lifeboat house on Blakeney Point and, glancing westward, the lifeboat station beside the pine woods at Wells next the Sea.

'I had better fix up his drip for breakfast,' said Mr Hopkin, jerking his head towards the figure in the bunk on the left side of the camper van.

213

Andrew Moncur

Mr Hopkin, who had unrestricted access to the stores at St Wilfrid's, had taken the trouble to prepare a box of supplies for Maurice Lovelace. He had brought everything necessary for the care of their travelling patient, down to nail-clippers and a toothbrush.

It took only a matter of moments to change his liquid feed bag. He checked to make sure that Maurice was breathing easily then he brushed his hair, parting it on the right. Mr Hopkin stood back for a moment, then parted the MP's hair again, this time down the middle.

Mrs Canty flapped her papers and read on:

It is the author's belief that treasure was hidden at that time – and hidden so successfully that it remains undiscovered to this day. Think of all that has occurred: the destruction of the holy house and the priory church, the remorseless passage of time and all the change that occurs over four and more centuries.

The odds are high against surviving the centuries of oblivion or coming unscathed through the last hundred years of revived enthusiasm for the Walsingham shrine, and all that it has entailed in terms of building work and development.

The flame of that revival was well alight in the Church of England of the 1880s. A new church was built at that time in Buxted, Sussex, with its lady chapel laid out to the exact dimensions of the wooden holy house created in Walsingham by Richeldis.

A boy who grew up there, Alfred Hope Patton, was eventually ordained a priest and in due course was offered the living of Walsingham.

Meanwhile the neglected slipper chapel a mile from Little Walsingham had been rediscovered. Its restoration was put in hand in 1894 by a Miss Charlotte Boyd who, unusually, supported a community of Anglican nuns at her home in Kent.

Miss Boyd then promptly went over to Rome. A pilgrimage to that chapel was organised by Roman Catholics in 1897; it would be another thirty-seven years before it was restored as

The Harlot's Prerogative

a place of pilgrimage for members of that church.

Back at the Church of England parish church, Father Patten had in 1922 raised a statue of Our Lady, copied from the ancient Walsingham seal. It became an object of devotion and pilgrims started to return. The priest resolved to rebuild the holy house on its original site in Walsingham although the exact whereabouts had long since been forgotten.

Father Patten and his companions sought guidance. They walked from the parish church to the centre of the village, knelt and prayed for a sign. Nothing was forthcoming.

However, the priest was subsequently offered a handy plot, then in use as a kitchen garden, to build his holy house sheltered by an outer chapel. It was dedicated in 1931 and extended to form the present shrine church six years later. Father Patten was clearly convinced by the discovery of a well and ancient footings that providence had led him to exactly the spot originally chosen by the Lady Richeldis.

Subsequent investigations have shown, without much doubt, that he was sadly wrong. The true site almost certainly lies to the south, across the road, over the wall, beyond the trees and smack beside the old priory ruins.

It is my hope that other treasures from Walsingham's past will soon be unearthed. Mysteries still remain in this place. For the pilgrim the task is to find the key. For what it's worth, I would recommend that the best place to start is the library of Keble College, Oxford.

Mrs Canty climbed stiffly out of the van and walked up and down on the dew-soaked Norfolk grass. Well, there's a strange thing, she said to nobody in particular. A reed bunting flitted by, with a white handlebar moustache visible against his newly-feathered black head.

She turned back towards the sunrise. They would soon be ready for the next move in Mr Lovelace's little journey.

Chapter Thirty-Two

On Friday morning Ellen Bright visited the district council's offices, an ambitious pile with the unmistakably flashy looks of a block of time-share apartments. It was perched on a hillside overlooking the North Sea resort of Cromer. Ellen called at the planning department and made a surprising discovery about the proposed theme park in Walsingham. At the same time, she stumbled across the likely whereabouts of Martha's Field. It made her feel rather foolish.

It was only at lunchtime, listening to the news on her car radio, that she caught up with the fact of the government's defeat. The prime minister was expected to go to the Palace during the afternoon; the Queen would dissolve parliament by proclamation. The country was facing a general election.

'Well, bugger me,' she said out loud.

Sitting members of parliament were preparing to return to the country to be adopted formally by their constituency parties, the first step in making ready to fight the campaign. Opinion polls suggested that the outcome would be remarkably close, with the outgoing governing party trailing at this early stage. However, as many as eleven in every hundred electors questioned declared themselves as 'uncertain', 'very uncertain indeed' or 'in a flat spin, actually' about their voting intentions. The battle would be lost and won in key marginals, said the BBC's political editor, straining his nasal passages with the power of his delivery.

'Never,' said Ellen to her radio. 'What an astonishing insight. He obviously knows how many beans make five.'

There was a brief report on the Commons vote which had led to political drama and the inevitable election. Ellen was startled – thunderstruck really – to hear the reporter say: 'The government's business managers had been counting on the support of sick MPs who were brought to the House for last night's critical vote.

'Their calculations were thrown into disarray when the Member for Walsingham and the Snorings, Maurice Lovelace, failed to appear as expected in the voting lobby. The MP, who has been receiving hospital treatment for injuries suffered in a road accident, has not been seen since last night's dramatic vote when the House broke up in disorder.'

Ellen Bright's lips formed the words with no sound emerging: 'Well, where the bloody hell is he?'

'Well, where the bloody hell is he?' said Sonia Marks, holding the telephone away from her ear so as to avoid drilling the little gold stud into the side of her head.

'The hospital says Maurice was taken by ambulance to the House of Commons last night. He was still in what they call a profoundly unconscious state – and he hasn't been seen since. The ambulance crew's trolley is still at the House. It's been detained by the Sergeant-at-Arms.' Ellen was unable to imagine how on earth it might lead them to the missing MP.

'Could he possibly have made his way up here and gone to the apartment?' she asked. 'What do you think?'

'What? A man in a coma? A man with a head cold would think twice before tottering up here from London. But, you're right, I should at least go round and check,' said Sonia. She would close the shop for half an hour and walk round to the gatehouse, although it was a lousy time to be turning away customers.

There had been a developing atmosphere of festival in Walsingham as the weekend of the great pilgrimage approached. Tomorrow would be really busy as visitors started to arrive in numbers.

The atmosphere in the Cabinet Room called to mind those gin-clear days on the North Norfolk coast when the January winds are cutting in from the east.

'We have the CCTV tapes from the hospital . . .' Sir Archie Miller was starting to explain.

'CC what?' The prime minister was notoriously ignorant about technical matters, refusing to absorb even the meanest detail.

'Closed-circuit television, Prime Minister.' Irving, from security, had stepped forward to intervene. He was a small man and there was something odd about his suit in that blue, shiny-silk material. 'We have the TV tapes from the St Wilfrid's Medical Centre and from our own surveillance cameras at Westminster, of course. We thought you should see this.'

Sir Archie sat down gratefully. Irving held the remote-control at arm's length and the television flickered into life.

It was a gritty picture in black and white. At first it appeared to consist of geometrical patterns of light and shade. Then a vehicle – some sort of van – came bounding backwards into shot and the shapes resolved into the outline of a building. It was the hospital.

A man climbed from the van and beckoned it towards him. It took another leap backwards and he fell over. Another figure, this time probably – no, definitely a woman – emerged from the driver's side and ran towards him. She helped him to his feet and seemed to dust him down. The pair then moved quickly to the left and out of the frame.

A series of numbers flashed across the screen. Then the two people reappeared, pushing a trolley. They heaved a rounded, body-shaped object into the back of the van. The man ran to the left with the trolley; then, after a couple of moments, he hurried back and joined his driver in the cab. The van pulled away, then stopped suddenly. The woman jumped out again and ran round to close the rear door. She returned to the wheel and the van shot out of the camera's view.

'Well?' The prime minister was like a peevish adder coiled to strike.

'It doesn't look good, I'm afraid,' said Irving, snapping off the TV. 'We have to assume, sir, that what we have seen here is Maurice Lovelace MP in the process of being abducted.'

In a photographic laboratory just off the Albert Embankment, in Lambeth, they were using a computer to enhance the images captured by the hospital's security camera. In a little while, if all went well, it would be possible to establish the registration number of the vehicle shown coming and going from St Wilfrid's.

The tapes obtained from the cameras at the St Stephen's entrance

The Harlot's Prerogative

at the Palace of Westminster were, in comparison, frankly disappointing. One had failed to function at all; it had probably been out of action for two or three days, the engineers decided.

A second had caught nothing of any significance except a sequence in which a Liberal-Democrat MP was shown committing an act of gross indecency with a House of Commons researcher right beside the doorman's box.

The third produced pictures of a woman in Arab costume leaving the St Stephen's doors. She swung to the right more rapidly than any home secretary and hurried away as though making for Parliament Square and Whitehall. It provided no clues at all which would help to establish her identity.

Chapter Thirty-Three

On Saturday morning the *Sun* splashed with a 'world exclusive' which also appeared in the *Daily Mail* and the *Telegraph*. The last ran the story across the top of the front page, above its main lead on the general election. 'Missing MP in hospital "abduction" mystery' said the *Telegraph* headline. 'Off his trolley!' said the *Sun*.

Ellen had the uncomfortable feeling of finding herself at the centre of events while at the same time being left behind by the news, hopelessly off the inside track.

She was worrying about that when she wandered outside and found a folded sheet of paper tucked under the windscreen wiper of her car, parked on the gravel drive at the side of the guest house. The message had been laboriously picked out in capital letters in blue felt-tip. Unfortunately, the note had been moistened by dewfall which in places had reduced the ink to a fuzzy smear.

'MISS BR ...' here it was blurred '... EET AT THE OLD BRIDEWELL. COME TO THE GATE, NORTH SID ...' obliterated '... R PARK. GO ROUND TO YARD. NOON. SUNDAY. HAVE INFORMATION ON MAURICE LOVE ...' there was another ink patch '... REAT DANGER. PLEASE TELL NOBODY, REPEAT NOBODY, FOR HIS SAK ...' There was one other legible fragment of a word: '... MOUSLY'.

Bloody hell, Ellen said to herself. Into every life a small adventure must fall. Was Maurice Lovelace in Walsingham? Could this be somebody acting on his behalf, asking for a meeting? Could it be the man himself? There was only one way to find out.

As for the secrecy, well. Apart from anything else the poor man must be terribly embarrassed. Government whips were clearly briefing the Lobby that Maurice was solely to blame for the collapse of the administration.

What was she to do about this bizarre invitation? For heaven's sake, it had the makings of an astonishing exclusive. There was no question about it. She was going to be there tomorrow.

It couldn't come quickly enough.

Meanwhile, she was going to take a recce round town and find out what the hell was up. Apart from anything else it would get her away from this place.

Veronica Legg had become unmistakably short-tempered, snapping like a mousetrap. She had a full house, a short fuse and it was obvious that Chef was playing up. 'He's in one of his moods,' Mrs Legg had announced at breakfast, 'so it's absolutely no use asking for more toast, thank you very much.'

It was quiet at the newsagent's when Neil Bugloss arrived to spend his golden pound coin. Or invest it, as he described the transaction to himself. The priest took no notice of the newspaper rack and the local morning paper's headline: 'Missing!' and the strapline: 'Who is behind bedside snatch of tragic MP?'

He pulled out the little red-backed notebook in his pocket.

Revelations 17, verse 1: And there came one of the seven angels which had the seven vials, and talked with me, saying unto me, Come hither; I will shew unto thee the judgement of the great whore that sitteth upon many waters.

And I saw a woman sit upon a scarlet coloured beast, full of names and blasphemy, having seven heads and ten horns. And the woman was arrayed in purple and scarlet colour, and decked with gold and precious stones and pearls.

And upon her forehead was a name, written, Mystery, Babylon The Great, The Mother Of Harlots And Abominations Of The Earth.

And here is the mind that hath wisdom. The seven heads are seven mountains, on which the woman sitteth. And there are seven kings: five are fallen, and one is, and the other is not yet come . . .

It was only at this point that Father Bugloss looked up from the page and to his dismay realised, from the wide and troubled eyes

Andrew Moncur

of the shopkeeper, that he had been reading aloud at the very top of his voice.

'Mrs Plumley!' he said. 'Mrs Plumley. What must you think of me? I was just doing a little mental arithmetic . . .'

She put down the box of one gross packs of peppermints, leaned across the counter and said quietly but firmly: 'There's no call for talk of harlots, Father Bugloss. Thank you very much. Now, you'll be wanting your lottery ticket.'

And so peace was restored, for the moment.

The village was alive with them. There were two carloads parked opposite the passageway leading to the door of Maurice's apartment and others, having been relieved by their friends, were stretching their legs in Knight Street and around Common Place.

Ellen Bright recognised one or two of them by sight. But she would have known them – feared by their breed, renowned for their deeds far from home – in any circumstances, anywhere, any time.

'What are they, then? SAS units?' asked Sonia.

'God, no,' said Ellen. 'They're reporters. And photographers as well, I suppose. What we have here is a full-blown stake-out of Walsingham. They think Maurice is here – or likely to show up here – and they are covering the place, round the clock.'

'Well, it's not like anything official, then?'

'It's far worse than that. People have no idea. This isn't like being pursued by plodding old jobsworths. These people are really sharp. They're serious.'

There was something else happening, too. Some kind of authority, the rougher sort, was present. She knew it instinctively but she said nothing about that.

That afternoon Ellen decided to take a long walk on the beach. It had become one of those fine pastel-coloured days when the country is a picture of slightly blurred blues and greens.

As she was leaving Little Walsingham she saw Sister Sigebert Buckley herding a small group across the road near the Shrine Shop; the nun was pushing one of them in a wheelchair heaped with rugs as though a fifth Ice Age had been forecast on the lunchtime news.

222

The Harlot's Prerogative

Sigebert waved and then made elaborate ear-trumpet gestures, pointing at her charges.

Her hard-of-hearing pilgrims from Scotland appeared to have arrived at last.

Ellen set off along the beach at Wells where the wooden beach huts stand in a long line on stilts. A party of perhaps a dozen people was playing a game on the sand, taking it in turns to toss steel bowls that clashed together. For some reason it reminded her of France.

Later, walking on the seaward side of the sand dunes covered with tall grass, Ellen sighted her first nudist of the year. He reared up out of the grass and stood on one leg, like a particularly ungainly stork. She was not to know that he was a staff photographer from *Health & Discipline* on the lookout for volleyball players.

Chapter Thirty-Four

On Sunday morning Ellen Bright had a poached egg on toast for her breakfast – although she had, in fact, asked for scrambled – and later sat down with the newspapers. The political writers were in a rage of excitement.

The *Observer* had struck back on Maurice Lovelace's behalf. 'Green Tory badger-lover snatched away from fray,' it said over a report suggesting that the only group which wanted to see the missing MP dumped as a candidate was the Conservative Right. It ran a leader suggesting that the prime minister was looking for a scapegoat, unnamed, for the manifold failures of an exhausted government.

'You remember I asked you about Martha's Field? And you'd never heard of it,' said Ellen.

'Did you, dear?' said Mrs Legg in her bored voice.

'Well. It isn't Martha's at all. It's Martyrs' Field.'

'Yes, everyone knows that, dear. It's where they want to build the theme park.'

'But that's all rubbish. Everybody's got that wrong, too.'

'Have they, dear? It was in the paper.'

'All that theme park stuff was just meant to get people steamed up. They really only want to build the hotel. That's all. It's the only thing that appears on their detailed planning application. They obviously wanted to float all that God nonsense and then be seen to be terribly reasonable and willing to back off – while settling for the one part they really wanted to build in the first place.'

'Yes, dear,' said Mrs Legg, ignoring every word Ellen had spoken.

At her hotel, a little over ten miles from Walsingham, Gwen Lightsome sent back her poached eggs on toast although she had, in fact, ordered them when she arrived for breakfast.

'I know I asked for poached eggs. Of course I asked for poached eggs. Do you think I'm some sort of idiot? I've changed my mind, that's all. Now go and find me some scrambled eggs,' she told the waiter. 'And you had better take away this toast as well. It's starting to look used.'

'Yes, madam. Anything else, madam?' he said. He would later be able to tell his mother that he had served Gwen Lightsome – *the* Gwen Lightsome – and she'd been, well, quite big close up. Not like she was on television at all, really. It had been dead funny, seeing her in that sort of tracksuit.

Later, when she had finished her breakfast, Mrs Lightsome walked across to the reception desk, interrupted the clerk who was dealing with another guest, slapped the counter and demanded to see the duty manager. When this young man was found she insisted, loudly, that her room was inadequate and must be changed.

'Did you hear what she called me?' The under-manager, whose name was actually Liam, spoke with a little tremor in his voice; he was perspiring freely. 'I told her. I said to her, I said, I'm not taking that sort of language from . . .'

'So, I'm to call a porter, am I? To transfer them to the Sandringham suite, yes? With a VIP bowl of fresh fruit in the sitting room, right?' The receptionist's hand hovered over her computer keys.

'Right,' said Liam.

Neil Bugloss had avoided watching the National Lottery live draw on television the previous evening. It wasn't difficult since he didn't possess a TV. The last one he had kept in his rooms had been a black and white set; it had broken down eight, maybe ten years ago and never been missed.

The truth was, he wasn't even aware that a lottery show occurred on television.

He resisted any fancy to check the numbers published in the newspapers on Sunday morning. He had other plans.

Mr Bugloss certainly didn't know it was a rollover draw with a jackpot of £20.5 million. He had never really considered the exact sum of money which would be required for his great purpose; it was sufficient for him to know that the Lord would provide.

* * *

Andrew Moncur

At a quarter to twelve on Sunday Ellen Bright walked into the car park beside the old Bridewell. It was relatively empty. She noticed a camper van parked close to the pay-and-display ticket machine. As she walked across the lot she noted a grey BMW in a parking bay; two men were sitting in the front of the car with the resigned stillness of those who have a long while to wait.

She had read the note over and again, trying to make sense of it. So far as she could tell, the writer wanted her to go to the gate on the north side of the car park and then find the yard. And, yes, there was a head-high gate in the brick wall at that end.

It clicked open and Ellen stepped through on to a driveway. To the left it ran up to the road; to the right it followed round the side of – what? An old red brick house?

Ellen turned right and walked past a couple of cottage gardens to an open gateway in the wall. Beyond she could see a patch of green. She was in what must have been the yard of the old House of Correction.

It was very quiet and still.

The building ahead was obviously a surviving part of the prison still in its original state. There were six barred windows, with flaking pale brown paint, on the ground floor; another seven on the first floor. There was a door of slatted wood and it was standing open.

'Hello,' sang out Ellen, torn between making her presence known and not wishing to draw unwanted attention to herself – or anyone else. Half a dozen starlings took off and flew to the safety of the roof. 'Mr Lovelace?' she hissed.

The little yard remained completely silent.

She stepped inside the door. There was a brick floor and gradually she could make out the arched ceiling and the flaking whitewashed walls. She felt a shiver start in the small of her back. Nothing much could have changed here since the block was built in the 1780s and abandoned in the 1860s. Behind her shoulder the unpainted stairway climbed to a half-landing, then on up into the darkness. On her left was a vaulted room with a heavy, studded door set with a trap and a grille.

To the right there was a corridor and, dimly seen, a row of doors. At the far end there was a faint light.

The Harlot's Prerogative

She glanced into the first door: it was a little cell with a sleeping platform and a high, barred window. There were rusted manacles hanging from the wall.

That was enough. She just wanted to get out into the sunlight. She turned and . . .

'Help!' The voice sounded like a child's. It was coming from the far end of the corridor – away from the outside door and the daylight and the clean air. She knew immediately she would have to do it. She must go down there to the place where some sort of a light was burning.

'Hello?' she called. Her voice was hoarse.

Ellen, drawing on all her courage, took it at a run. It was the last door in the corridor. She swung round the frame and peered inside. A stub of candle was burning on what looked like a box standing against the wall. She took in the bare details: it was another cell, only this time lined with wood panelling from floor to ceiling. There was no light from any grille. There appeared to be some sort of wooden shutter high on the end wall where the bars ought to have been. There was nobody in the room. The cell door was massively heavy.

It swung shut behind her with an immensely solid crash. She could do no more than raise her hands to her mouth and suck in breath. Somebody must have been out there in the corridor, hiding behind the door and waiting to spring the trap.

Ellen Bright was confined on her own in the silent cell. More than that, it was the dark cell – as she would shortly find out. It was the very worst place that a system of cultivated cruelty could provide for the malefactors in its punishment wing.

It was the last resort to which they turned if the treadmill, for heaven's sake, had proved to be an insufficiently harsh penalty to cool the convict's courage.

In the impenetrable blackness of the dark cell a woman could scream herself insane – as happened from time to time, a catastrophic destruction of the spirit noted with interest by the prison medical officers of the day. And she could do so without troubling the smooth-running of the jail.

Ellen Bright, to her credit, did not even waste her breath.

Chapter Thirty-Five

The cell was nine feet long and six feet wide with, as far as could be seen, an arched roof of beautifully interlocking brickwork. The door was heavy and forbidding. Ellen put her weight against it: it was massively immovable in its frame.

There was about half an inch of candle stub still to burn, planted on a saucer on the little box seat fixed to the floor. There was no other furniture. The light was very poor: she could make out the shape of the wooden window shutter but it was well above the top of her head. Jumping up, she could touch it with her fingertips. There was no hope of opening it.

The cell had been admirably designed for its silent purpose; it was built by people who knew not only how to contain but also to crush. Very soon it would be plunged into total darkness.

'Oh, God. What a place,' Ellen said aloud.

Then she hooked her bag off her shoulder and found her mobile phone. Her fingers tapped out the number.

'Ready when you are,' she said. 'I'm in the cell at the end of the row on the ground floor. OK? Right. Thanks.'

She had made her arrangements the previous day after carrying out her reconnaisance of the village and taking a careful look at the place proposed for her rendezvous.

'Well, I'm not a complete bloody idiot,' she had said, outlining her plan during a phone call on Saturday evening.

There was a faint sound of footsteps in the corridor beyond the cell door and then to her relief – she didn't mind admitting it – the door swung open. Sister Sigebert Buckley was standing there, beaming.

'It was only secured with a stick,' she said, holding up what looked like a length of stout broom handle.

'Thank you, Nicky.'

'I ran round just as soon as you phoned. I'm not even puffed.'

228

The Harlot's Prerogative

'Did you see anybody?'

'No. But there was a car roaring away up the drive. I think it came out from behind the wall over there. I made a note of its number.' There was a blue ballpoint scribble on the back of her strong hand.

Ellen nodded. The candle flame soared up for a moment, flickered and died.

'Come on. I'll make you a cup of tea,' said Sigebert. 'We've got some very interesting people staying at the hospice.'

'Are they deaf?'

'Well, some of them are. But the ones I'd really like you to meet have arrived from London, seeking refuge.'

'So, you're Mrs Canty?' Ellen Bright took her hand. The older woman had a good firm grip and strikingly clear blue eyes.

'Yes, dear. And this is my friend, Mr Hopkin . . .' She gestured to him to step forward across the little sitting room. 'Don't worry about the limp. I ran him over the other night. He'll live.'

Mr Hopkin bobbed and nodded and gave Mrs Canty a crooked little smile. He shook Ellen's hand and winked at her.

'And the man himself? Where's the patient?' Ellen raised her eyebrows in query.

'Mr Lovelace? Oh, he's all right. The sisters have been doing a wonderful job with him. Young Stephanie there, the what-d'you-call-it . . .'

'The novice.'

'That's it. Stephanie's been praying at his bedside. Oh, you've never heard such prayers. She told me she'd done the litanies – what a lot of litanies. You've no idea. The litany of the holy name. The litany of the sacred heart. Oh, yes, and the blessed Virgin. And another one. She's been saying the rosary, the Hail Marys and the Glory be. I'm sure he's loved all that.'

'I'm sure he has,' said Ellen.

'And Sister Sigebert's been reading to him. What book was it she was reading to him, Mr Hopkin?'

'*The Guinness Book of Rugby Records*, I think.'

'Yes, that's right. He'll have been lapping that up,' said Mrs

Canty. 'Me and Mr Hopkin have been trying to work out where they hid the lost treasure of Walsingham. Mr Lovelace seems to think he knows, to judge from his book. Do you know about his book, dear?'

'No, I'm afraid . . .'

'We just wanted to get him away from London for a few days, you see, so he'd have a chance to get better without being dragged around the Houses of Parliament, casting votes and things.'

Ellen regarded the pair closely. There was not a hint of cunning or guile about them.

'Are you aware that it's caused a bit of a stink?' she asked. 'In the papers, I mean.'

'No, dear,' said Mrs Canty. 'It's very quiet here, you know. We don't get to see the news. We've hardly been out at all.'

'Well, I can tell you everyone's got rather worked up. The whole of Walsingham's full of reporters – and I'm fairly sure that the police are swarming around the place as well.'

'Ooh, my giddy aunt,' said Mrs Canty. 'Do you think we ought to be moving on? What do you think, Mr Hopkin?'

'Shall I go fetch the camper van?' he said.

'The camper van in the car park? With the red roof?' Ellen asked. Mr Hopkin nodded.

'That's the last thing you should do. I'm absolutely certain the police are staking it out. They must have good reason to think that vehicle's involved with the disappearance of Mr Lovelace. That almost certainly means they know you're in town.'

'Then what can we do?' Mrs Canty sounded more interested than alarmed.

'Listen,' said Ellen. 'I've got an idea.'

And in a few minutes they had settled on a plan of action.

Sonia Marks sat back on the kitchen chair. 'Well, that sounds good to me,' she said.

Ellen had known she could count on her help. She was convinced the news story of Maurice Lovelace's disappearance would be a nine-day wonder – or even more short-lived than that, given the way the election campaign was already gathering pace.

The Harlot's Prerogative

If he could just be removed from view for a few days the press would soon be occupied elsewhere, pursuing the main political news. As a story it would simply be left behind. The government itself would hardly want to keep up the hue and cry.

'It means slipping him away from Walsingham. There's too much attention here,' said Ellen. 'The problem is, every inch of the village is under scrutiny – and, I guess, every road in and out. Still, as I say, there is a way.'

'Hold on,' said Sonia. 'What about you? You're a journalist. You could be telling the world you've found him.'

'What, breaking the big news in *Home & Beauty*? I could sell the story to one of the tabloids, I suppose. But it would feel like thirty pieces of silver.'

The Little Sisters seemed serenely confident that Maurice would return to the land of the living. They differed only in their guesswork about how exactly he might regain consciousness. Sister Thomas Figge remembered a coma patient who had slowly inched back to normality over a period of weeks, having first shown a flicker in an eyelid and, several days later, a twitching of the fingers.

Sister Augustine Bradshaw, on the other hand, recalled the case of a deeply unconscious youth who had suddenly sat bolt upright, opened his eyes and asked for a beer and a hot curry.

There was simply no way of knowing which way any individual would jump, Ellen was told.

She had been worried that the nuns might be deeply involved in the next day's big pilgrimage. Sister Sigebert had quickly put her right. 'Oh, no,' she said. 'That's the other lot, the Anglicans. You shouldn't worry your pretty little head about them. We certainly don't.'

Later, as the light began to fade towards evening, Ellen took a short drive. She wanted to ask a question, a simple enough matter.

The car was parked in front of the house, its number plate corresponded with her note.

'I just need to know how you could do something so cruel?' she said when the freshly painted door was eventually answered.

There was a prolonged silence while Mrs Westlake, the chairman

231

of Maurice's constituency association, looked at her with hatred in her eyes.

'All right,' she said at last. 'I wanted you out of the way. You and everything you stand for. I want to clear you away, all of you. People despise you. Do you know that?'

'But, I can't see . . . Why me?' asked Ellen, trying – and failing – to hide the chill passing through her.

'It's everything you represent. If we could be rid of you – you press people, reptiles – for only a day or two then Maurice could be adopted again in the constituency; his future would be secure. It's the least I can do for him . . .'

'What?' said Ellen, 'You did that for the sake of Maurice Lovelace's career?'

'It's the very least I can do.'

'I'm sorry. That's simply . . .'

'I was able to do very little for him as a boy,' said Mrs Westlake. 'It was the circumstances.'

Ellen looked at her very steadily.

'You mean . . .'

'What I mean has nothing to damn well do with you,' she said, her face still strangely opaque. Then she slammed the door again.

That night Ellen read the Lovelace history of Walsingham. She lingered over the final page, describing Maurice's discovery in Keble College library: a beautifully illuminated breviary of fifteenth-century origin.

On its flyleaf it bears the words: *'Iste liber pertinet dno Ricd Vowell priori de Walsyngham'*. The book had belonged to the much-despised last guardian of the holy house, Richard Vowell, the appeaser who presided over the destruction of the ancient shrine.

The endpapers are filled with notes in his own hand. Some are arcane, others merely surprising. There is, for instance, a detailed instruction on the use of the priory's curative bath – absolutely not to be visited by anybody alone and unattended

– and elsewhere the words of a service for St Dorothy, the patron saint of gardens.

The lines which had held Maurice's attention were these: 'Such are the wrackes of Walsyngham, gone bye, whose fairest jewelle now in Martyres field doth lye.' The word 'jewelle' had been heavily underscored.

It was Maurice Lovelace's belief that this was no recantation, no expression of regret for the author's part in the betrayal of the subprior, Nicholas Mileham, so widely thought to have been sent to his execution on the testimony of Prior Vowell himself.

'No. In my view these words are a guide, a clue, left to those who might be drawn to Walsingham in years to come – and in a happier, more peaceful age,' Maurice wrote.

'I am persuaded that Prior Vowell bought time and favours from a tyrannical regime, at the most dreadful expense. He did so in order that the object or objects he venerated most might be hidden away and preserved. I submit that he points us to the place where one day they will be found.'

Chapter Thirty-Six

The village was starting to swell with the bank holiday crowds of pilgrims, coming to make their devotions to Our Lady of Walsingham. Others were arriving to deplore this idolatory, this bobbing and praying to plaster saints, and to register their protests.

The battle lines would become clearly drawn as the day of pilgrimage wore on. On the one hand an archbishop of the Church of England, a dozen mitred bishops, enough priests in birettas to choke an entire street; all the panoply of crozier and cross, of cope, candle and mace, flaming torch and censer. On the other, like small unyielding rocks against which all this flood tide would break, fundamentalist protestants with their banners and slogans.

They would stand in the middle of this festival and preach against it. Before the end of the day visitors to Walsingham would hear hymn-singing deployed as a weapon.

The argument is all the more bitter, of course, because this is a matter of Christian versus Christian. It was only in the planned theme park that anybody thought it remotely necessary to give lions a place on the fight bill.

Through it all would glide the Virgin herself, borne at shoulder height in a rich cope and on a sea of lilies.

But early on bank holiday Monday, while the dew was still wet on the grass, there was still time for a little calm before the storm.

In the holy house itself, within the Anglican shrine church, glowing with candles in glass holders of red and blue, Father Neil Bugloss was making his own singular offering. The statue was raised above the altar against a golden reredos, richly decorated in the style of a celestial Wurlitzer organ. Above loomed a tester like the canopy of a four-poster bed.

It was in the tradition of Walsingham to bring great riches to the shrine of Our Lady.

*   *   *

The Harlot's Prerogative

'Has it occurred to you that geography is all-important in this business of divine visitation? Think about it. If the Lady Richeldis had been living only a mile and a half down the road when she had her visions in – whatever year it was – then all these people would be coming today to pay their respects to Our Lady of Great Snoring.' Reggie Lightsome, his hands resting on the steering wheel, looked pleased with himself.

'What?' snapped his wife.

'If she'd had her vision in Great Snoring instead of Walsingham then we'd all . . .'

'For Christ's sake, Reggie. Where are we?'

They had come to rest at a junction; narrow lanes went winding off between high hedges in both directions. The council had helpfully installed a signpost saying 'By-road' to the right. And another indicating 'By-road' to the left.

'By-road? What help is By-road? They might as well say Get Lost,' snapped Gwen Lightsome. 'Look, we've got to get to Walsingham, find the photographer and pick up a cripple. So can we just move it!'

Reggie was craning round to see whether the signpost indicated where, exactly, they had just come from. 'By-road,' it said.

'It's got to be the left,' he said, swinging the vehicle into the lane where the banks were a jungle of hemlock and goose grass. A little alarm was sounding somewhere low in his brain stem, its message disregarded for the moment in the higher centres: there was grass growing along the middle of the road.

The four-wheel drive occupied at least three-quarters of the lane's width. They had decided back in London that since they were coming to the country it would be necessary to have some kind of rough terrain vehicle with bull bars, headlamp grilles, roof storage racks, spare jerry cans, searchlights and a four-speaker CD player. Well, there was a certain amount of mud on the tarmac. And there was really quite a lot of grass sprouting in the middle of . . .

'There's grass growing in the middle of the road,' said Gwen, sitting bolt upright. 'How can we be going to Walsingham when we're on some bloody farm track?'

235

Andrew Moncur

'Everything's perfectly all right,' said Reggie in that infuriating tone men use when everything isn't.

'How do you know where we are?'

'I'm heading west towards the sun.' There was something horribly self-satisfied in his voice.

'Reggie. It's nine o'clock in the morning. The bloody sun rises in the bloody east.'

They drove on in silence for a moment.

'I'll find a place to turn round,' he said.

Just then, bounding over the crest of a small rise, a white pick-up truck came bursting into view. They could make out a flat cap above what might have been a sack of potatoes in the driver's seat; there was a coat-hanger aerial on one wing. A brown and black terrier was leaning out of the truck, his facial hair combed straight back by the rush of the slipstream.

It seemed not to have occurred to Reggie Lightsome that he was on an exceedingly narrow lane. It had possibly never crossed his mind that roads could be allowed to exist on a scale too small to permit converging vehicles to pass.

The oncoming truck had by now slowed and pulled its nearside wheels on to the verge. Reggie ploughed on without deflecting from his course, straddling the centre of the lane; his speed was unchanged.

The truck was heaved still further on to the bank, tipping to a dangerous angle and scooping cow parsley on to its bumper bar. Reggie thrust forward on his majestic path, not yielding an inch. When God made the world he patently gave Mr and Mrs Lightsome the inalienable right to drive on regardless.

They passed the truck, by now at a standstill in the hedge, without a flicker of recognition. Not a finger was raised in acknowledgement. As the two vehicles passed – the one in the undergrowth, the other enjoying untrammelled right of way – there was a gap between them of several microns.

The terrier watched spellbound, without so much as a bark.

The little old lady in the brown fluffy hat was wearing a body-length tabard with slogans painted on back and front. '*Thou shalt*

The Harlot's Prerogative

not make unto thee any graven image,' boomed her bosom and stomach. *'Wise men still seek Jesus, not booze,'* said her rear quarters.

She was standing in the Common Place with a phalanx of her friends ranged beside the sixteenth-century village pump, a building which had suffered a little from local exuberance during celebrations to mark the Relief of Mafeking in 1900. Today a knot of fundamentalists had gathered there to voice their bitter opposition to the cult of Our Lady of Walsingham.

'Behold the Waltzing Ham show with its wobbling high doll,' one banner declared. A woman in a raincoat held up another: *'Remember the protestant martyrs.'* A breeze was getting up and tugging at their placards.

A Pentecostal preacher, a tall, gaunt man with a hard-edged voice, had already started to declaim. He thundered at pilgrims and priests gathering on the far side of the square. 'Repent! Repent! Each one of us,' he cried in a sepulchral tone, 'is heading for the time of our departure . . .'

'Good!' shouted a priest with a boxer's nose. 'Don't let us delay you.'

A plump young nun in the traditional habit of the Mildredine order slipped through the crush, ran down a side street and let herself in through the private door to the hospice. Sister Christopher Bagshawe had a report to deliver.

'You were right,' she said, breathlessly. 'The police are on all the roads. It's easy for them. They're stopping all the traffic – only pedestrians are being allowed through.'

'And did you see any photographers?' asked Ellen.

'There's a whole bunch of them in the Common Place, outside the Bull. TV camera crews as well.'

'Right. Let's go.'

The four-wheel drive, all-terrain, great white hunter-style land cruiser was standing motionless in the middle of a fiord. The river Stiffkey was playing wetly around its cross-country tyres. Thirty or so ewes were gathered on the far bank, chewing and staring.

'I am not one to criticise, Reggie. You know that, don't you?' Gwen Lightsome brought her hands together carefully on her lap.

Andrew Moncur

'I think you'll agree that I like to take a constructive approach when little problems arise. Isn't that so?'

Reggie Lightsome, in the driver's seat, nodded miserably.

'Then get me out of this god-forsaken swamp, you complete toss-potting wanker. And I mean now. Now.' Her words were all the more menacing for being spoken so quietly.

Reggie took off his ox-blood brogues and his wool-mixture socks. He rolled up his new twill trousers well above his white and gingery knees. Then he opened the door and, shrinking from the coldness and the invisible leeches and worms slapping about beneath the surface, he stepped into the water.

'I'll go and find somebody to give us a tow,' he said, waving his shoes in the air.

Mrs Lightsome said nothing. She looked straight ahead through the windscreen: across the lapping water, over the meadow, beyond the teeming hedgerows, the oaks, the fields of standing barley, high above the set-aside, the gamekeeper's patch of corn, the rabbit warren and the broad-leafed woodland. Way up there a solitary swan was flying free, its neck outstretched.

The bugling cry of the great bird seemed strangely reminiscent of something or other. She could not think what.

The procession was forming up at the shrine church. The Priests Associate of the Holy House were assembled in alb and white stole; members of the College of Guardians adjusted their mantles and chains; the beadle took up station in his red skullcap and robes; the Guardians' cross was raised; the Sea Cadets guard of honour fell in, shining with blanco. Incense was starting to scent the air. Then, above all, the statue itself, crowned and robed in a mantle of cloth of gold, was borne up on the shoulders of four clergy in dalmatics, their finest robes. The wind caught at their vestments. Candles were blown out.

It was as though they were all taking part in a subdued carnival. They were to walk in procession through the centre of Walsingham, enter the priory grounds through the ancient gatehouse and gather on the site of that lost church, beyond the big beech trees, for an open-air mass celebrated by the archbishop.

The Harlot's Prerogative

In the Common Place they were warming up for a battle of nakedly aggressive hymn-singing. On the pilgrims' side it would be a salvo of:

> Jesus is Lord!
> Creation's voice proclaims it,
> For by his power each tree and flower
> Was planned and made . . .

The entrenched opposition front line would reply with a withering burst of:

> There is power, power,
> Wonder-working power
> In the precious blood of the lamb . . .

Veronica Legg, who had strolled into the village to watch events, leaned against a wall and observed the scene.

Over there was Father Bugloss, inspecting his cadet guard of honour. He motioned them forward to take their places on either side of Our Lady. Then he walked round behind the image where he seemed to be adjusting the Virgin's cope. No, he was attaching something – a slip of paper – to the edge of the garment. Mrs Legg could not know this, but it was his votive offering.

He believed, he truly believed, that he would live to see the rebuilding of the ruined Priory of the Annunciation of the Blessed Virgin. If it took a lottery rollover he would not complain. It would happen; it was the purest matter of faith. Neil Bugloss turned and walked to his position immediately behind the bearers.

And then the procession slowly started to move, unwinding itself from the shrine grounds.

Mrs Legg always found it a curiously un-English spectacle; there was to her mind something foreign about this enthusiasm for a dressed-up statue. If she screwed up her eyes this could be a town in Spain; if she screwed up her imagination, it was in medieval England. It was the Walsingham of 500 or 800 years ago when bed and breakfast was a very different experience.

Andrew Moncur

'*For by his power each tree and flower* . . .' Real poetry was a wonderful thing.

There was a sudden movement. Something was wrong. The front of the column was advancing towards the Common Place and the statue itself was swaying out on to the road when a commotion began near the head of the procession.

The tractor rolled through the fiord, throwing its bow wave against the door panels of the rugged, all-terrain, cross-country vehicle which remained stationary in midstream.

'Hoofy hoo!' the tractor driver shouted at Gwen Lightsome, who was not so much walking on water as sitting on it.

'Wait, wait. What did you say?' She suddenly sprang alive, leaning out of her window to wave at the tractor man. 'What did you say?'

'It's a bootiful voo,' the driver shouted over the roar of his diesel.

'Oh, bugger off,' said Mrs Lightsome.

Chapter Thirty-Seven

The TV cameraman and his sound recordist had been shooting some stock footage in a desultory way, passing the time as much as anything. They were not to know that their crowd scenes from Little Walsingham would make the *News at Ten* that night.

A nun in full habit was propelling a handicapped person through the Common Place. It was just possible to make out that it was a man, bundled up in rugs in her wheelchair. The sister had a plump, pink face and a serene smile which remained in place as she steered carefully through the onlookers towards the roadway.

The camera followed her for a moment and then panned across the square, lingering on the banners around the pump. In a moment the procession would come up the road.

A piercing cry went up from somewhere among the sea of faces. It might have been a shout of: 'Look! It's him!' or possibly 'it's sin'. The camera swung back in time to catch a surge in the crowd. The same voice piped: 'Maurice Lovelace!' A flying wedge of men and women who had been standing near the Bull pub began instantly to push their way into the crowd. The nun had broken into a run, charging full tilt down the road with her wheelchair and passenger – aiming straight for the head of the approaching column.

Behind her the crowd, responding to the panicky shoving from behind, started to surge across the road. The tall preacher who had been urging repentance on the pilgrims now tightened the belt of his raincoat. He was used to trouble around his pavement pulpit. The lady in the tabard gripped the pole of a banner and planted herself ready for action like a guardsman in a British square.

A quick-thinking policeman rushed to place himself between the two opposing camps, throwing his arms wide as they surged together. At that moment a woman behind him started to unfurl her end of a banner – '*No popery*,' it said – and lost control of the

241

pole. It swung round wildly and smacked the policeman a telling blow on the back of his head.

His colleague, a policewoman, came steaming in to help and began to grapple with the banner – and suddenly the fighting started. Someone was screaming. The priest with the squashed nose made a terrible whooping noise and hurled himself at a Presbyterian bus driver from Dalkeith. A Nonconformist bicycle wholesaler from Norwich threw a great milling punch at an Anglo-Catholic dentist who had travelled to Walsingham by coach with a church mothers' group from Sale.

It was unfortunate that one of the first blows caught a visitor from the Republic of Nauru who was a member of both the Exclusive Brethren, a strict Calvinistic sect, and the Nauruan rugby league team. He reacted with shocking speed. It would take a large number of police eventually to restrain him; they would then find that he enjoyed diplomatic immunity.

The treasurer of a Congregationalist church somewhere on the Black Country fringes of Birmingham tried to restore peace and was hit on the nose by a Church of England curate from Lincoln. A Pentecostalist from Stafford punched an Orthodox Serb from Halifax who knocked him down and then took a swing at a Lutheran librarian on holiday from Ontario. A special constable in a moment of panic lashed out at a friar in sandals, damaging his spectacles.

A Salvationist from the Brighton Citadel was slapped by a lay-reader from Oswestry and turned the other cheek, whereupon he was slapped again. Most frighteningly of all, a party of low-church peace women from Leighton Buzzard attacked a quintet of choristers from a particularly camp high church in Blackheath, south-east London.

There was a good deal of wrestling and people were caught up in an awful, mindless crowd movement which carried them backwards and forwards in the middle of the road. Several women threatened to faint and an elderly priest from Cambridge had to be helped into the Shrine Shop where he was laid down on the floor.

While these ugly scenes were taking place the procession itself was separately halted by a strange little incident.

The Harlot's Prerogative

Mrs Legg had been watching her friend, Father Bugloss, walking behind the lily-decked image. Then a gust of wind caught his lottery ticket offering, detaching it from Our Lady's cape and spiriting it into the air. It was carried up and over the priest's bowed head. Veronica Legg did not waste a second.

'Neil,' she roared in her most powerful songster's voice, with terrific vibrato. And all those within earshot dropped to their knees.

It was an astonishing moment which could easily have gone to Mrs Legg's head. The entire column was brought to a standstill. Even the mace-bearing beadle went down ponderously, still holding his staff, the symbol of his office, over his right shoulder.

In the confusion nobody noticed where the slip of paper had ended up. Many people, though, saw the nun with the wheelchair, her seated charge being thrown about like a doll as she careered down the road.

They watched her corner the chair on two wheels – for a second it looked as though it would overturn – and then cut through a gateway into the grounds of the shrine church.

The press photographers and several fit-looking young men in plain clothes caught up with her there. They were surprised to find that the figure in the wheelchair, far from being the missing Member of Parliament they sought, was totally unknown to them.

'This is Mr Evangeltine Hopkin,' Sister Christopher Bagshawe explained politely in response to their brusque questions. 'Say how do you do, Mr H.'

'How do you do,' said Mr Hopkin.

They were never able to establish who, precisely, was responsible for starting all the trouble by shouting out Mr Lovelace's name.

A party of Norwegian pilgrims paying a visit to the shrine was later gratified to see Mr Hopkin rise from his wheelchair and walk.

They said afterwards that a golden oriole had flown out of a bush and perched on the vacant seat. It began singing, in its flutelike voice, an elusively familiar tune. One of the group was back in Stavanger before she recalled the name of the song: '*Disse Dumme Ting*'.

* * *

Sister Sigebert Buckley came flitting around the garden wall. 'All clear,' she hissed. 'We can go across.'

Three women were grouped around the figure in the wheelchair; the youngest of them was arranging a blanket over the seated man's knees.

'There's a road block just up at the junction where they're stopping all the cars,' whispered Sigebert, 'but all but one of the policemen have gone running off into the village. If we time it right he won't see us at all and we'll be clean away. It's exciting, isn't it?'

'Hang on,' said Ellen. She checked to make sure that Mrs Canty was prepared for a quick dash. Stephanie Beard, the novice, had a little blue veil pinned to her hair. She was carrying a small suitcase.

'Virgin most clement, Virgin most faithful, Mirror of righteousness, Seat of wisdom, Mystic Rose, Tower of Ivory . . . pray for us,' murmured Stephanie.

'We'll hold on here for one more minute,' said Ellen.

'Whatever you say,' Sigebert replied. 'You're the boss.'

Maurice Lovelace's entire frame bucked wildly.

'Bloody hell,' said Ellen. 'Say that again.'

'Whatever you say. You're the boss.'

This time Maurice let out a prolonged grumbling moan.

Mrs Canty bent over the chair and gave him a quick peck in the middle of his forehead. 'Brilliant,' she said.

Sister Sigebert took charge of the chair, pushed back her sleeves and waited for the nod. Then the oddly assorted group trotted out of the alleyway, bumped over the kerb, sprinted across the road, raced up the pavement and jogged into the safety of the yard opposite; the wheelchair was manhandled over every obstacle by the big nun.

It took a matter of moments to load their patient and climb aboard themselves for the thirty-minute journey which would complete their breakout from Walsingham.

They were using the one route which the watchers had utterly overlooked: the miniature train hauled by a scaled-down steam locomotive on the narrow gauge rail line linking the pilgrim town to the coast at Wells next the Sea.

The guard's whistle blew.

The Harlot's Prerogative

'Boss,' said Mrs Canty. 'Boss,' said Stephanie Beard.

Maurice Lovelace raised a feeble hand and groaned. The nun, the novice, the cleaning lady, the journalist and the reborn MP slowly receded from view, shrouded in steam.

'By the time we reached the other end of the line he'd spoken his first words,' said Ellen, making her report to Sonia Marks.

'Which were?'

'Am I in heaven?'

'So has he lost his marbles?'

'Not at all. It was very touching. He said all his life he'd been lonely – and now, at last, he was surrounded by women. It had to be paradise.'

'Did he say anything else?' Sonia asked.

'Only a request: please, no more litanies.'

They were surprisingly comfortable in the caravan. Ellen had booked it for a week at low season prices but Maurice would decide in a matter of only a day or two when he wanted to make his return to life. It would not be long delayed.

They had been astonished by the speed of his recovery. 'It's a miracle,' Ellen said.

'Oh, come off it,' said Sister Sigebert Buckley, of the Little Sisters of St Mildred. 'Damned good nursing, more like.'

Maurice Lovelace appeared to have emerged from his long ordeal refreshed and without so much as a headache.

'I think that Constance Verity might pick up her career again. It's more profitable than politics,' he had announced after being brought up to date on current events.

'By the way, Ellen,' he said. 'When's your birthday?'

'That's funny,' said Stephanie Beard. 'He asked me the same question.'

'Was that a winning ticket? Should you have picked up the top prize in the lottery?' Veronica Legg asked when, at last, the time seemed ripe.

'I haven't the faintest, Veronica,' said Father Bugloss, stretching out on the chesterfield in her private sitting room. 'I didn't feel the need to check the numbers.'

Mrs Legg looked into the fire. There was a long pause during which they both listened to the ticking of her clock.

'It doesn't make any difference,' he said eventually. 'It will happen one day, I know it. That's all that matters.'

Mrs Canty returned the following weekend to collect the camper van and on touching the driver's door handle was immediately approached by two police officers, almost whooping with pleasure.

They and their colleagues had been watching the van throughout the week and had retained their sanity only by running a sweepstake, the winners being those on duty when the driver finally returned. It emerged that they had carried out a dawn raid on the home of Mrs Canty's indignant neighbour as soon as the vehicle had been identified from the security camera's tape, cleverly enhanced. The camper had soon been spotted in Walsingham.

It was difficult for them to bring any charge against Mrs Canty. She could hardly be accused of abducting her own employer when he was so eager to commend her actions. Besides, by the time the police were able to interview her, the search for Maurice Lovelace had been discreetly wound down.

The election campaign was by then running at full throttle. The prime minister had been persuaded that it did not enhance his administration's reputation for competent management to have the voters reminded daily that it had managed to lose one of its own backbenchers, bringing all this trouble on its own head.

'Do you realise that you have been instrumental in bringing down a British government?' the chief superintendent had asked during a cheerful interview at Fakenham police station.

'No, dear,' said Mrs Canty. 'Oh, that is a nice cup of tea. You obviously warm the pot properly. It makes all the difference, doesn't it.'

Mr Hopkin returned to St Wilfrid's after the long weekend and nobody even realised he had been away. However, his long-term girlfriend's suspicions had become aroused on the Saturday night when she tried, and failed, to phone him at work.

'You said you wasn't going to be there and you wasn't,' she said accusingly.

'That's right,' said Mr Hopkin.

'I've got my eye on you,' she replied.

Mr Hopkin touched the folded, slightly water-stained scrap of paper in his pocket and smiled a very broad smile.

Gwen Lightsome made a highly lucrative arrangement to transfer her picture byline and her celebrated column to *Mother's Own*, which was being given a radical make-over by its recently appointed editor. The new man was committed to giving the magazine a younger, fresher, bolder, sexier appeal. In short, he wished it to resemble more closely all its rivals.

The Lightsome move left the way clear for Constance Verity to resume her briefly interrupted career at *Home & Beauty* to the intense pleasure of her many faithful followers at that award-winning weekly. She was actually given an extra half-page which she used to assure readers that the problems they described were entirely normal. They might occasionally require the attentions of a doctor but, more usually, they could cope with a brave smile and a dab of petroleum jelly.

Hearts could be lightened by a courageous, uplifting word or even a little burst of verse. Miss Verity had more time and energy to devote to her journalism now that other duties had been discarded.

Muriel Oliver and her restored assistant, Juliet, began a collection of their favourite items from the page; Juliet pasted the cuttings on the side of the little blue two-drawer filing cabinet which sat behind the *Monstera deliciosa* Swiss-cheese plant.

It was almost exactly a year later, when they were digging trial bores in Martyrs' Field for the Walsingham hotel project, that Maurice Lovelace's thesis was finally proved. Nothing would come of the hotel, as it happened, owing to a combination of geological and financial complications which were to prove insurmountable.

However, the diggings fulfilled at least one useful purpose. At a depth of four feet the site workers struck an object which proved to